Caroline was dangerously near to tears and Jimbo, receiving distress signals right down at his end of the table, sprang to his feet and offered Sheila Bissett more wine, thus diverting her from Caroline. Katherine Charter-Plackett intercepted a glance between Suzy and Peter. She leant towards Muriel and whispered in a loud voice, 'What's between the gorgeous rector and that red siren? There's something going on.'

Educated at a co-educational Quaker boarding school, Rebecca Shaw went on to qualify as a teacher of deaf children. After her marriage, she spent the ensuing years enjoying bringing up her family. The departure of the last of her four children to university has given her the time and opportunity to write. Her latest novel in paperback in the Turnham Malpas series is *Intrigue in the Village*, and in hardback *Whispers in the Village*, also available from Orion.

*By Rebecca Shaw*

TALES FROM TURNHAM MALPAS
The New Rector
Talk of the Village
Village Matters
The Village Show
Village Secrets
Scandal in the Village
Village Gossip
Trouble in the Village
A Village Dilemma
Intrigue in the Village
Whispers in the Village

THE BARLEYBRIDGE SERIES
A Country Affair
Country Wives
Country Lovers
Country Passions

# The New Rector

*Tales from Turnham Malpas*

REBECCA SHAW

**ORION**

An Orion paperback

First published in Great Britain in 1994
by Orion
This paperback edition published in 1996
by Orion Books Ltd,
Orion House, 5 Upper St Martin's Lane,
London WC2H 9EA

Ninth impression
Reissued 2005

Copyright © 1994 Rebecca Shaw

The right of Rebecca Shaw to be identified as the author
of this work has been asserted by her in accordance with the
Copyright, Designs and Patents Act 1988.

All rights reserved. No part of this publication may be
reproduced, stored in a retrieval system, or transmitted, in
any form or by any means, electronic, mechanical,
photocopying, recording or otherwise, without the prior
permission of the copyright owner.

A CIP catalogue record for this book is available
from the British Library.

ISBN 0 75282 750 2

Printed and bound in Great Britain by
Clays Ltd, St Ives plc

www.orionbooks.co.uk

# INHABITANTS OF TURNHAM MALPAS

| | |
|---|---|
| Sadie Beauchamp | Retired widow and mother of Harriet Charter-Plackett. |
| Willie Biggs | Verger at St Thomas à Becket. |
| Sir Ronald Bissett | Retired trades union leader. |
| Lady Sheila Bissett | His wife. |
| James Charter-Plackett | Owner of the village store. |
| Harriet Charter-Plackett | His wife. |
| Fergus, Finlay and Flick | Their children. |
| Toria Clark | Village schoolteacher. |
| Pat Duckett | Village school caretaker. |
| Dean and Michelle | Her children. |
| Jimmy Glover | Poacher and ne'er-do-well. |
| Revd Peter Harris MA (Oxon) | Rector of the parish. |
| Dr Caroline Harris | His wife. |
| Muriel Hipkin | Retired solicitor's secretary. Spinster of the parish. |
| Betty McDonald | Licensee of The Royal Oak. |
| 'Mac' McDonald | Her husband. |
| Sharon and Scott | Their children. |
| Patrick Meadows | Nuclear scientist. |
| Suzy Meadows | His wife. |
| Daisy, Pansy and Rosie | Their children. |
| Neville Neal | Accountant. |
| Liz Neal | His wife. |
| Guy and Hugh | Their children. |
| Michael Palmer | Village school headmaster. |
| Sir Ralph Templeton | Retired from the Diplomatic Service. |
| Vera Wright | Cleaner at nursing home in Penny Fawcett. |
| Rhett Wright | Her grandson. |

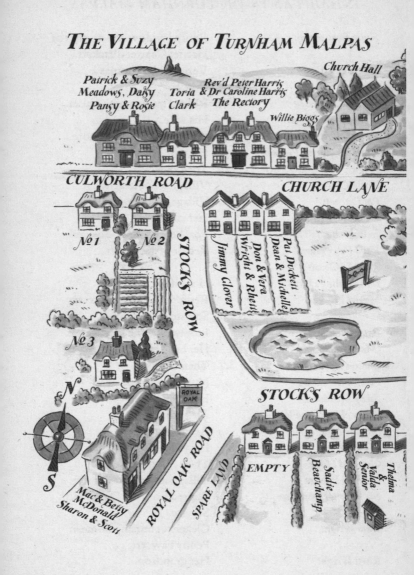

St Thomas à Becket

Muriel Hipkin

FOR SALE

Liz & Neville Neal Guy & Hugh

GLEBE COTTAGES

GLEBE HOUSE

CHURCH LANE

Jimbo & Harriet Charter-Plackett Fergus, Finlay & Flick Village Store

JACK'S LANE

School House Michael Palmer

STOCKS ROW

Swimming Pool

Turnham Malpas School

SHEPHERDS HILL

Sir Ronald & Lady Bissett pond

Methodist Chapel

SPARE LAND

BECK

TURNHAM

footbridge

FD'01

# Chapter 1

Muriel Hipkin turned over in bed to look at her floral china bedside clock. It said a quarter to eight – another fifteen minutes before she needed to rise. It was Easter Sunday today, such a special day in the Christian calendar, and this particular Easter Sunday was extra special, for the new Rector would be taking his first service. The Reverend Peter Alexander Harris MA (Oxon) was young and full of vigour, so different from dear Mr Furbank. She'd always had hopes of dear Mr Furbank, but now he'd died and so suddenly, too, and it was too late. Too late for lots of things.

Her tiny bedroom caught the first shafts of sun each morning and she lay revelling in its warmth. The neat floral curtains with their tiny pattern matched the neat floral bedspread. The carpet was cream with a tiny pattern on it, too. This was the first house she'd ever lived in where the choice of colours and furniture had been her own, her very own. Before, it had always been Mother's choice – nice, sensible dark reds and browns, lifeless and 'practical'. That particular bondage had been laid to rest four years ago. Muriel had been a willing slave but it wasn't until her

Mother passed over Jordan that she realised how she had been bound hand and foot. Her money kept the house and fed them, her money paid the bills for the special foods and the extra warmth, but she'd made none of the decisions.

Released from her chains, she'd returned to the village of Turnham Malpas where she had been born, and bought this 'starter home' – except that for her, it would be the starter *and* the finisher. No moving up to better things. This was it – till she needed constant care in a home, heaven forbid. The house was tiny. It had one living room out of which a square was taken to provide a minute kitchen. In the back corner of the living room was a spiral staircase which led to the small landing, hardly bigger than a doormat. Upstairs was one bedroom, and one miniscule bathroom. Not even a space for the vacuum cleaner, which had to live under the spiral stairs. Its compensation was that it was built alongside the churchyard. Glebe Cottages, the little row was called. No one else wanted Muriel's house, with its view of the ancient graves and the lych gate and the church, but it had a large garden which curved comfortably around the churchyard wall. Muriel loved gardening, and hers was the pride of the village. She'd won so many prizes at the annual Village Show the two years she'd been entering, it was becoming embarrassing. Maybe this year she wouldn't enter anything at all and give everyone else a chance.

Eight o'clock. As the church clock chimed the last stroke, Pericles came tip-tapping up the stairs. His bright brown eyes sparkled with delight as he flung himself on Muriel's bed. His snow-white fur contrasted sharply with his bright black nose.

'Off the bed, Perry, you naughty dog! Get off.' He leapt down and sprang about the bedroom, looking for slippers or shoes to race off downstairs with. Muriel got up and

2

chased him out. Looking through her bedroom window, she could just see the back garden of the village store. Eight o'clock on Sundays, James Charter-Plackett – new owner of what was the village shop, but which now gave the appearance of being a miniature Harrods Food Hall – stood naked on the side of his brand-new pool and dived in, shallowly, for the pool was not really deep enough but it was the only way he could force himself to take his morning exercise.

Harriet Charter-Plackett, also naked, followed him in. Muriel could just glimpse them as they stood side by side on the pool edge. She'd once seen her father undressed when she was nursing him through his last illness and had been somewhat surprised, but James, or 'Jimbo' as he preferred to be called, was the first man she'd actually had a chance to take a good look at. This cavorting naked in the garden had caused a minor scandal when the couple first started doing it, but the locals now accepted it as one of the idiosyncrasies of a townie. Besides, they liked the revival of their village shop. Mrs Thornton's fly-blown cakes and tired lettuces and the cigarette ash dusting everything was no longer acceptable in 1990. After all, you had to move with the times, hadn't you? It was time for a change.

Muriel glanced at her slim figure shrouded in its long cotton nightgown – white, of course. In school photographs Mother had only to look for the palest blob of a face to find it was Muriel. She was still a pale blob. Pale skin, pale blue eyes, pale fair hair, and that was going paler still now it had white streaks in it. In strong sun she was almost obliterated. At boarding school (only a minor one – her parents couldn't afford one of the better ones) she had been taught to undress without the necessity of revealing any part of her anatomy. It was unseemly to expose oneself, the

Anglican nuns had declared. Muriel often wondered how much their teaching had influenced her relationships in later years. They'd taught her embarrassment and shyness and modesty to such an extent that she had never been able to communicate properly with the opposite sex – except for dear Mr Furbank, of course. Some people might have sniggered that maybe he wasn't of the opposite sex, anyway, and that was why she got on with him so well. She straightened her shoulders; she must correct her habit of stooping.

Her bathroom was dedicated to cleanliness. Crisp clean towels, snow-white, lay in regimented rows interspersed with fresh face cloths. They were all crisp to the touch for they'd been blowing on the line for the best part of a day getting dried and 'freshened up'. She actually had seven face cloths, one for each day of the week. All white. That way you knew when they were clean. The walls were white, the bath, basin and lavatory were white; the floor had white tiles, the curtains were white, the ceiling, the taps, the towel rail . . . all virginal, like Muriel. She had an all-over wash first thing in the morning, after having been in bed all night.

Baths she kept for evenings. She would lie in the scented water with the bathroom light turned off, and just the moonlight creeping into the corners of the room. She would dwell on life and its meaning, though she never had many answers. Sometimes she pondered what her life would have been like if she had married. Children, perhaps four. All nice clean little girls with pretty faces and nice blonde curly hair. Clever at school and well-mannered, not like that young Sharon McDonald from The Royal Oak, all boldness and flashing hips and eyes. Her girls would be sweet and well-behaved. She would prepare lovely meals for her husband each evening when he came home from the office. He would have a military moustache and fair hair, he'd be tall and fresh-complexioned, and he would be gentle and amusing to be with. Occasionally, though, when soaking in the bath she would see her life endlessly unfolding before her and would weep at its barrenness and isolation. Then, like the good Christian that she was, she would count her blessings and begin to scrub herself vigorously so she would go to bed immaculately clean.

Everything clean, as on every day in the week, Muriel descended the spiral stairs with care. Another ten years and she could have problems with those stairs. Perry dashed to the door to be let into the garden. She'd taught him to relieve himself in one particular spot so that she could disinfect the area each day. He was usually very good. She warmed her blue and white teapot, which matched her breakfast set, with boiling water, preparing it lovingly for brewing her tea. Muriel loved the delicate blue flowers which danced up the spout and around the lid. The handle of her cup had flowers climbing up it, too. She'd chosen the set with a picture in her mind's eye of her little dining table, hardly bigger than a card table, in the window of her living room. The small silver toast-rack awaited its load, the honey pot, matching, gleamed alongside the silver sugar bowl with its air of Georgian gentility, also matching. A bowl of All Bran followed by toast and honey – her breakfast unchanged since her chains fell off – was augmented by a banana this Sunday morning. A little treat to mark the special day.

When the kitchen was tidy again Muriel glanced at the clock. Time for Pericles' walk. The back door locked, she took his lead from the hook behind it – a hook shared with her neat white and blue flowered apron which matched the tea cosy and the oven gloves. Hearing the rattle of the lead,

Pericles began chasing round in circles, yapping. Poodles did yap a lot, but she didn't mind. The gardens at the front of Glebe Cottages were open plan so she had to watch that Pericles didn't forget his manners.

Straight ahead was Jacks Lane, which ran between the school and the back garden of the village store. On school days she chatted to the children on their way to school and they loved to pat Pericles and ask her why he had such a funny name. Today being Sunday, the school was silent, resting from its labours. Over the wall she could see poor Mr Palmer sitting reading his newspaper on the garden bench. His schoolhouse came with the job. Muriel always pitied him – a widower in such tragic circumstances. Of course the village had stood by him, but there were murmurs which wouldn't be stilled. He'd stayed on with the stuffing knocked out of him, but for all that the children loved him and he was an excellent head teacher.

There must be nearly forty children in the school now. It had dwindled to five at one time and the County said they would close it. Then in moved these townies with their families, fancying a country life, and then the Big House had been turned into a home for children at risk, so they, too, had helped to fill up the school. What they were at risk from, Muriel wasn't quite sure. That tale Willie Biggs the verger had told her simply didn't make sense. She read things in the papers which she couldn't make head nor tail of, but there you were, they still needed loving like all children.

'Morning, Miss Hipkin. I got four eggs this morning.' Finlay Charter-Plackett was sitting astride the stone wall surrounding his parents' garden.

'Oh, good morning and A Happy Easter to you, Finlay!'

'Did you get an egg, Miss Hipkin?'

'No, dear, I've no one to give me one.'

'Here – have this Cadbury's creme egg. Mummy's got plenty in the shop.'

'I couldn't, dear, really I couldn't. Your mother wouldn't like it.'

Harriet Charter-Plackett, now fully clothed, emerged from between the conifers and looked over the wall into the lane. 'That's all right, Miss Hipkin, of course you must have it. I like my children to be generous. Happy Easter to you.'

'Oh, thank you very much. I shall eat it this afternoon with my cup of tea. Bye bye.'

Pericles was in a hurry to be let off the lead. She crossed Shepherd's Hill and went into the opening onto the spare land behind the tiny Methodist Chapel. There she undid the little dog's lead and he raced off to his favourite spots. It seemed ridiculous that he could find such enjoyment every day from sniffing the same clumps of grass. The new coat of paint on the chapel walls had helped to improve it but, oh dear, it *was* so bleak and austere. Muriel much preferred the gentle beauty of her St Thomas à Becket, with its stained-glass windows, the banners, the altar and the flowers. There would be Easter lilies from the glasshouses at the Big House this week. A bit severe, but a delightful change from the usual fussy arrangements done by Lady Bissett. How could anyone be knighted for being a trades union official and be called Sir Ron? Sir Ronald and Lady Bissett. Before the knighthood he'd always been known as Ron Bissett. Now it was Sir Ronald. How could he justify accepting a knighthood? It went against everything he had ever stood for, surely? Lady Sheila Bissett believed she had assumed the mantle of the squire's wife, but only in her own mind; everyone else knew she'd been serving behind the bar in

The Case Is Altered in Culworth before she married, and unfortunately had never left it behind. She carried the aura of it with her wherever she went.

'Good morning, Miss Hipkin. Happy Easter to you.'

Muriel blushed bright red. Lady Bissett's Pomeranian sniffed at Pericles.

'Good morning, Lady Bissett, and A Happy Easter to you, too.'

'See you in church later on. Bye bye.'

It was so embarrassing. Of course Lady Bissett couldn't read her mind but she felt as if she could.

Muriel glanced at her watch and decided to take the short cut across the green as time was running short. No ducklings yet on the pond. The oak, well the Royal Oak, was coming into bud again. Two years ago, it had looked as if it were dying but it had perked up again. When the Royal Oak died, the village would die, too – that was what everyone believed. But the village was beginning to throb with life again, with new people, new ideas. As she waited to cross Church Lane, the new rector – Peter, he asked everyone to call him – crossed from the Rectory into the churchyard. He waved to her and called a cheery 'Happy Easter!' She waved back and for a moment wished it was dear Mr Furbank; she could have made him very happy. The two of them there in the Rectory tending the Lord's garden and watching His little flowers grow. In our dear Lord's garden. Ah well, you couldn't put back the clock.

The morning service began at ten o'clock. The children were already in their places when Muriel entered. Willie Biggs gave her a wink. That man would never improve. Dear Mr Furbank should never have given him the job; he was misguided there. Muriel wore her navy suit with the Sunray pleated skirt and a buttercup-yellow blouse. Her navy straw had buttercup-yellow flowers decorating the brim; she only ever wore it on Easter Sundays. One of her navy gloves had developed a hole but they would have to do. No one would notice if she carried it and wore the other. Organ music flooded the church. Just as Mrs Peel the organist arrived at a particularly triumphant bit, Sir Ron and Lady Bissett came down the aisle to take their places. In less polite circles his stomach would have been described as a beer belly. He had grown his white hair quite long and wore it brushed back without a parting, while his florid face and heavy jowls implied good living, which earlier stalwarts of the trade union movement would have scorned. Muriel found his hale and hearty personality overwhelming.

The church was filled this morning, partly because it was Easter and partly because the whole village wanted to hear the new rector.

The processional hymn began and they all stood. Peter wore a beautiful surplice decorated with heavy antique lace. He made an impressive figure with his thick hair forming a bronze halo around his head. His broad shoulders seemed designed to carry any burden asked of them, and at six feet five he towered above the verger and the choirmen as well as the boys. He ought to be a bishop, Muriel thought. Suzy Meadows, mother of three and new to the village, thought he was sizzlingly attractive. Daisy, Pansy and Rosie sat beside her in front of Muriel wriggling and giggling. Muriel wished they hadn't decided to sit near her, they were so distracting in their loveliness. So sweet and so alike, except for their size. Daisy was five and round, Pansy four and very thin and Rosie three and just right. All pretty and blonde like their mother. Patrick Meadows never came to church. He worked somewhere in one of those secret nuclear places and never joined in family life at all.

After the hymn had been sung and the congregation was settling down, in came the rector's wife, looking harassed and breathless. She was so feminine and pretty. Her dark curly hair was cut short in a no-nonsense style, but the curls still made themselves evident. She had a clear ivory skin and bright blue eyes. She rushed down the aisle, sat in the rectory pew and hastily knelt on the specially embroidered kneeler with symbols appropriate to a rector's wife. It hadn't had any use while dear Mr Furbank had been there, for he'd lacked a wife all the thirty years he'd been the incumbent. Muriel had been delighted that at last there was to be a rector's wife, but her hopes had been dashed when she'd learned that Caroline Harris was a hospital doctor in Culworth. Full time, too. No babies or Mothers' Union for her – she belonged to the new breed.

An inspirational sermon followed by uplifting singing and a new modern anthem from the choir made a beautiful Easter morning service. Muriel realised that dear Mr Furbank's sermons had become very dull. She had only enjoyed them because she loved his beautiful enunciation and the gentle aspect of his face.

Peter shook hands enthusiastically with the entire congregation as they left, saying that next Sunday he hoped they would all stay for coffee afterwards in the church hall and he would do his best to get round to see every member during the next few weeks. Willie Biggs winked at Muriel and said out of the corner of his mouth, 'Not quite like the old rector, is he? Got a bit more go, like. You won't be coming with your jars of lemon cheese for this one. He plays squash and runs, he does. Smarten us all up, he will. Bashing tambourines and kissing and hugging we shall be before long, mark my words.'

Lady Bissett came pouring out of the church, hand outstretched.

'My dear Peter, welcome to Turnham Malpas! We're so glad to see you – you're like a blast of fresh air. You've met my husband, of course, but I haven't yet met your dear wife. Ah, here she is. My dear Mrs Harris . . .'

'*Dr* Harris, actually.'

'I'm sorry, Dr Harris. I'm Lady Bissett and this is my husband Sir Ronald.'

Caroline Harris turned to look at Sir Ronald, and Muriel saw a mischievous light come into her eyes.

'I seem to recognise you from the television. Aren't you a TUC person?'

'Oh, he's often on the telly, er – television, aren't you, Ron . . . ald?'

'Frequently. When you've held public office it's hard to keep your face off it.'

'Surely you must be the one who orchestrated that massive strike at the engineering works in Bradley?'

'In all truth I actually tried to stop it, Mrs . . . Dr Harris.'

'Oh, it didn't come across like that on our television,' Caroline said, then she turned to Muriel, still smiling and said: 'You must be Miss Hipkin. Willie Biggs tells me that your family has been in this village since the Conquest.'

'Well, I wouldn't say quite as far back as that, but my ancestors worked in the gardens and the park for generations at the Big House, then when Lady Templeton had to sell up after the war my family moved away and now I've come back to live here again.'

'You must come and have tea with me one day and tell me all about the village. I'll call in and let you know which day I shall be at home and we'll get together.'

Before Muriel could thank her for her kindness, Lady

11

Bissett had edged her way between them and thanked the rector's wife for the invitation. Short of being extremely rude, Dr Harris had to concede the point and include Lady Bissett in her invitation. It quite took the pleasure out of it for Muriel, but then she remembered her Christian duty and smiled her delight.

Pericles was standing behind the door when she got back from morning service. He'd been terribly sick on the mat. She rushed him out into the back garden, where he was incredibly sick again. Considering what a small dog he was, it was amazing how much he'd had in his stomach. Cleaning the mat put her off her dinner so she put her thick cardigan on and sat in the back garden with him instead. He lay all afternoon looking extremely sorry for himself. About three o'clock, she made herself a cup of tea, put her Cadbury's creme egg on a plate and carried the tray into the garden. She had a small table out there which she used for potting up but with a scrub it served as a tea table in the warmer weather. The creme egg did taste lovely – very rich and rather sickly and very indulgent. But she didn't have many pleasures. From her chair, Muriel could just see over the wall into the churchyard. Sunday afternoon was the time when most people who cared took fresh flowers to the graves. The churchyard tap was alongside the gardener's shed near the wall. It was far enough away not to block Muriel's view but near enough for her to see what was going on.

Michael Palmer the headmaster was putting fresh water in the vase from his wife's grave. He came every Sunday, winter and summer. You'd never think he was only forty-five – he looked a good ten years older. Up the path came Sharon McDonald from The Royal Oak. A right little madam, thought Muriel. That skirt couldn't be any shorter nor tighter, and that T-shirt was surely meant to sit equally on her shoulders, not be dragged over to one side so that her whole shoulder was exposed. A man would have to be blind not to notice the flagrant exhibition of her feminine charms. Sharon stood provocatively in front of Mr Palmer, her shrill voice carrying on the wind.

'Hello, Mr Palmer. Remember me?'

'Why, of course, Sharon.' He straightened up, holding the vase full of water in one hand and the flowers in the other. 'It's some time since you were in school but I remember you quite clearly. I don't see you around nowadays.'

'No, I work in Culworth, in Tesco's. Boring, but there's not much else. How are you? Still teaching in this godforsaken little dump?'

'Still teaching, Sharon, yes I am. I like it here.' He set off to walk to the grave. Sharon followed, teetering along the rough path in her stilettos. As he crouched down to arrange the flowers, Sharon bent over and rested her hand on his back. Muriel couldn't hear what she said but she saw Michael stand up quickly and move out of her reach. He was shaking his head and protesting. Their conversaion lasted a few more moments, with Michael Palmer still backing away and shaking his head. Sharon seemed to find their conversation a huge joke, and her laughter carried across the churchyard towards Muriel. It sounded cruel. Mr Palmer turned on his heel and marched away with the wrapping paper from the flowers still in his hand. Muriel knew he always put it screwed up into a ball in the bin provided by Willie Biggs. He must be upset. A man of meticulously regular habits, was Mr Palmer. She knew because she played the piano for the singing in the school on Monday and Thursday mornings.

Sharon wandered aimlessly across the churchyard. She

saw Muriel watching so she put her thumb to her nose and waggled her outstretched fingers in Muriel's direction. Muriel turned away. How rude that girl was. Her parents ought to teach her better manners. Still, what could you expect? Running The Royal Oak left Mr and Mrs McDonald little time to spare for Sharon and her brother Scott. He was a rude, arrogant young boy. Mr Palmer said he was very clever but Scott didn't care enough to bother.

Pericles took a turn for the better so Muriel walked him out and then went inside to make a substantial tea for herself. She didn't usually go to church in the evening unless it was something special; instead, she watched the religious programmes on TV, and then perhaps a good play afterwards. TV was her live-saver. Mother wouldn't have it, even though Muriel had offered to pay. Old people can be very tyrannical.

Easter Monday dawned clear and bright but there was nothing of interest planned by Muriel for this day of leisure. Just after she got back from walking Pericles there was a knock at the door. Muriel tucked Pericles under her arm and opened it. Caroline Harris stood there smiling.

'I know you probably have a very busy day booked, with it being a Bank Holiday, but could you possibly fit in afternoon tea with me?'

'Why, good morning, Dr Harris. How nice of you, I'd love to do that! Thank you.'

'Good – come about three. If it's warm we'll sit in the garden. Peter is away today so I shall be glad of your company. See you later, then. Your daffodils do look lovely. I shall be glad of your advice regarding our garden: I'm afraid it's very overgrown.'

For her outing, Muriel chose her pale cream blouse with a brown tweed skirt and a toning brown cardigan – well, rust really. She brushed her hair and tortured it into a French pleat – the style she'd adopted when it was the height of fashion and had never troubled to change since. In honour of the invitation she put on a tiny amount of orangey-brown lipstick. She stepped gently along Church Lane, past the lych gate and Willie Biggs', where she noticed the curtain twitching as she went by, and rang the Rectory bell.

The door was opened by Caroline Harris, her three Siamese cats standing by her feet, their long tails winding around her legs.

'Come in do,' she said warmly. 'I've got some scones in the oven and they're nearly ready. Let's go in the kitchen while they finish cooking.'

Dear Mr Furbank had not been good at housekeeping and Muriel was dreading the embarrassment of his unkempt kitchen; however, Caroline Harris had worked wonders in the few days since they had moved in. The walls had already been painted – a bright melon colour – copper pans gleamed in racks, the old cooker has been burnished to within an inch of its life and a large pine table had replaced the nasty gateleg thing that dear Mr Furbank had used for dining. A huge fridge freezer stood where there had once been a grubby mesh food cupboard. The floor had been sanded and stained, and Indian rugs covered it in a deliberately haphazard manner.

'Why this is beautiful!' Muriel said, looking around with pleasure. 'You've worked miracles in here, and in such a short space of time, too. I love the curtains. Are they Indian?'

'Yes, they are. I went there for six months, working with the down and outs in Calcutta, and brought loads of things back. It's what Peter refers to as my Indian period. Milk and sugar?'

'Just milk, thank you.'

Caroline carried the tray into the garden. It was laid for two.

'Lady Bissett isn't coming, then?' Muriel asked tentatively.

She answered, 'No,' in a manner which rejected any further queries, and then added: 'Will you call me Caroline? I much prefer it. Now, tell me all about your family and what you do in the village, Miss Hipkin.'

Muriel launched herself on a potted family history and then on a brief history of the village. She'd only been back three years but she'd caught up on forty years of happenings in a very short time. Finally, she remembered herself and exclaimed, blushing: 'Oh dear, I've gone rambling on and you've told me nothing about yourself.'

'Miss Hipkin, there isn't much to tell,' Caroline laughed. 'Peter and I have been married five years. I've thrown myself into my work to compensate for the fact that I can't have children. We're both very disappointed but there you are. It's my fault and nothing can alter it.'

A door slammed in the Rectory and Peter himself came into the garden, bearing a mug. He leant over Caroline and kissed her, cupping her chin with his spare hand. 'Mind if I join you?' he said, addressing them both.

'You're back early,' his wife remarked.

'Yes, I am. How are you, Miss Hipkin?'

'Very well, thank you. I should like it very much if you would both call me Muriel. It seems more friendly.'

'Certainly we shall.' Peter took a huge bite out of a scone as he said this, then, with his mouth full: 'I thought Lady Bissett was coming today as well?'

'No.' Caroline offered no further enlightenment regarding Lady Bissett so Peter turned to Muriel.

'I shall tread very carefully about making changes here,' he told her, 'but changes there will have to be. We need to do more to encourage the local children. Do you have any ideas?'

'I have often thought that there are a lot of little ones on the farms and in the more isolated houses who could well do with one of those nursery schools. That way they get used to mixing with other children before they actually start school. I play the piano for the singing on Mondays and Thursdays for Mr Palmer and I do notice that the new ones have great difficulty learning to join in.'

'What a perfectly splendid idea. We could use the church hall, couldn't we?'

Muriel considered this and then said, 'It would take some manoeuvring, because there is a yoga class and a ladies' quilting group which meet regularly in the mornings – and Lady Bissett has a flower-arranging group there, too. But I'm sure the timetable could be adjusted.'

'I shall see to that immediately. All we need is someone willing to organise it. I'll talk to some of the mothers with small children, as they might do it as a group rather than having just one person in charge. What do you think, Caroline?'

'The Council will have something to say about facilities. Perhaps it could start as a mother and toddler group until proper permission has been obtained.'

Peter stood up and went to kiss his wife on the top of her head. 'What would we do without your common sense?'

Shortly after this, Muriel left. Pericles would be getting restless, she said, and thanked them for a lovely afternoon. Peter accompanied her to the door.

What a charming young man he was. Just what the village needed.

# Chapter 2

Peter Alexander Harris prayed in his church every morning from six-thirty until seven o'clock. Having dealt with the spiritual he then attended to the physical and ran a circuit of roughly three miles round the parish. Turning in at the Rectory door, he jogged straight up to the bathroom and took a shower, singing vigorously whilst he did so. As soon as the singing stopped Caroline began preparing his breakfast: two Weetabix, with full-cream milk and a banana chopped up on the top, followed by a boiled egg with wholemeal toast and plenty of butter and marmalade. Having concluded his daily ritual he then turned his attention to Caroline.

'Come here, my darling girl, and spend some time with me before you disappear into the vampire department.'

'Vampire department? Peter, that is dreadful! Don't let any of your parishioners hear you say that, or they'll get terrible ideas about what I do.'

'Tell me why you didn't let Lady Bissett come to tea on Monday.'

'It's not often I take an instant dislike to people, but I'm afraid Sheila Bissett and I will be clashing swords before

18

long. If she conducted herself as the person she really is I could quite like her, but instead she gives herself such airs. She honestly believes she is the modern equivalent of the squire's wife. I know for a fact she used to work behind the bar in The Case Is Altered in Culworth.'

'Who told you that?'

'Willie Biggs. If you need to know anything about anybody, ask Willie. I've made a point of becoming a friend of his.'

'How have you done that?'

'By diagnosing his ailments for him.'

'Caroline!' Peter tipped her off his knee and pretended to slap her bottom for her. Caroline laughed, kissed him full on the mouth with a lingering relish which reminded Peter how much he loved her, and dashed off to the hospital. Peter cleared the table, washed up and went into his study.

Hearing a noise not unlike the chattering of a brood of nestlings, he glanced out to see what it was, and passing the window was the girl he had noticed in church on Sunday. Her silvery-blonde hair was held back by an Alice band so that her charming rosy-cheeked face could be clearly seen. She had a long, perfectly straight nose, round curving cheeks and brilliant blue eyes. Her colouring was echoed by the three little girls who were walking hand in hand beside her. One was round, one very thin, and one just right. All three had long plaits swinging behind as they hopped and skipped on the pavement. Their mother looked up at the study window and raised her hand in greeting. For some unexplained reason, Peter's heart almost stopped beating. He waved back and then bent his head to open the post. His heart righted itself and he tried hard to concentrate on his work, but couldn't. He was being quite ridiculous. His post that morning was considerable – most of it addressed to the now deceased Revd Arthur Furbank.

The phone rang. 'The Rectory, Peter Harris speaking. How may I help you?'

'It's Michael Palmer here, Headmaster at the village school. Could I possibly come round some time in the next day or two, and have a chat with you? We are a church school so you'll be very much involved.'

'Certainly, I shall be delighted. This is the first time I've been directly concerned with education and I'm looking forward to it. Now, there's no time like the present, is there? I would be free to see you about eleven this morning. How would that suit you?'

'Fine, I'll see you then.'

Peter put down the receiver, leant back in his chair and contemplated the study. Hanging above the fireplace, in which a two-bar electric fire tried defiantly to warm the room, was a crude peasant-like painting of the Virgin Mary. The only thing that was good about it was the face. Who did it remind him of? – Caroline? No, not his darling girl. Then he knew who it was. The over-bright blue eyes and the rounded cheeks reminded him of the girl who'd been in church on Sunday and who had caused his heart to jolt only moments ago. Peter's self-discipline enabled him to push his feelings into the background. He leapt up, took down the painting, and placed in face downwards on top of the filing cabinet. Above the fireplace there was now a light buff-coloured square where the picture had hung. Peter moved another picture from the wall and realised that the wallpaper was very dirty indeed. So were the bookshelves which were waiting for him to unpack the tea chests full of books stacked against the far wall. The carpet was threadbare and dirty, the desk where he worked grimy and slightly sticky to the touch. He should never have agreed to take the Rectory as it stood. He ought to have insisted on furnishing it himself. Caroline had worked wonders with the kitchen; this, being his domain, he would have to work upon by himself.

Within ten minutes of rolling up his sleeves, Peter had removed all the pictures from the walls, and unplugged the ancient electric fire. Once it had cooled down, he put it, flex and all, into the bin. The desk, filing cabinets and the sofa – ancient and falling apart – had all been pulled or pushed into the hall. The easy chairs had been stacked against the hall wall, too, and all that remained was the removal of the carpet. As he began to roll it up, thick dust fell from it and made him cough. He opened the study window and waved his arms about trying to dispel the clouds of dust and found himself once more face to face with Suzy Meadows returning home with Pansy and Rosie. His heart jolted again as he looked into those sweet, Madonna-like features.

'Good morning, Mr Harris. I'm Suzy Meadows, this is Pansy and this is Rosie. Say good morning, you two.' The tiny girls smiled and hid their faces in her skirts.

Peter's voice boomed out onto the pavement. 'Good morning, Mrs Meadows. I'm just—'

'Call me Suzy – everyone else does.'

'Suzy, then. I'm just clearing out the study. Sorry for the dust blowing about.'

'The binmen come on Tuesdays. If you're quick they'll take anything you don't want – and if it's the rector they'll most likely do it for nothing. They'll be along here in about half an hour.'

'Right, thank you. Most of it needs to go.'

'There's a furniture place in Culworth if you're needing some replacements. I bought a lovely pair of hall chairs there for an absolute song. They've always got plenty of easy chairs and things.'

'Thank you for your advice. Hello, Pansy and Rosie. What have you done with your sister?' Neither of the two girls offered a reply so Suzy answered on their behalf.

'Oh, she's gone to play with Hugh Neal in Glebe House. They're both learning the recorder at school and Liz Neal has promised to help Daisy with it. Be seeing you soon, Mr Harris. Bye!'

'Bye.' Peter watched her disappear down the road and recognised his feelings for what they were. Shatteringly, for a man so devoted to his wife and his Church, he felt disastrously attracted by her. Why, he had no idea. It was just one of those things which happened and over which one appeared to have no control. Peter left the clearing of the study and went across to the church. Here, surely, he would find help before it was too late. How could such a thing have happened to him? Every cleric, young in years, had his quota of young women who made sheep's eyes and for a while became devoted to the Church until they realised they were making no progress, but this was it in reverse. He knelt before the altar and prayed. '*Dear God, help me a miserable sinner . . .*'

Willie Biggs, needing a rest from labouring in the graveyard, crept quietly into the church by a side door and sat munching his morning break in the gloom by one of the pillars. His Mars bar was nearly finished when he spotted the rector, head bent in prayer. Funny that, he thought – only halfway through the morning and needing to recharge his batteries. Already been here for half an hour first thing. The man must be troubled. Willie kept silent and still, hoping Peter wouldn't see him when he went out and Peter didn't, because he went across to the organ and, switching it on, began playing a jaunty hymn tune. Willie, whenever he heard the organ being played, always thanked the good Lord that it no longer required him to work the bellows at the back. Years he'd done that, till some benefactor or other, needing to put in a good word with God before departing this life, had paid for it 'to be electrocuted' as Willie described it. My word, he thought, now that Rector can't half play. Mrs Peel'll have to look to her laurels and no mistake. The music throbbed through the church with a kind of lively triumph which Willie found quite moving. Brass band music was more to his personal taste, but he mightily appreciated the beauty of the rector's playing.

Peter concluded his performance with a flourish, switched off the organ and quietly made his way home. He heated a pot of coffee and carried the tray with two cups on it into the sitting room. As he put down the tray the doorbell rang.

Standing on the step was Michael Palmer, schoolmaster extraordinaire of Turnham Malpas for the last twenty years. What had been meant as a stepping stone had become a millstone, and here he was still teaching a new generation of children, holding onto life by the merest thread. His square, weatherbeaten face topped by thinning hair smiled benignly at Peter, who stood looking down upon him from his great height, Michael reaching only five feet six in his socks. The two men shook hands and Michael winced at the strength of Peter's grip.

'Delighted to meet you, Mr Harris. Or shall I call you Peter?'

'Yes, please. Coffee?'

'Thank you, black, please. It seems odd using your Christian name. We always knew the previous incumbent as Mr Furbank – it would have felt impudent to have called him anything else. It was time we had some new blood;

he'd been here far too long. Sorry for being outspoken, but it's the truth. Mr Furbank took a great deal of interest in the children but I'm afraid he didn't have the right touch and I had difficulty preventing the children from giggling at his absent-minded ways. He came into school every Friday morning to take prayers and then gave the children a little talk of some kind. I don't expect you to follow exactly in his footsteps, so I wondered what kind of presence you would like to have?'

Peter took a sip of his coffee whilst deciding how to answer. 'I should very much like to take prayers one morning a week, but how about if it was held in the church?'

'What a good idea.'

'I'm very keen to encourage the children of the village to come into church and centre their lives around activities here. I intend to start Beavers and Brownies as soon as I can find suitable helpers, and also Muriel Hipkin has suggested that a playgroup would be a good idea. She feels that a lot of the children come into school at five not having any real experience of joining in with other children and knowing how to share. How would you feel about that?'

'I should be delighted – it's a perfectly splendid idea! There are quite a few children from the farms hereabouts who come to school quite afraid of what they have to face. A playgroup would be excellent. Where would you hold it?'

'I had thought of the church hall.'

'If we can get permission from the County we could hold it in the school itself. I have a spare classroom and the facilities like toilets and equipment would all be available with very little extra expense. I'll have a word with my assistant – she takes the infants so she would be more

24

involved than me. I'm sure she'll be delighted.'

'Does your wife help in the school?'

For the moment Michael didn't answer. He carefully placed his cup on the little table, took out his handkerchief and dabbed his moustache dry. Peter noticed his hand was shaking as he put the handkerchief away.

'My wife died three years ago.'

'I'm so sorry. Please forgive me, I didn't know. What an intrusion.'

'Not at all – how were you to know? She did teach, but over in Culworth. No, my assistant is Toria Clark, one of the new breed with plenty of energy and fresh ideas. The children love her.'

Peter put down his cup and offered Michael more coffee. The two of them talked for another hour about the village and the possibilities of change. Peter sensed that Michael was a fine schoolmaster, and Michael thought what a blessing it was for Turnham Malpas that Peter had accepted the living.

To keep himself occupied and push his current problem to the back of his mind, Peter had raided Caroline's plentiful supply of paint in the garden shed and, having washed the walls and paintwork, was finishing putting a muted shade of antique gold on the study walls when he remembered he needed to go to the village store to buy meat for the evening meal.

Jimbo Charter-Plackett stood by the door discussing politics with Sir Ronald. Jimbo was wearing his butcher's apron and straw boater, a get-up he'd adopted to give style to his store. He raised his boater as soon as he recognised the Rector.

'Good afternoon, sir, welcome to Turnham Malpas Village Store. It's an honour to serve you. See you later,

Ron . . . Sir Ronald.' He waved a dismissal to the self-appointed squire and made room for Peter to enter. 'Perfectly ridiculous man. Now, Rector, what can I get for you?'

'Caroline has asked me to buy lamb chops for dinner tonight.'

'Come this way.' Jimbo led him to the meat department. The Charter-Placketts had bought the next door cottage and by pulling down walls and reorganising the space available, they had made an excellent store out of what had originally been a small village shop in the front room of a large cottage.

'I have never seen such an incredible shop in such a small village before,' Peter exclaimed. 'Is there anything you *don't* sell?'

'Not much. You name it we sell it – and if we don't, we soon will.'

'Forgive me for asking, but how on earth do you make it pay?'

'Well, we don't sit here waiting for people to pass the door. We run a mail–order business selling farm products to the nation, and also have a catering business providing food for weddings and the Hunt Ball. This year, we've won a contract for catering for the VIPs at the Game Fair in the next county. I buy almost all our fresh food from the local area and all our cakes in the freezer and on the counter are made by local farmers' wives, so I provide work for the people hereabouts as well as giving a good service to the local inhabitants. I pride myself that there are not many villages with as good a village store as Turnham Malpas. Now, these four chops are on the house, Rector – a small token of our delight at having youth in the Rectory for a change. We loved the old boy but he should have gone years ago. When it comes to the Harvest Supper, Harriet and I would like to provide all the meats free of charge as our contribution.'

'How extremely kind and generous of you, James.'

'Jimbo, if you please. Here, put this box of sugared almonds under your good lady's pillow with love from Harriet and me.'

'You're more than generous, Jimbo – she'll be delighted. Must press on, got to finish painting my study. Thank you very much indeed.'

The lamb chops, delicately flavoured with rosemary and grilled to a turn by Caroline, were a gastronomic delight.

'These chops are a vast improvement on the ones we used to buy in the supermarket, aren't they, darling?'

Caroline, chasing the last of her mint jelly round her plate, nodded her agreement. 'Everything in that shop is fresh,' she enthused. 'The fruit, the vegetables, the cakes, the meat, the cheeses . . . it's a positive wonderland. They must have to work terribly hard, Peter, to keep it all up to scratch. That Jimbo is a bit of a lad, you know. Willie tells me that they swim "nakkid" every day in their pool at the back.'

'Naked, eh? I bet that set the village tongues gossiping.'

'In fact, one could get quite carried away with Jimbo. Harriet must have her work cut out keeping an eye on him.'

'Caroline, really! Is there any of that cheese left that we had last night?'

The sugared almonds came to light when Caroline searched under her pillow for her nightgown.

'Darling, what a lovely surprise! I do love you for it.'

'Don't thank me, thank Jimbo Charter-Placket – he gave them to me for you. Said I should put them under your pillow. Maybe it's a secret method of his for getting his evil

27

way with Harriet.'

'Well, you can have your evil way with me right now.
Hurry up.' She put the box of almonds on her bedside table
and lay on top of the bed 'nakkid' with her arms outstretched in welcome.

Peter made love to reassure himself that everything was
well between his darling girl and himself, but as he fell
asleep the face of Suzy the Madonna floated into his mind.
He rubbed his forehead to push her away.

# Chapter 3

The busy life she led keeping her three girls well cared for, compensated Suzy for the lack of her husband's companionship. He was the archetypal mad scientist. She knew it when she married him so she'd no right to complain, but at the time it had seemed an endearing quality. Now, with lawns to mow and decorating to be done and the new sitting-room fireplace still laid out in pieces on the floor waiting to be fitted, Suzy was feeling bleak. Daisy, Pansy and Rosie were the delight of her life; without them she would have left Patrick by now. She'd willingly given up her career to have babies and had wallowed in motherhood for five years, but right now there was a powerful feeling that her life lacked purpose. Then she laughed at herself. Considering the mound of ironing waiting to be done she didn't need to be looking for anything else to do. But the window wide open and the girls playing in the garden and the daffodils in the narrow-necked glass vase on the kitchen window didn't provide the deeply satisfying feeling that had always lifted her spirits. Lonely, that's what I am – lonely, she thought. She stood ironing Patrick's shirt and felt that this was the closest she came to him nowadays.

He'd provided her with the babies she wanted, and then almost departed this life. Self-absorbed and erratic, he hadn't wanted sex for nearly a year, and she was only thirty-two. Agreed he was forty-five, but the difference in years hadn't seemed to matter to start with, although now it seemed like a yawning void. Maybe all men went off sex when they got to their middle forties – it wasn't really something she could discuss with the mothers from the school. Even the girls all looked like her and not a bit like Patrick. Anyone would think she'd had three virgin births. It seemed as though he'd had nothing to do with them right from the first.

Suzy contemplated how many other wives stood ironing, wondering where their husbands had gone. For all practical purposes they might as well be dead. Perhaps there were thousands of women all over Britain who felt as she did this morning. A new hairstyle, a pretty nightgown, expensive perfume, a special candle-lit dinner when the girls were all in bed . . . she'd tried everything. And it had all been a total waste of time. She held Rosie's tiny socks to her face and enjoyed their warmth and the recalling of Rosie's delightfully happy personality. How she loved them all. For their sakes she had to keep going.

She heard the front door open and then bang shut. Patrick stood in the hall looking shattered. He'd come home to pack a bag en route to America to read a paper at a conference there. The researcher who should have done it had been taken ill and he'd stepped in at the last minute. She made him some sandwiches which he ate while she packed his bag. He was in a tremendous hurry and after he'd left she realised she didn't know which hotel he would be staying at. Still, he would only be gone three or four days at the most; not much could happen during that short period.

The next time she heard someone at the door it was Miss Hipkin. She couldn't expect anything of a world-shattering nature from her.

'Good morning, Miss Hipkin. Do come in.'

'Good morning, Mrs Meadows. Have you a moment to spare?'

'Yes, of course. I'm just going to make a drink for myself and the girls. Would you join us?'

'Oh yes, please. There's nothing I'd like better.'

Muriel stepped eagerly into the hall of Suzy and Patrick's house. Laura Ashley had had a field day here. Muriel loved the delicate grey carpet and the complementary wallpaper. These old houses really were worth the effort of doing them up.

The three little girls stood shyly in the hall watching their visitor. Muriel made a special point of remembering children's names as she felt it was so important to them. Daisy knew her from the infant school music lessons.

'Hello, Daisy and Pansy, and you, little Rosie.'

'Hello, Miss Hipkin. Have you come to see me?' Daisy enquired.

'Well, your mother really, but I'm delighted to see you, Daisy. Are you enjoying the holidays?'

'Want to get back to school, I like that best. After the summer holidays Pansy will be going too.'

'Yes, I know. I saw Mr Palmer putting her name on a list only the other day.'

Suzy brought the girls Ribena and wholesome-looking oatmeal biscuits. Muriel and Suzy had coffee.

'Mrs Meadows . . .'

'Suzy, please.'

'Well, Suzy then, I've come on a little fishing expedition. Peter, you know, Mr Harris is wanting to start a playgroup for the little ones. They are hoping to have it in the church hall, although that's not definite, but they will be looking for someone to lead the group and for other helpers as well. It occurred to me that you might be interested in running the group. I know you were a teacher before the babies came along and I thought you would be an ideal person. Mr Harris, Peter, you know, doesn't know I've come to see you, so it's all very secret at the moment.'

'You must be the answer to a prayer. I would *love* to do it. What an opportunity! I could bring Rosie with me because she's the right age. Oh, Miss Hipkin, I could kiss you! In fact, I will!'

Suzy stood up, took Muriel by the shoulders and gave her a hearty kiss on each cheek. 'Seeing as we're in the Common Market you can have a continental kiss.'

Muriel hadn't been kissed since she couldn't remember when. Her mother hadn't been one for kissing, and there wasn't anyone else. She blushed bright red.

'It isn't definite yet, because Mr Harris doesn't know I'm here, but if you seriously mean you want to do it then I'll have a word.'

'Oh, I do, I do. It will be such an advantage for the children to have a playgroup. Just think of all the children on the farms and the ones from the Big House. Those poor little mites will be in their seventh heaven.'

'This coffee is lovely, thank you very much for it. I'll go and see the rector now and tell him of our plan. Dr Harris says she thinks it will have to be a mother and toddler group until we get proper permission from the County. We must walk before we run. Bye bye, dear girls.'

'Bye bye, Miss Hipkin,' they said, their mouths full of crumbly biscuit.

'My head's exploding with plans, Miss Hipkin. I shan't

be able to sleep tonight for thinking about it.'

'Mr Meadows won't mind, will he? I know some men can be funny about their wives having jobs outside the home.'

'Oh, don't worry about Patrick. He probably won't even notice I'm doing it. Anyway, men don't mind wives having jobs nowadays. Let me know as soon as you can about the playgroup. Liz Neal would probably help as well.'

'Of course, I'd forgotten about her. Bye bye . . . Suzy.'

Muriel stepped along past the infant teacher's cottage to the Rectory and rang the bell.

Peter answered the door wearing his decorating trousers and an old shaggy jumper relegated to the bin by Caroline but rescued just in time.

'Come in, Muriel, you've caught me finishing painting my study. How do you like the colour I've chosen?'

'Lovely, it's really lovely. I'd no idea this room could be so light. What a difference! The white woodwork sets it off so nicely. It takes courage to choose such strong colours. I'm afraid my house is white or magnolia and that's that. I've really come to see you on parish business. You remember we were talking about starting a playgroup? Well, I think – with your approval of course – that I've found the very person to be the leader.'

'That's excellent, Muriel. Who is it?'

'Suzy Meadows. She can take little Rosie with her and when I mentioned it she jumped at the chance.'

Peter turned to look out of the window to hide his consternation. Muriel awaited his grateful thanks.

'She used to be a teacher, you know, before the girls were born and I think she would enjoy getting back into the fray, so to speak.'

'What a good idea, Muriel. I should never have thought

33

of asking her. Are you sure it won't be too much for her with those three girls to look after and her . . . husband?'

'This new generation of women are much more energetic and determined than their mothers used to be. She's very keen.'

'Very well. We'll get the ball rolling. I'll make arrangements to meet her and get down to brass tacks. Thank you for being so inspired, Muriel.'

'Not at all. I'm looking forward to it all starting. Good morning, Rector. I'll see myself out.' And Muriel shut the Rectory door behind her.

Her next stop was the village store, where both Harriet and Jimbo were working. As Muriel entered, Harriet was serving Sharon and Scott from The Royal Oak.

Sharon was choosing her shopping with a disdainful expression on her face. 'You haven't got no convenience foods, have you, like what we sell in Tesco's. Lovely Chicken Kiev and things all ready to pop in the oven, we have there. Scott, put that KitKat down. Mum said you weren't to have no more chocolate today.'

'Shut up you, I'll do as I like.' Scott picked up the KitKat, tore off the wrapper and began eating it.

Jimbo fumed. 'You'll have that to pay for, Sharon.'

'He can pay for it himself, I'm not paying.'

'Can't, our Sharon. Haven't got no money.'

'Wait till I get you home, I'll tell Mum about this.'

'If you do I'll tell her about where you were last night.'

Muriel felt compelled to intervene. 'That's not the way to talk to your sister, Scott. You should pay for it. Come to think of it, you shouldn't have taken the chocolate in the first place if your mother says you shouldn't.'

'Shut up, Miss Prim Hipkin. Miss Neat an' Tidy, Miss Dull an' Boring, mind your own business.'

34

'Well really.' Muriel blushed bright red. This nasty little boy had spoken out loud something she'd been thinking about herself for quite a while. But it was disconcerting to hear the truth from one so young.

Jimbo marched round from the cheese counter, took hold of Scott by his collar and removed him from the store.

'Out, you, and stay out. You can come back in when you've apologised for your bad behaviour. And if your father wants to know why I've sent you packing, ask him to come round to see me.'

Sharon didn't even have the grace to apologise for her brother. She paid for the goods she'd bought and sauntered out of the shop, putting her tongue out at Muriel as she went.

Harriet sat Muriel down on a chair and gave her a coffee from the machine provided for customers.

'Sit here, Miss Hipkin, and drink this. I'm sorry he was so rude. The parents are to blame, not him – remember that.'

Jimbo was fuming. 'And you remember, Harriet, that Scott McDonald is not allowed in here until he has apologised – and I mean it.'

'Jimbo, The Royal Oak is a very good customer of ours.'

'I know, I know, but I won't have him in. He'll be shoplifting next.'

Muriel found her tongue. 'He's very difficult in school, you know. Mr Palmer has to keep him on a tight rein. He always plays up in music lessons.'

'Doesn't get enough attention at home, I suppose.' Harriet had turned away to press on with collecting ingredients for some cheesecakes she was making for the freezer.

Jimbo went into the meat department to find some trimmings from a hindquarter of beef that he'd just cut into joints for a customer. He presented them to Muriel in a smart dark green plastic bag with 'Turnham Malpas Village Store' printed on it.

'To Pericles from Jimbo with his compliments.'

'How kind you are, Mr Charter-Plackett. Pericles will enjoy himself. You indulge him too much.'

'Not at all, it's my pleasure.'

After Muriel had made her purchases she wandered off home. As she paused to check the road before she crossed, Scott McDonald approached from the green and, ramming something into her shopping bag, ran off laughing. When she looked inside she found his KitKat wrapper. He'd quite spoilt her day. It had begun so well, solving the problem of the playgroup leader and admiring Peter's colour scheme and looking forward to shopping for her little bits and pieces – and now Scott had ruined it all. She couldn't demean herself by speaking to Mr McDonald. She didn't go into The Royal Oak: ladies didn't. She had to hope it would all blow over. However, Pericles enjoyed his fresh meat and eventually her usual cheerfulness reasserted itself.


Muriel's visit had left Suzy Meadows all of a dither.

'Come on, girls, we'll go round to Mrs Neal's and tell her about the playgroup. I know it's not official but I'm bursting to talk to someone about it.'

Rosie shrugged on her anorak and asked her mother what a playgroup was.

'A school for little girls and boys who are not old enough to go to Mr Palmer's school.'

'Where?'

'In the church hall, I expect.'

'Oh.' Rosie popped her thumb in her mouth whilst she sorted out her feelings about it.

Liz was pruning her roses in the front garden. Guy and Hugh were racing madly about on their bikes.

'Liz, I just had to come round. Muriel Hipkin has told me that the rector is thinking of starting a playgroup in the church hall and she is going to suggest me as the leader.'

'I know, I know.'

'How do you know?'

'Peter's been round to see me this morning. It's not going to be in the church hall – well, it might be to start with – but then with any luck it will be moved to that spare room in the Infants.'

'Liz, has he asked you to be leader?'

'Of course not, I'm not a teacher. He just wanted to know if I would be willing to help you, and help form a committee.'

'Would you mind working with me?'

'I'd love to. We both need some kind of outlet and this would be just the thing. Hugh, leave Pansy alone – she doesn't want to ride your bike. Stop it, please. Let's all go inside and get Chinese Checkers out or something. Come on, all of you.'

When Suzy left Liz's house she decided to take the bull by the horns and call on Peter.

He answered the door and invited them all inside.

'I hope you don't mind me coming to call,' Suzy began rather shyly. 'Have I caught you when you're busy on anything? No? Well, Miss Hipkin has been round to ask if I might be interested in starting a playgroup and I've come to say yes, I'd be delighted.'

Peter had lifted Pansy onto his knee and given her his watch to play with. Rosie was trying hard to get it off her.

'Let me see if I can find something for you to play with.' He opened a drawer in his desk and took out paper and a pencil. 'There you are – draw me a picture. I would be delighted, too, if you would do it,' he said, finally meeting Suzy's bright blue eyes. 'We need enthusiasm but we also need expertise, and it will make it much easier for us to get the use of the room in the school if the person in charge is known to be properly qualified for the job. I envisage a really lively playgroup doing a real job, not just keeping the children out of their mothers' ways. Would that be how you would feel about it?'

'Yes, of course. It will make Toria Clark's job so much easier if the new intake have had the experience of a good playgroup. Liz Neal is very willing to help. I don't know about charges, though. I'll ask around some of my friends in London and see what they pay.'

'I hadn't thought about charges, but of course there will have to be one. You ask around and I'll draft a letter for the Council and get someone to come down and view our facilities. If we can have it in the school that would be the best. If not, the church hall.'

'I won't keep you any longer, Peter. Come along, girls. Isn't it exciting? I can't wait to get started!'

'My daddy's gone to America this morning.' Pansy looked up at Peter as she told him her news.

'Oh, I see. Will he be away long?'

'No, just three or four days.' Suzy took hold of Rosie and set off for the door.

Peter saw them out and stood watching them walk along the pavement. They lived next door but one. He heartily wished it hadn't been Suzy who was the most suitable candidate for the job.

Two days later Suzy, her head full of lists and jobs to do towards the successful opening of the playgroup, answered a knock at the door. Expecting it to be Muriel with more news about the project, she had a shock when she found a policewoman and what looked like two detectives standing there. The older man showed her his warrant card and then asked if she was Mrs Patrick Meadows.

'Yes, I am.'

'May we come in?'

'Yes.'

They stood looking at one another in a group in the hall.

Finally the policewoman said, 'I'm afraid we have some bad news for you, Mrs Meadows. It's your husband. I'm sorry to say he has died.'

'*Died?* You must be mistaken – he's in America. No, no, you've got it all wrong. It must be another Patrick Meadows. My husband is giving a paper to the Commission. He'll be home tomorrow – won't he?' Her voice trailed off as she recognised the embarrassed sympathy in the faces of the officers.

The policewoman took her into the sitting room and helped her to a chair.

'I'll go and make a cup of tea for you, Mrs Meadows. Where are the children?'

'How do you know I've got children?'

The policewoman pointed to the bottom bookshelf where the children kept their books.

'They're at my mother's for a couple of days. I'll make the tea.' She started to get up out of the chair but the WPC gently pushed her back down again and disappeared into the kitchen. The two detectives stood in front of her. The younger one was looking about the room as though expecting clues to come leaping out of the walls.

Suzy managed to find some words to say. 'How did he . . . how did . . . what happened?'

'He died in his car.'

'You mean he had an accident?'

'Well, no, it appeared to be intentional.'

'Intentional? What do you mean, "intentional"?'

'He used the exhaust pipe and a piece of hose.'

'You mean *suicide*? Patrick wouldn't commit suicide. He's not that kind of person!'

'In view of the top secret job he was doing, Mrs Meadows, could we be allowed to look through his papers and belongings to see if we can find a reason for what has happened? If not today, perhaps another day when you're feeling more able to cope.'

'Where was he when he . . . he . . . did it?'

'He was found this morning at first light. He'd parked his car on the cliffs near Flamborough Head in Yorkshire.'

'Oh well, it definitely isn't Patrick then, because he went to America three days ago. I packed his case for him.'

'He never actually left the country, Mrs Meadows. He had no passport, no currency, no ticket – nothing to indicate that that was what he intended to do.'

'He said he was going. He never told lies – he was scrupulously honest.'

'Had he been behaving oddly recently?'

'He always behaved oddly. Everyone thought he was odd, but it was normal for him. His mind was always preoccupied with his work; he didn't socialise or bother with the children. There was nothing different about him that day he left.'

'We found this letter addressed to you. I'll put it here on the mantelpiece and then you can read it when you feel ready. If there is anything in it that might throw light on his state of mind or why he did it we'd be glad to know.'

'Thank you. That's his desk over there. You can look in it

40

if you wish.'

Suzy laid her head back, unable to grasp what had happened. Her mind was racing over the happenings of the last few weeks before Patrick had left for America. Had there been some clues which she'd failed to recognise? Suddenly she shot bolt upright. 'However am I going to tell the children? Oh dear God, what am I going to do?'

The matter-of-fact voice of the policewoman broke in with a kindly, 'Here's your tea, Mrs Meadows.' She didn't notice that the tea was scalding hot, she was so thirsty. The senior one of the two detectives had begun searching Patrick's desk: methodically, drawer by drawer, file by file, letter by letter. His filofax was in the top drawer. Suzy knew when she saw the detective begin to look through it that Patrick had never intended to go to America. He took the filofax with him whenever he left the house. It was filled with names, addresses and messages, all necessary to his work. So he had acted out of character, even before he'd left for work that last morning.

'He was frightened – that was it. He was frightened that morning when he left,' Suzy told the policewoman in a shaking voice. 'I don't know what he was frightened of, but he was.'

'Did you do much entertaining of people from the office or the laboratories, Mrs Meadows?'

'Well, sometimes we did, but not often. Patrick wasn't a very social being. Occasionally we had people from abroad. They stayed here – they liked the idea of the typical English village.'

'What nationality were they?'

'Middle Eastern sometimes, or European, and once an American.'

'Was everything all right between the two of you? You

know, were you close enough for him to confide in you?'

Suzy felt as though she was carved out of wood. Her face didn't work properly and she'd lost her voice. There was no part of her of which she was in command. All control had gone. Slowly tears began to trickle down her face. Not huge rolling streams of tears but a steady trickle like drizzling rain. She knew she'd have to get to the lavatory quickly or she was going to wet herself. She found herself in the cloakroom, where she suffered violent diarrhoea. It must have been almost ten minutes before she had sufficient control to leave. The policewoman knocked on the door twice to ask if she was in need of help but Suzy's voice had gone and she couldn't reply. Finally she came out and went back to the sitting room. She sat trembling uncontrollably. The room was so cold.

'We'll leave now, Mrs Meadows. I'm taking this filofax to the station to see if I can find anything that might be of help. I'll give you a receipt for it. Debra will stay with you. If there's anything you think of that might be of help, tell Debra and she'll let us know.' The three of them went into the hall and Suzy could hear them quietly talking. Debra came back in, took off her jacket and sat down in the chair opposite her.

A few minutes after the detectives had gone the door-bell rang. Debra answered it. Whoever was at the door was invited in and stood talking in the hall. The sitting-room door opened and framed in the doorway with his head bent because of his height stood Peter Harris. He was wearing his white marriage cassock. He appeared to Suzy like an angel sent from God to comfort her.

'Mrs Meadows, I saw the police car outside so I came to see if you needed help. The policewoman has told me what's happened. I'm so sorry.'

Peter took her hands in his and automatically rubbed them to bring some warmth to them. She smiled at him. 'Thank you for coming.'

'I'm sorry I'm wearing this cassock, I've been conducting a service. Do we know why it happened?'

Debra explained that they knew no reason for it but that Mr Meadows had left a letter for Mrs Meadows. She seemed glad of an opportunity to mention it as though anxious to know what was in it, but sensitive enough not to suggest opening it.

'Would you like to open it while I'm here, Mrs Meadows?' When Suzy nodded Peter picked up the letter and handed it to her. She gave it back to him and asked him to read it to her.

'I really can't do that, Suzy: Patrick meant it for you. It will be very private. Perhaps we'd better leave it till later when you feel more yourself.' He held her hand and she held his as though by doing so she held onto reality.

'I shan't have a funeral service for him. It would be an absolute mockery if we did. He had no time for the Church. I'll just have him cremated. No hymns, no prayers. There'll be no afterlife for him, Peter. He's finished. Give me the letter.'

'"Suzy,"' she read. '"*The research I have been doing for the last three years has proved to be based on a total misconception, a complete falsehood. I am so appalled by my colossal mistake, that I have destroyed all my notes and the paper I was preparing, so no one will find out what a horrifying waste of time these last three years have been. I might as well never have lived at all. I can't face my colleagues, so I am obliterating myself.*"'

'Peter, here – you read it.'

He took the letter expecting to read a loving farewell. He'd read suicide notes before, but this was the cruellest.

Hot tears began falling on the hand Suzy held. He looked into her face and saw her Madonna-like features crumpled with grief. He held her close whilst the tears fell. Gradually the tears lessened and Suzy spoke.

'Did you notice, Peter, that there was nothing in the letter about me or the children? Nothing about what will happen to us now, or how we shall live? Nothing about "how much I have loved you or sorry for what has happened"? Losing him is bad enough, but to know he hadn't a thought for us is what really hurts.'

'I think you need someone to be with you. We ought to get your mother to come and bring the girls home.'

'Oh dear Lord, how on earth can I tell them? What words do you use? "Your father's killed himself because he can't live with himself any more? He didn't care a fig for you all"?'

'Perhaps your mother could help you to find the right words. Whatever you say it won't be easy, I'm afraid. We should contact Patrick's parents. I'll tell them for you if you would like me to.'

'His parents both died when he was in his twenties. He has no one, except a distant aunt who never bothers with him. Will you ring my parents and get them to come and bring the girls? The number's here.'

After a pause she said, her voice trembling: 'I'll sit here waiting. I don't know what I'm waiting for, but I am. Patrick will be home soon. He's always early on Thursdays.'

# Chapter 4

First thing next morning, before she left for the hospital, Caroline placed a vase of flowers on Peter's desk with a little note telling him how much she loved him. She looked out of the study window to see what the weather was going to be like. Outside on the pavement were four or five photographers and press reporters, grouped around Suzy's door. Their cars were parked haphazardly on the village green. So the ghouls had arrived. She could just imagine the headlines: '*Nuclear physicist dies. Was it murder?*'

'Peter, come here a minute. Look at this.'

He was horrified. 'This simply won't do. I'm going out to stop it. First I'll ring the police – they ought to be here.'

'I'll ring them. You go out and have a word.'

Peter swept out of the Rectory door and down the pavement, his cassock swishing angrily as he walked.

'I would be most grateful if you would kindly move away from here and leave Mr Meadows' widow and her children in peace.' The reporters clustered around Peter, holding their microphones up ready to catch his words.

'Can you give us some information about Mrs Meadows? How many children has she? Did she realise something was seriously wrong? Will she come out for an interview?'

'Have you not listened to what I said? I asked you to move away from here. Get in your cars and go. Please.'

'Now, sir, you can't expect us to leave a headline story like this, the public have a right to know. A top nuclear physicist is found dead in his car . . . something must be *very* wrong. Could be a breach of national security.'

'Has his wife been playing away?'

'Is it marriage problems? You'll know, sir, being the Vicar.'

They all clamoured around him.

'Can you get us an interview?'

Peter towering above them all caught a glimpse of the little girls watching from a downstairs window and the hurt this must be causing them made him angrier still.

'Come into my study and I'll tell you everything I know,' he promised, saying the first thing that came into his head just to get them away.

'Right, sir, you lead the way.'

Having got them away from Suzy's house, Peter then had to think what on earth he would say when they reached his study. At the same time, he remembered why he was wearing his cassock: the children from the school were coming to church for their morning prayers. As he opened the Rectory door to let the reporters in, the police arrived. The local sergeant, beefy and belligerent, made his views known.

'Now then, gentlemen and ladies, we don't want Mrs Meadows troubled by all of you stood about. Have some consideration, if you please. Those cars will have to be moved. It's an offence to park on the green, and I shall put the owners on a charge if the vehicles are not moved

46

immediately. Constable, you can stand on duty outside Mrs Meadows' house. Let's have these cars moved pronto, if you please. The Royal Oak will be open soon so you can go and sit in there for a bit. They've got a car park, too.'

When the group of eager journalists had dispersed, he turned to Peter. 'Thank you, sir, for moving them on. Never thought they'd be on to it as quick as this. Reckon they must be telepathic.'

'Mrs Meadows needs to be protected from these people. She has quite enough to contend with.'

'You're absolutely right, Rector. I'll see to it. Nice to meet you, sir, sorry it's in such difficult circumstances.'

'Thank you. Must be off, got a service to take.'

There must have been almost thirty children gathered in the church for their Friday morning prayers. Muriel Hipkin was seated at the piano playing gentle 'settling down' pieces. She'd often fancied trying out the organ but felt it was beyond her. In any case, Mrs Peel would have had something to say about that; she jealously guarded her position of organist. Michael Palmer stood as Peter entered the church and the children followed suit. Everyone, that is, except Scott McDonald, who was feeling anti-everything that morning. Muriel frowned at him but he stuck out his tongue and ignored her.

Peter, well practised at attracting everyone's attention, had Scott out at the front as his assistant before he knew where he was. He cooperated wonderfully and displayed an intelligence at odds with his usual silly behaviour. However, as he passed the piano on his way back to his seat he made a rude gesture to Muriel. She turned her bright pink face to the music and played the tune for going out. That boy really was obnoxious. She didn't like using that word

47

about a child but it fitted him exactly.

Peter argued with himself as to whether or not he should go in to see Suzy again. Best not, he eventually decided. He might find himself holding her hands in a most un-rector-like manner, and that would never do. As he settled down at his desk to commence his notes for Sunday's sermon he noticed the flowers and the note propped up against the vase.

'*To my dearest Peter, to keep you cheerful till I get back. All my love, Caroline.*'

He leant forward so that he could appreciate the scent of the flowers. It was gestures like this which made Caroline so endearing. The two of them were like one person and he never wanted to spend even a single night away from her. If he lost her through death like Suzy had lost Patrick, his life would be over. A large family would have completed their happiness, but God in His wisdom had seen it differently. Perhaps if Peter had had children he would not have been able to devote his life so entirely to the Church. He'd never replaced the crude painting of the Madonna which he'd taken down that day, but nevertheless the image of her face kept reappearing in his mind. Suzy – a rather ridiculous name, but it suited her. She might move away then he would have a chance to forget her. He recollected her face crumpled in grief. Why on earth hadn't the man said something in his letter about how he felt? Why hadn't he said the kind of things Peter had read in other suicide notes, like: '*You will be well provided for,*' or, '*The insurance policies are in the bottom drawer,*' or '*I love you. Please forgive me.*'? There had been nothing of his relationship with his family at all. Peter pushed to the back of his mind thoughts about Patrick's relationship with Suzy. If he was as icy-cold in his life as he had been in his letter of death, maybe their marriage had not been idyllic.

The phone rang.

'Caroline here. Is everything all right with Suzy? I had to dash, I was running late.'

'Yes. The police have moved the reporters on and there's a constable outside the door. Darling, can I come into Culworth and take you out to lunch?'

'I'd love that – what a nice surprise! See you about twelve-thirty outside Casualty. Bye, darling.'

When he got back from his lunch with Caroline, Suzy's mother called round to say that she and her husband were taking Suzy and the girls to live with them for a few days. They'd be leaving tomorrow. Could Peter call in this afternoon while they took the children out and advise their daughter about Patrick's cremation? Suzy didn't want the girls to overhear, as she had no intention of them going to it . . .

It was about three o'clock when Peter saw the girls set out with Suzy's parents. He waited five minutes and then went round. The constable had gone and the reporters were nowhere to be seen. Suzy answered the door. He'd expected her to be in black but she was wearing a bright pink shirt and white trousers, with her hair tied up in a pink ribbon. Only the dark shadows under her eyes showed her distress. She took his hand and drew him in. They discussed Patrick's cremation. The police had told her that it would be some time before his body would be released: post mortem etc, etc.

'I want no one there. I'll go by myself. I shall put his ashes in the bin. No, no, it's no good protesting, I shall do just that. And I'm staying in this house. The children are upset enough without moving them to a strange place. And,

Peter, I don't want you at the cremation. No one – just me. Then I can forget him. Do you know, we had not made love for over a year? Fancy that. I've not told anyone that but you. Don't really know why I'm telling you. Yes, I do. Yes, I do. Please comfort me, please.'

Suzy reached out her hand as she finished speaking and took hold of his arm. Peter lifted her hand and held it to his cheek, then turned it over and kissed the palm.

# Chapter 5

Muriel, taking Pericles for his afternoon walk, had stopped for a rest on the seat under The Royal Oak on the green. She'd seen Peter go into Suzy Meadows' house and had decided to have a word with him when he came out. She needed to know if Suzy wanted help with the children. Muriel quite fancied having the three of them for the afternoon some time. Poor little mites. She hoped they were too young to understand fully what had happened. Little Rosie in particular would never remember her father. He'd always been strange, had Patrick. It really wasn't surprising that he had committed suicide – though with so much to live for at home, how could he leave them all?

The sun had gone in and it had become quite chilly. She decided that she was only making an excuse to have some one to talk to. That was it – she was so lonely she had to make up excuses to talk to people. What must it be like, to be grateful for a moment of peace and quiet? Fancy being so busy, so very busy that being left alone felt like a bonus.

That was it, then. She would march purposefully across the green, down Shepherd's Hill and cross the spare land and walk by Turnham Beck. Pericles liked rooting about on the banks. Do something positive, she had read in a magazine article. Yes, *positive*. Her brown walking shoes made quite a brisk noise as she set off determinedly for the beck.

It must have been over an hour before she came back into Shepherd's Hill and turned up Jacks Lane. As she came out at the top of the lane and crossed to her house she glanced towards the rectory and saw Peter leaving Suzy's house. Poor dear, she must be very distressed. How thoughtful of the rector to spend so much time with her. Muriel waved enthusiastically to him but he didn't see her. It must be very draining, she thought, dealing with people who are bereaved.

The following Tuesday was not one of Muriel's better days. She played the piano at the school from 10.30 to 11.30; half an hour for the Infants and then, while they were out at play, half an hour for the Juniors. The first half hour she always enjoyed. Toria Clark was a lovely, lively girl just right for tiny ones, but the Juniors were another story. How Mr Palmer controlled them she didn't know. So calm he was, and yet they did as they were told.

Muriel had very nearly been late for school. She'd begun baking early for a coffee morning, but somehow the cakes had not been ready to come out of the oven and she'd had to wait around. Finally, she'd got to school. She usually put her coat and her keys in the tiny teachers' room, but being late she'd left them on top of the piano. Halfway through the Juniors' lesson, half a dozen infants had come running in, shouting: 'Miss Hipkin! Peri-what's-it is in the play-ground.' They were closely followed by what appeared to be the entire Infant Department. Miss Clark also came hurrying in, hoping to retrieve the Juniors' singing lesson before it was too late.

Pandemonium reigned. The entire school rushed out to help catch the errant poodle, but by that time, Pericles was over the wall and well on his way down to the beck. With a booming command, Mr Palmer stopped the children from crossing Shepherd's Hill just in time, and ushered them all back into school. Meanwhile, the singing lesson forgotten, Muriel stumbled on the rough ground as she hurried after him. 'Pericles, Pericles!'

She shouted in vain. He scampered on, leaving her well behind. Tears began to run over the edges of her eyes and trickle down her face. She hadn't anyone who cared, apart from Pericles, and even he had decided to desert her. She struggled on, calling his name. Just as she had given up on him and decided to sit down on the grass and wait, Sir Ronald appeared with Pericles tucked under one arm and Lady Bissett's Pomeranian under the other.

'Found him digging a big hole down by that rabbit burrow in the bottom field. 'Fraid he's dirty, Miss Hipkin. Now, now, don't take on so. He's safe and sound.' He handed Pericles to her and she thanked him profusely. Muriel didn't enjoy being under an obligation to such a common man but she had to tolerate it.

'Thank you very much indeed. How he got out of the house I don't know. I do appreciate your kindness, Sir Ronald. Thank you again.'

When she got back to school the caretaker was getting the hall ready for dinners.

'Sorry to trouble you, Mrs Duckett. I left my coat and keys on top of the piano.'

'Here's yer coat but there ain't no keys with it, Miss Hipkin.'

'Oh, there are. I left them there.'

'Only yer coat. There ain't no keys whatsoever.'

Muriel looked under the piano and moved the chairs about in the hope that they had been knocked off in the excitement.

'I've just put all them chairs ready for dinners, do you mind!'

'Sorry, Mrs Duckett. Maybe I never locked the house at all – perhaps that's how Pericles got out. Oh dear, I do hope I haven't been burgled!'

'Don't put that Prickles down in 'ere, this floor's clean.'

'Sorry. I'll be off then.'

She hurried home to find the back door wide open but the front door locked and no sign of her keys. She spent most of the afternoon worrying herself to death. She must pull herself together. Sixty-four didn't mean you were in your dotage. The keys must be at school somewhere. Her spare ones were hidden under a plant pot in the back garden. She'd use those till the others turned up. What a mercy she'd hidden the spare set in case she ever locked herself out.

The next two nights were uncomfortable ones and she didn't sleep at all well. On the Thursday when she went to school to play for movement lessons, Michael Palmer greeted her, jangling her keys in his hand.

'Look what I've just found amongst the music in the piano stool. I was sorting out what we needed for this morning and there they were.'

'Oh, thank you, Mr Palmer. What a relief! How foolish of me.'


The postman rarely called at number 1 Glebe Cottages, but on the mat the next morning was a lovely thick envelope. Inside was a gold-edged invitation card. Harriet and James Charter-Plackett invited Miss Muriel Hipkin to dinner to celebrate James's fortieth birthday. Formal dress. Never, ever, had Muriel attended any event at which the gentlemen wore dinner jackets. The incident of the keys dwindled into insignificance. Two weeks today, no – two weeks and one day. What on earth should she wear? And what should she buy Jimbo for his birthday? Equally important, who else had been honoured with an invitation? Her finances were stretched to the limit just living from day to day; extra expense caused havoc. The only answer would be to dip into her capital. After all, this *was* the highlight of her year. Surely she could afford to live dangerously for a while? A visit to Culworth and the Building Society was a must and while she was there she would look for a suitable present and for a dress.

Wednesday would be the best day to go. Monday didn't seem the right day for shopping in her mind; there was too much washing and ironing to do and tidying of the house after the weekend. Tuesday and Thursday she was needed at the school, and Friday morning she played for the morning prayers in the church, which meant that she would miss the only bus into town. So Wednesday it was.

Tuesday evening there was a knock at the door and on the step stood Caroline Harris.

'Hope I'm not intruding. I felt like a chat – have you the time?'

'Of course! Do come in. Shall we have a cup of tea, or would you like a sherry? I do have a very nice one. It's years old and very good.'

'Sherry would make a delightful change from the gallons of tea I drink at the hospital. I swear if there was a shortage of tea the whole place would grind to a halt. What a lovely house you have, Muriel. That does sound rude but I can't help but comment.'

Muriel disappeared into the sideboard cupboard and re-emerged with a bottle of sherry and two very attractive crystal glasses. A little tray with a neat white cloth on it and a china plate with dry biscuits arranged in a circle completed her hospitality.

'I heard all about Pericles escaping,' Caroline said. 'I'm glad you found him safe and sound.'

'Well, actually, it was Sir Ronald who found him. He'd been digging for rabbits – Pericles, that is, not Sir Ronald.' They both giggled at the prospect of Sir Ronald digging for rabbits.

Caroline took a sip of her sherry and a nibble of her biscuit, dusted the crumbs from her skirt and cleared her throat.

'We've had an invitation from Jimbo and Harriet to Jimbo's fortieth birthday party.'

'So have I – isn't it exciting? I'm going into Culworth tomorrow to buy a present for him, though I haven't any idea what to get.'

'I'll give you a lift if you like. I always leave by eight-thirty – would that be convenient?'

'Oh yes, it would, then I'll come back on the bus.'

'Muriel, I do hope you won't take offence, but have you decided what to wear?'

'That is a problem. I have nothing at all suitable, because I've never been to a smart dinner like this. One can't wear a nice wool dress, one must be a little fancy.'

'Look, I don't see any point in you spending money on a dress you'll not get a lot of wear out of. You and I are about the same height, so how about if I lend you one of mine? If I've given offence I'm sorry. It was just a suggestion.'

'Not at all. Do you really mean that?'

'Of course I do. Because we're new here no one's seen my

smart clothes so they will never know. Look, it's dark outside so we wouldn't be noticed – why not sneak across now and have a try on?'

'What a splendid idea. Mr Harris won't mind, will he?'

'Of course not. He'll be glad to be of help.'

It was embarrassing for Muriel to be undressing in Caroline and Peter's bedroom. They'd not got round to decorating it yet, but on the old carpet Caroline had spread a huge off-white rug which felt luxuriously comfortable to Muriel's stockinged feet. On a chair in the window was Peter's running kit, and his trainers lay on the floor beneath. Caroline's nightgown – a peach-coloured silk confection – lay on the bedspread beside Peter's Paisley pyjamas. It felt almost indecent to see their night-clothes in such close proximity, as if she was peeking into their private life. Out of dear Mr Furbank's huge old wardrobe came three delightful evening dresses.

'This black one with the bead decoration on the bodice would look good on you, Muriel, don't you think?'

'It's beautiful. The beadwork is quite splendid but for someone my age, I think the arms would be too bare, don't you?'

'Ah, but you see there is a long-sleeved jacket to wear over the top for dinner. It's in the wardrobe somewhere – ah, here we are. Try it on.'

The beaded dress fitted Muriel exactly. If she'd been to a shop, this would have been the very one she would have bought. When Caroline fastened the tiny georgette bolero over the top she gasped at the change in herself.

'Why, this is wonderful! Do you really mean that I can borrow it? I shall have to do something with my hair.'

'When I've worn it before I've used this hair ornament to hold my hair back. Look, like this.'

The black velvet clasp holding her hair smoothly back from her face suited Muriel beautifully. All she needed was to find those black court shoes she'd had since the sixties.

'I'm going to wear this cream thing, I think. Peter loves me in this.'

Muriel had changed back into her own clothes and stood looking at herself in the long mirror of dear Mr Furbank's wardrobe. Given half a chance and the money, she might have made something of herself, but it was too late now. The two of them wrapped the dress and jacket in a carrier bag and went downstairs. Peter was on the phone. 'Yes, certainly I'll come round. Yes, straight away.' He hung up and turned to Caroline.

'Darling, that was Suzy Meadows. She wants me to go round. She didn't go to her mother's after all. Will you come with me? Sorry, Muriel, good evening. I'm forgetting my manners.'

'I was going to have an early night, Peter.'

'I'll say good night to you both, and thank you, Caroline, for thinking of this. I'll be here not one minute later than eight-thirty tomorrow.' Muriel held the carrier bag up in thanks and swiftly made her way out of the Rectory and home past Willie Biggs' cottage and St Thomas à Becket, and into her own Glebe Cottage. There she stood with her back to the door for a moment holding the bag up out of Pericles' way as he jumped and pranced celebrating her return.

Upstairs she carefully took the dress out of the bag, and laid it on the bed. Her clothes were off in a jiffy and the dress back on again. She tried it first of all without the bolero. There was a small hint of her brassière strap showing white against the black. Dare she wear it without a brassière? Since no one could see her at the moment she tried it without. Her size 34A brassière would not be missed, she thought. Who would know? No one but herself. Dare she? Why not! Lots of girls did nowadays, she'd noticed. The georgette bolero gave the finishing touch. She brushed her hair back and put the black velvet clasp in. She'd buy a little gift for Caroline tomorrow – some of those special Belgian chocolates from that expensive shop in Culworth. She would like that.

What Caroline *didn't* like, was Peter wanting her to go to Suzy's at this time of night.

'You've never asked me to go visiting with you before, darling.'

'We didn't live in a little village like this before. I want you to be there, in case she needs a sedative or something.'

'It's not ethical for me to be dishing out drugs to other doctors' patients, you know that. Anyway, I'll come.' She reached up and kissed him on his lips, pushing her tongue against his teeth, enticing him to kiss her properly. He put his arms round her and kissed her as though he wouldn't be seeing her for a thousand years. His hands gently massaged her back and then slid down and pressed her body to his so that from toe to head she felt welded to him.

'Never forget that whatever might happen, I love you more than life itself. My love is always there for the asking.'

'Peter, I love you too, from now and for ever. I can't imagine my life without you. Now come on, down to earth if you please.' Laughingly Caroline pulled herself free and said, 'We're only going next door but one. Come on, she'll be wondering where you are. We'll finish this conversation in bed when we get back.'

When Suzy opened her door to them she was hysterical. She flung her arms around Peter, clutching his coat and alternately crying and screaming. Caroline's matter-of-fact voice in the background saying, 'Suzy, let us in or all the neighbours will be round,' brought her head up with a jerk.

She produced a handkerchief from her sleeve, wiped her eyes and drew back.

'I'm so sorry.' This was said more to Caroline than to Peter. 'I know I'm being ridiculous but the press will not leave us alone. They've been pestering my mother, they keep ringing me, they've been to the school where I used to teach, they've even found out where I went to school and have been asking friends what I was like at school. Nasty suggestive things like, "Was she very interested in boys? Did she have a lot of boyfriends? Did she take drugs?" They're trying to dig up dirt about me for their articles. I just need someone to consider my feelings. I'm sorry for asking you to come.' She burst into tears again and sat down with her head almost on her knees.

Caroline rooted about in the sideboard and found a bottle of brandy.

'What you need, my girl, is some brandy and a good night's sleep. Here you are – drink it slowly.' Caroline stood over her while Suzy, protesting, drank each and every drop.

'I don't want it.'

'Well, it'll do you good. Now to bed if you please, while you're feeling warm inside. I'm not going to leave you; I'll spend the night on the settee.'

Suzy vehemently shook her head. 'No, no, I can't have you do that for me! Please, I shall be all right.'

Caroline insisted and got her way. She found a pillow and a duvet and arranged them on the settee.

'Be a darling, Peter, and go home and bring me my night things. Or you stay here and I'll go.'

'No, I'll go.'

When he got back Suzy was tucked up in bed and Caroline was reassuring her that she would listen for the children. She peeped into the two bedrooms where the girls slept and wished she had to go the rounds in her own house every night before *she* went to bed . . . Peter came back to the house, gave her what he'd brought, kissed her and quietly left.

When, finally, the body was released for cremation, Suzy was free to put Patrick in the bin as she'd said she would. Caroline tried to persuade her to have the ashes buried at the crematorium, arguing that at the moment she felt that was what she wanted to do, but in later years she might think differently. Suzy disagreed.

The day the urn came home, she waited until it was dark and the children were in bed, then she put the urn in a Sainsbury's plastic bag and marched through the village to the beck. She couldn't quite bring herself to put the ashes in her own bin, so she was going to use the Council bin by the little footbridge. Watching the water flowing by, however, she decided it would be preferable to scatter her husband's last remains over the surface of Turnham Beck and let them rush away, eventually down to the sea perhaps and out into the world.

Suzy turned for home, feeling as though a door had been shut on a part of her life. There was nothing to do now but step forward into the next stage. Patrick's pension would be adequate if she lived carefully, and what with the playgroup and things she would be busy enough. Perhaps one day she might meet someone else whom she could love. But not yet. She needed to live for a while entirely for herself. For a start she'd find someone to babysit for her, perhaps Toria

Clark would do it, and she would attend Jimbo's birthday party. Why not? She'd be a person again wholly unto herself, not having to worry about Patrick causing offence with his withdrawn, offhand manner.

# Chapter 6

Muriel had wrapped the pen she'd bought for Jimbo, written the card, washed her hair and manicured her nails, using that little manicure set in the leather case she hadn't bothered with for years. She'd taken a long lingering bath, and Pericles had been turned out in the garden for nearly an hour so he'd be all right till she got back. Her borrowed dress was laid out on the bed, her court shoes were gleaming and now she was putting some perfume on. 'Panache' it was called. Not the most expensive, but delightful just the same. A touch behind her ears, a touch on her wrists – well, perhaps more than a touch – and some at her throat. The clock said six-thirty. Oh dear, an hour before she needed to be there. She was ready much too soon.

Muriel lay on the bed in her underskirt reading this week's book from the mobile library – *A Horseman Riding By*. A most enjoyable story; what a lovely young man he was. When her little china clock said seven o'clock Muriel got up, refreshed herself with more Panache, put on her dress, tied the little bolero beneath her now unrestrained bosom, eased on her court shoes, picked up the evening bag she'd used at the annual Young Conservatives' Dance all those years ago, kissed Pericles on the top of his head and sallied forth to Jimbo's party.

She'd done that unforgivable thing, arrived first and too early. Seven-thirty for eight, the invitation had said, and look what she'd done – arrived at twenty-five past seven.

'Come in, Muriel, come in. Delighted to see you!' Jimbo kissed her warmly on both cheeks. 'You're not a customer tonight, you're a guest so I can call you Muriel and give you a kiss. I must say, you're looking stunning tonight. Where did you pick up that little number?' Muriel blushed. 'You three come here and greet Miss Hipkin.'

Out of the sitting room popped the boys Fergus and Finlay and then little Flick, all dressed in their best. 'Daddy, Daddy, can we give Miss Hipkin her sherry?' Flick asked excitedly.

'Don't worry, Muriel, they're not staying up for the dinner, just long enough to welcome everybody and then off to bed. We like our children to be sociable beings and to know how to behave. Yes, you may, gently now.'

'I'm much too early, I am sorry.'

'Not at all, it's good to see you. Harriet has everything under control. Excuse me while I attend to the wine.'

The children took Muriel into the sitting room. The boys led her to a chair and Flick brought her a sherry.

'How did you know I like sherry?'

'Daddy said you would. The others will want gin and tonics but he says you belong to the old school and you'd want sherry.'

'Oh, I see. Are you enjoying school?'

The boys pulled funny faces but Flick said, 'Oh, yes! Miss Clark is lovely. She's so funny, she's always making us laugh. She's not coming tonight, though. She's sitting in for Mrs Meadows.'

'Is Mrs Meadows coming, then?'

'Oh, yes. Mummy said it would do her good to mix a little.'

'How old are you, Flick?'

'Six, why?'

'You seem to know a lot of what goes on.'

'Mummy and Daddy think we should know. Anyway, I listen when I shouldn't.'

At that moment, Harriet came in with her mother and mother-in-law.

'Muriel – can I introduce my mother-in-law, Katherine, and of course you know my mother Sadie.' She took them to shake hands with Muriel and left them talking.

Katherine settled herself importantly in the chair next to Muriel, leaving Sadie Beauchamp to stand beside her.

'So, Muriel, you're one of the village people, are you?'

'I live in the village, yes.'

'All this seems rather a bore to me. Jimbo should never have organised this party. I've only come because I didn't want to let him down. He had a great career in a merchant bank, you know, doing famously until he got this idea that he would leave the rat race as he called it and come down here to be a grocer.'

Muriel felt bold enough to be controversial. Perhaps the sherry had gone to her head and not to her knees as usual.

'I'd hardly call him a grocer. He and Harriet have a very good busines here. They're doing—'

Sadie indignantly interrupted: 'Sometimes, Katherine, you are extremely rude. They are making a great success of this business! I'm here every day, so I should know, and I can also see that Jimbo is in much better health than he was.'

'Allow me to know what is best for my own son.'

65

Sadie's gin and tonic began trembling in her hand. 'What's more, the whole atmosphere here is much better for the children. There's no more of that keeping up with the Algernons and the Arabellas; it's much better for them at the village school.'

Katherine snorted and turned her attention to making Muriel feel small.

'What have you done with your life – Muriel, is it?'

'I was a secretary to a solicitor until I retired. Now I live in Glebe Cottages.'

'I must say, you know how to dress – rather surprising for a village person. Though I don't suppose you get much chance to wear an ensemble like that. Who is this gorgeously handsome man coming in?'

Sadie smiled and told her he was the rector.

'The *rector*? What a perfect waste of a man. He should be in a city parish heading for a bishopric. His wife looks very stylish. I assume it *is* his wife, and not his mistress. One has to be so broad-minded where the clergy are concerned nowadays.'

Muriel stood up to welcome Caroline and Peter and introduce them to Jimbo's mother. Sadie they already knew from church. Muriel took this opportunity to escape and spend some time with Suzy, who had just arrived with Michael Palmer. Suzy was wearing a bright scarlet skin-tight dress which revealed more than it concealed. Muriel felt it was hardly suitable for a new widow. Which indeed Suzy knew it wasn't, but she was in a defiant mood. Mustn't cast a cloud over the festivities: Jimbo had a right to enjoy his party.

Harriet gently guided everyone into the dining room, so the children reluctantly went off to bed while the adults settled themselves at the table. How Harriet had ever found the time to lay the table, let alone provide all the wonderful food, Muriel could not understand. The table had been spread with a delicate pink cloth, down the centre of which were small glass candle-holders, each containing a pink candle gently illuminating small pink and white flower arrangements – just the right height not to obscure the face of the person sitting opposite you. There were three crystal wine glasses at each place setting, and a pink linen napkin arranged in the shape of a swan. The hors d'oeuvre were already in place. She knew Sadie came every day to help, but even that couldn't explain how all this food had been cooked to such perfection.

Peter and Caroline were seated opposite Muriel, and on either side of her she had Suzy and Katherine. Next to Caroline was Lady Bissett, with Sir Ronald next to his wife. It seemed an unfortunate choice to have Sheila and Caroline together, but Harriet wasn't to know they didn't get on. Jimbo sat on one end, with Harriet and her mother at the other. In between were Michael Palmer and Liz and Neville Neal; Neville being Jimbo's accountant.

The food was unusual and quite superb, and by the time Muriel had chosen hazelnut meringue for her dessert she'd no idea how she would find room for it. Three different wines at one sitting had made her very talkative and the wine had also loosened the tongue of Lady Bissett.

'We shall be very busy next weekend, shan't we Ron . . . ald?'

'Yes, indeed. We have Neil and Glenys coming for the weekend, you know.'

Caroline stopped eating her zabaglione and, all innocence, asked: 'Neil and Glenys? Should I know them?'

'Of course you know Neil and Glenys Kinnock! He's going to be the main speaker at the Labour Party rally in

Culworth. We suggested they stayed with us – typical English country weekend and all that. Give them a chance to relax.' Sir Ronald had answered her in all seriousness, but Lady Bissett guessed Caroline was being provocative.

Peter gave Caroline a nudge but she ignored it, continuing: 'I do hope there won't be an overspill in the village, and that we shan't be inundated with banners and marchers. I understand that the rally is quite crucial as far as the Party is concerned.'

'No one will even know they're here – it's being kept secret. Well, the police know, of course. Thanks to his position in the Party they have to check out where Neil is.'

'I see.' Caroline put down her spoon and leaned over towards Lady Bissett, enquiring confidentially: 'Do they have any particular quirks which Central Office have had to tell you about?'

'Quirks? Certainly not. They're very nice people.' Lady Bissett turned to Peter. 'We do hope that now you're settled in here we shall soon be hearing the patter of tiny feet at the Rectory, Peter.'

After a short pause Caroline answered on his behalf. 'That you will not be hearing . . . Sheila.'

'Oh, you're one of these modern women who doesn't believe in having children, is that it? You're a career woman then?'

'It is a matter entirely between my husband and myself, and no concern of yours. I think you are being offensive.'

Peter interrupted with a kindly, 'To our great regret we are unable to have children, Lady Bissett.'

'It will soon be the Village Flower Show, Lady Bissett. What do you have in mind for it this year?' Muriel strove to change the conversation, but Sheila Bissett would have none of it.

'Being a doctor I would have thought you would have known what to do about it. There's all kinds of ways nowadays, you know. I don't know where I'd be without my Bianca and Brendan.'

'I have no need to resort to having children in order to justify my existence.'

Caroline was dangerously near to tears and Jimbo, receiving distress signals right down at his end of the table, sprang to his feet and offered Sheila Bissett more wine, thus diverting her from Caroline. Katherine Charter-Plackett intercepted a glance between Suzy and Peter. She leant towards Muriel and whispered in a loud voice: 'What's between the gorgeous Rector and that red siren? There's something going on.'

Muriel was horrified. Fortunately Caroline was occupied getting her feelings under control and missed Katherine's comment, but Peter didn't. He looked very distressed.

Neville sat back, well satisfied with his meal. 'Harriet, that was wonderful! You ought to open a restaurant, you know. You've got the talent and the experience.'

Harriet playfully put her hand over his mouth, as she spotted a sparkle come into Jimbo's eyes when he overheard the remark.

'Be quiet, Neville. Don't put any more ideas into his head, there's enough there already. No, Jimbo, down, boy, down. I'm not falling for that one.'

Neville continued making his point. 'There's that cottage next to Sadie's house going for a song, *and* it's got spare land at the side for a car park. Sadie would be very handy for keeping an eye on it, wouldn't you, Sadie? It would make an excellent restaurant, right opposite the village green and all.' They all burst out laughing but Jimbo didn't laugh; he made a note of it in the filing cabinet he called his mind.

After coffee and liqueurs they retired to the sitting room, where Jimbo had two bottles of champagne on ice. They all sang Happy Birthday to him whilst he opened the bottles.

'Your very good health, Jimbo. Here's to your fiftieth!' Peter said and they all applauded. After that they danced, played games and had a thoroughly riotous time. At midnight Peter said he really must go as he had early service tomorrow, and he and Caroline offered to escort Muriel home. Jimbo went with them to the door. He took Muriel by the shoulders and gave her a huge kiss.

'Thank you so much for my splendid pen. I shall treasure it as a gift from a lovely lady who did herself proud tonight.' Muriel felt bold enough to kiss him back.

Jimbo then kissed Caroline and whispered in her ear. 'Take no notice of my old hag of a mother. I don't. She isn't worth the candle – OK?'

She smiled, took Peter's hand and they went off into the night. The moon shone and the sky was full of stars bright and clear, a perfect ending to a lovely evening.

'Good night, good night and thank you for seeing me home.'

'Good night, Muriel, see you tomorrow.' Both Caroline and Peter waved to her as they turned down Church Lane towards the Rectory. Peter was gripping Caroline's hand tightly. Caroline remained silent. She knew how Peter longed for children and she longed for them, for his sake. The hurt engendered by Sheila Bissett was beyond endurance.

When they were safely tucked up in bed Caroline in a small tight voice offered Peter a divorce.

He sat up, shattered by what she had said. 'A *divorce*! Why?'

70

'Because you want children and I can't give them to you, that's why. Then you could marry someone who is able to give you children. How I would live without you I don't know, but for your sake I would have a jolly good try.'

There was a moment's silence before Peter answered.

'Caroline, I'm not worthy of you. I married you because you are the light of my life, not for the sole purpose of procreation. You make me feel very small. Don't ever dare suggest such a thing again. That is, unless you yourself truly want a divorce, though heaven help me if you did. Who'd want me anyway? There's only a saint like you could put up with me.'

'That's not true, you're very eligible. In fact, you're really rather superb. I saw Katherine Charter-Plackett looking you over!'

'Her tongue's too sharp. It's time she engaged her brain before she speaks. I'm giving you a good night kiss and then I'm going down to my study to have a word with the Lord.'

'You can have a word with Him here, if you wish.'

'No, you'll distract me. I need to think. Good night, my love.'

Peter went down to his study and wept.


Muriel, having waved them goodbye, unlocked her door and found Pericles looking worried. She hurriedly popped him into the back garden and left him there while she made herself a cup of Ovaltine to help her sleep. What a wonderful evening she had had. The food, the company, the wine, the kindness, everything. She'd never forget it. She opened the drawer to get a teaspoon out and found the cutlery in disarray. The knives were where the forks usually were, and the spoons where the knives ought to be, and the forks where she kept the spoons. How

71

ridiculous! She must have been so excited about the party that she'd mixed them all up. It left an odd feeling in a corner of her mind.

# Chapter 7

Mrs Duckett the school caretaker was the first one in the village to voice an opinion about the change in Muriel.

'Failing, that's what she is. Never seen such a change in a person. One minute as fit as a lop, bit too prim and proper, mind, but still fit as a lop – and now what is she like? I reckon she's got that disease Asmizler yer read about in the papers. This Tuesday she couldn't play a right note to save her life. Mr Palmer looked real fed up.'

Her neighbour Vera Wright nodded in agreement. 'She was in the store the other day and couldn't remember what she'd come in for – and I'll tell you another thing. I think she's neglecting herself.'

'Neglecting herself? What do you mean?'

Their heads drew closer over the fence. 'Haven't yer noticed she's losing weight?'

'No I hadn't, but come to mention it you could be right.'

'She's never been the same since that Jimbo's party you and I didn't get invited to. Good customers we are as well.'

'That dog of hers needs putting down. He's getting old and smelly. Mucky things, dogs. Perhaps she's got a disease off 'im. No self-respecting dog would want to be called

Prickles or whatever his name is. Going round The Royal Oak tonight?'

'Might. See how the money stretches when I've done me shopping. Our Rhett's eating me out of house and home. Must be 'aving a growing spell. Yer bring yer own up and then get landed with bringing yer grandchildren up as well. It's not right. Our Brenda was sex-mad and look what that got her – our Rhett.'

Mrs Duckett locked her back door and went off to put the hall to rights for school dinners.

Muriel was just finishing putting the music away.

'Got yer keys have you, Miss Hipkin?'

'Oh yes, thank you, Mrs Duckett. I'm much more careful than I was. Now, where's my cardigan? Oh, here it is.'

'Tell yer what, Miss Hipkin, I don't think you're looking too good. Aren't you well?'

'Oh yes, I'm quite well, thank you. Yes, quite well.'

But she wasn't and Muriel knew it. And she knew why. It was the worry that her memory was going. It had started with little things, but they were a matter for concern. First there was the cutlery. Then another time she'd put a cake out to cool on the rack and when she came back home it had gone. She blamed poor Pericles but she knew he couldn't have reached it. Then she always made her bed when she went upstairs to clean her teeth after breakfast. One morning she came back from school and the sheets and blankets were all pulled back as if she'd just got out of it. Another time she came home and her ornaments had been changed round. Mother's delicate china figures were all back to front and her own little cottages, lovingly collected these last three years, had been arranged along the edge of the hearth instead of being on the shelves she'd bought specially for them.

74

True, these were only minor incidents but she had come to the conclusion that her brain was softening, as her mother used to say. Before she knew it she would be in a home and her lovely life which seemed to be perking up at long last would be finished.

Muriel went to church and prayed about it. Peter had been playing the organ when she got in there, so she'd let his lovely sad music carry her along. Eventually, he switched it off and came to sit beside her. He took her hand and said, 'God bless you, Muriel. Are you happy to be by yourself or would you like some company?'

'I'd like you to stay and talk if you would.'

'I have the feeling that things are not right at the moment. I was so glad when you agreed to give Mrs Meadows—'

'We all call her Suzy.'

'—Suzy, help with the playgroup. It doesn't do not to be busy, you know.'

'I know that, Peter, and I am busy with one thing and another, but just lately things haven't been right for me.'

'Can you tell me about it?'

'It's all silly, just women's talk. I'll be off now.'

She picked up her bag and fled from the church. Willie Biggs, cutting the grass in the churchyard, watched her escape. Something funny there, he thought, something funny. Peter emerged from the church and made his way down the path to the Rectory.

'Rector, I got some nice geraniums. What do you say I make a flowerbed hereabouts and put 'em in? They're all pink-coloured. Can't abide them bright red things – go against nature, they do.'

'Sounds wonderful, Willie. How's the back?'

'Fine, sir, thank you. Fine. That stuff Dr Harris recommended is grand. Will you thank her for it? I'm not troubled at all now – which is more than I can say for that Muriel Hipkin. What's up with her, do you reckon?'

'Don't know, Willie, and she won't tell me.'

'We went to school together, yer know. We were in the Infants. Her father was head gardener at the Big House. Married above himself, and Muriel was the result. Used to play with Sir Tristan's boys when she were young. Pretty little thing she was. Now she's all spinsterish and that. Pity, really. So, geraniums it is, sir, then?'

'Yes, please. Could I buy some from you for the Rectory garden as well? My wife thinks it's time I made inroads into the weeds.'

'If you're in need of help there, Rector, we might be able to come to some arrangement the two of us?'

'I'd be very glad if you could spare the time, Willie. I'm getting much too involved with the parish to find time to do it. Some amicable agreement could be reached, I'm sure. By the way, that shed in the graveyard needs clearing out. Could you put it on your list?'

'Anything for you, sir. Top of the list it will be. Morning to you.'

'Good morning, Willie.'

Come Saturday afternoon, Willie began clearing out the shed. It was surprising what had collected there. Gardening tools that would have done well on the 'Antiques Roadshow'. Old buckets, old vases, string, old wrapping paper from flowers and – surprise surprise – a plastic container from supermarket sandwiches. Who in their right mind would want to have a picnic in this old shed? There were also two Coke tins and two empty crisp packets. 'Well I never, what next?' muttered Willie. By the time he'd finished there were two full bags of rubbish for the bin men. He stood them out on the path, straightened his back and then noticed

Mr Palmer from the school filling his vase at the tap.

'Afternoon, Mr Palmer. Don't usually see you here on a Saturday.'

The headmaster looked up, startled. 'No, you're right, Willie. I thought I'd come earlier this week.'

'Sunday as regular as clockwork you are, sir. Wish some others would care for the graves like you do. It's a pleasure to look at your wife's. Three years it is now, Mr Palmer. She'd have wanted you to find someone else, you know.'

'That's as maybe. Good afternoon, Willie.'

After he'd gone Willie perched himself on the edge of a tombstone and lit his pipe. He rested his elbows on his knees like he did when he was going to have a good think. Three years. He remembered the fuss there'd been. It was the Saturday of the Village Show. Boiling hot day it'd been. Sun beating down, one of the best attended for years. The flowers in the marquee had been wilting with the heat. Lady Bissett had upset all the flower arrangers by taking it upon herself to spray their arrangements with a secret concoction of her own to freshen them up. There'd been some very unpleasant things said that afternoon. Tempers got even more frayed when the ice cream ran out and the little steam train they'd hired had blown up – something to do with the pressure gauge. And it wasn't only the pressure gauge on the train that had got steamed up. Revd Furbank had had the money from the coconut shy stolen from under his very nose. Nice gentle old chap, but he didn't know what made the world tick nowadays. Can't leave a thing about, not even in old Turnham Malpas. Willie blamed the boys from the Big House. A leopard won't ever change its spots.

The late Mrs Palmer had been in charge of the maypole dancing. She'd brought a group over from her school in Culworth, as the village school couldn't muster enough children. Muriel Hipkin had seated herself at the piano which the men had dragged out of the school and into the field, right job that was. She was warming up with a few of her jolliest tunes, the maypole was in place, the children were all ready in their costumes, and the crowds awaited the start. Muriel played a few more tunes, and still Mrs Palmer hadn't appeared to set the ball rolling. The children were getting restless. All apologetic, Mr Palmer went home to see if he could find his wife – and he'd found her, all right. Hanging from the big beam in the school hall. If Stella Palmer had set out to cause a sensation she couldn't have chosen a better moment. And nobody ever found out why. He was a decent enough chap, Michael Palmer. Mightn't set the world on fire, but you can't have everything. He was kind. Maybe that was it – he was *too* kind.

Willie saw Muriel come out into her garden. He went and leaned over the church wall.

'Them daffodils is finished now, Muriel. They wants tying up.'

'Thank you, Willie, that's my next job.'

'You'll never guess who I met in Culworth the other day.'

'Oh?'

'You know where the Market Square just bends a bit and there's that dentist's surgery right on the corner? Well, I'd been 'aving another fitting for me new teeth and who should I bump into on me way out, but Sir Ralph Templeton.'

Muriel perked up a little at this. 'Really? How on earth did you recognise him?'

'He recognised me. Said I 'adn't changed a bit, but since it must be more than forty years since he last saw me I must be wearing well. He's still got all that thick bushy hair 'cept it's snow-white now. Tanned he is, been out in the Far East for years and now he's retired and come back to live in England. In all those years he's never married. Remember that time he put a jumping cracker inside Miss's boots when she'd put 'em by the stove to dry out? He were a lad, he was. Didn't we laugh!'

'What was he doing in Culworth?'

'Visiting some friends, he said. Wanted me to go for a drink but I knew I'd miss me bus if I did. I've been clearing out the shed – amazing what yer find in there. Rector wanted it doing. He's a grand chap, he is. Yer know where yer are with 'im. Mr Furbank couldn't talk to yer, somehow – he never had that touch. Rector's worried about you, Muriel. He reckons yer not yerself at all these days.'

Willie left a pause but got no reply.

'I'll get on then if yer not talking.'

He turned his back on Muriel and heaved the bin bags off to his dustbin corner.

Muriel sat on her little seat by her rose arch, tickled Pericles behind his ears as he settled down beside her and pondered on her predicament. If she told someone, they would have her certified. If she didn't tell someone, she would go mad. Maybe she was already mad and didn't know it. Perhaps one would be the last to realise. If she did one more stupid thing she would give up playing for the school. Last week she had made an idiot of herself with constant wrong notes, wrong timing – and even the wrong tune, once. She couldn't expect Mr Palmer to put up with it much longer. She didn't profess to be a pianist as such but she could play some lively tunes for her age. That was it – her age! She was trying to be twenty-four when she was sixty-four. One glimpse of her reflection in a shop window and she despised herself. She was nothing but a faded elderly spinster, dragging out her life because she was too much of a coward to commit suicide. Death would bring its own reward. Paradise. What greater prize could one have than entering paradise? What an incentive, Thy face to see. Surely the good Lord would let her in? She'd been well-behaved all her life. For this to happen just as she was feeling needed and beginning to enjoy her life . . . One can't even gas oneself nowadays. That would have been a gentle way to go. Drowning? Jumping off the church tower? But she got vertigo simply going up to take the bell-ringers their cocoa on New Year's Eve. She'd never reach the top. In any case, Peter would be so upset . . .

This last incident was ridiculous, but she'd done it. How could anyone leave the oven on at full blast with the door open and all the rings on as well? To say nothing of the gas bill. The house was positively steaming when she got back. She'd had to open all the windows and the doors to cool it down. She hadn't even intended to cook a Sunday dinner seeing as it was 82 degrees. Tomorrow when she went to church she would take particular notice of what she was doing and check everything before she left. That way she'd know when she got back that she hadn't done it. Maybe she had a ghost. Maybe someone from years past resented the cottages being built on church land. There'd been plenty of opposition when they were built – from the living, never mind the dead. If that was it, Peter would have to exorcise it.

Sunday morning came. The sun shone brilliantly as it had done for two months now. Before it got too hot, Muriel watered her most precious plants with water from the butt. She enjoyed turning the little tap on and watching the water come running out. When she'd finished she lifted the lid to check how much water was still left: floating in the top was a drowned cat. A drowned ginger cat. A fully grown, drowned ginger cat. A beautiful fully grown drowned ginger cat! Someone's pet, someone's beloved pet in her water butt. The horror of its drowning whilst she'd been going about her affairs ignorant of its agony, was more than she could tolerate.

She fled out into Church Lane, past the church gate and on to Willie's front door. She banged and banged but he wouldn't answer. Of course – he'd be in the church opening up. She turned round and headed for the church door, hastening up the path, shouting: 'Willie Biggs! Willie Biggs!'

He emerged, wearing his cassock. 'What's the matter, Muriel? What's up?'

She grabbed his arm and began to gabble, trying to tell him about the cat. 'Come on! You've got to come. Please help me, please.' When she showed him the cat she was shuddering with the horror of it.

'Now sit down,' he told her kindly, alarmed at her reaction. 'It's only someone's old cat got in here by mistake. Wasn't your fault.'

'The lid is always on tightly in case children get in the garden. Someone's put it in there, I know it. It's a nasty trick, a vile evil trick.' She began sobbing.

'I'll find a plastic bag to put it in. 'Spect there's one in your kitchen somewhere.'

She watched Willie invade the seclusion of her neat pristine kitchen with his big heavy shoes on, tramping on the small white tiles, defacing them with footprints, the footprints turned here and there whilst their owner found the place where a score of plastic carrier bags were stored, all neatly folded inside a Tesco's bag.

'I'll put it in here and get rid of it in the church bin.'

'It's got a collar on,' Muriel shrieked as he lifted it out.

'So it has. I'll take it off and we'll see whose cat it is. Why, it's Mr Charter-Plackett's cat!'

'Oh no, I can't tell him, I can't tell him. You tell him, Willie, you tell him.' Her voice was frantic.

'I'll have to tell him after church then, 'cos I'm running late. Won't do for the service to be late. You make yourself a cup of tea and then come to the service. Don't sit here by yourself thinking about it. Do as I say, now.'

'Yes, yes I will.'

She didn't hear a word of the service. Her mortal remains sat in the pew but the real Muriel was in the rafters avoiding looking at Jimbo and Harriet and the children. Oh, the children would be so upset about their pet. Such dear children they were, never a mite of trouble in school. There was Caroline sitting in the Rectory pew, wearing a lovely lemon-yellow dress with big splashes of apricot and soft brown on it. What a dreadful thing that Katherine Charter-Plackett had said. 'Red siren' indeed. As if Peter would get involved with someone else when he had Caroline. The scent of the flowers was delicious up here in the rafters. It was like being in some heavenly garden. No weeds here. No need to water the plants. No discovering dead . . . no, she wouldn't think about that. Mrs Peel is excelling herself today. Was it the 'Trumpet Voluntary' she was playing? Heavenly music for a heavenly day. The cherubs, decorating the arches in the roof, had joined her and were swirling about in a kind of celestial maypole dance. She'd loved maypole dancing as a child. The patterns you made with the ribbons so intricate and then you danced again and unravelled them. All her ribbons had got tangled and they wouldn't come straight.

The church was emptying. The chosen of the Lord had

walked firmly down the aisle, accompanied by His servants singing a hymn of praise. The sun shining through the ancient coloured glass of the windows had cast strange streaks of reds and purples on their white gowns. They were like Technicolor angels. She must have done it, she must have done it and here she was about to see the face of her beloved Lord.

Caroline took immediate action.

'Peter, we must take her to Casualty. There's something seriously wrong here. She doesn't even know I'm speaking to her. What can have happened?'

'I can tell you that, Dr Harris.' And Willie related the story of the cat.

'Whatever's been worrying her these last few weeks, the cat has been the final straw. Whoever would do such a thing to poor Muriel – or the cat, come to that? She wouldn't hurt a flea.'

'Someone's got it in for her, that's for sure.' Peter tried to rouse Muriel but she sat as though carved from stone.

He and Caroline drove Muriel to the hospital while Willie went across to the Charter-Placketts' to break the news.

'Orlando? How could that have happened?'

'I don't know, Mr Charter-Plackett, but I've got him in the churchyard shed. Here's his collar, sir.'

Jimbo went white when he saw poor Orlando's bright red collar. 'Hardly dare tell the children, but I must. We'll have to have a funeral service and bury him in the garden. I'm surprised at Miss Hipkin, having a water butt without a lid.'

'She did have a lid and she kept it on all the time – tight-fitting it was, too. She only found him 'cos she was wondering how much water she had left in it.'

'It was deliberate, then. How could anyone do such a thing? I'll go in and break the news to the children and Harriet, and then come across and pick up poor Orlando. We left London to avoid dreadful things like this.'

# Chapter 8

On the Monday morning, Jimbo was busy freshening up the displays for the coming week. He hummed to himself while he planned the menu for a dinner party he'd been asked to do for a customer in Culworth. They weren't his kind of people but you can't pick and choose your customers in this business. Harriet sped through the shop on her way to pick up the fresh vegetables they prided themselves on supplying. As she opened the outside door she was brushed aside by the angry figure of Betty McDonald from The Royal Oak.

In her hand was a letter. Her face, normally red, was even more so; now in fact, it was almost puce.

Harriet gathered herself and said, 'Good morning, Betty. Is that your order?'

'Order? *Order?* You'll be lucky if I set foot in here ever again. Where is that two-timing blackguard? You come from London with your fancy ways and your new ideas and before we know where we are you're cutting our throats.'

'Cutting your throats? What do you mean?'

'Where is he?'

'Is someone wanting me?' Jimbo emerged from amongst

the bananas hanging along the rail above the vegetables. His face was devoid of expression. Harriet with a sinking feeling began to suspect he'd been up to something she knew nothing about.

'Wanting you? I'll swing for you before long. How dare you do it!'

'Do what?'

'You know full well what I mean. This – this is what you've done!' She smashed her hand onto the letter she was holding and it nearly tore in half. 'This letter is informing me that you have applied for planning permission for a restaurant in old Phyllis Henderson's house, and a car park right on the corner. I'll fight you every step of the way, every single step. If you open up I might as well say goodbye to my morning coffees and my ploughman's lunches and my farmhouse soup. The damage to my business will be devastating.'

Harriet held out her hand. 'Let me see this letter, please.' As she read it her face grew stormy. 'How dare you do this without consulting me? How dare you? Jimbo, I shall never forgive you for this. Have you bought it already?'

'Now hold on a minute, Harriet. I've made an offer subject to planning permission. A chap's got to make progress, he can't just stand still.'

'Stand still? A chap's got to make progress? I'll give you progress, Jimbo. Not one foot will I put inside that restaurant if this goes through. Not one foot. So think on that.' She flung out of the door and the little bell, the delight of Jimbo's heart, rattled till it nearly fell off the door. Then the Charter-Placketts' Range Rover crashed into life and roared off down Stocks Row as if it was the M4.

Betty was triumphant. 'See, even your wife is against the idea!'

'Leave Harriet to me, she'll come round. If it all comes off I shan't be doing ploughman's or farmhouse soup so you've no need to worry about that. I'll be catering for a different part of the market.'

'Don't try to sweet-talk me. It can only do harm. I know – I've been in the licensed trade too long not to know serious competition when I see it. I shall get a petition up and ask everyone to sign it. You won't win this one.' And Betty McDonald marched out of the shop, whereupon the poor bell had another fit as she smashed the door shut.

Jimbo chuckled to himself. He'd have that restaurant before he was much older, and it would turn out to be a right money spinner. It was definitely a box of sugared almonds under Harriet's pillow night tonight. He'd soon have her eating out of his hand: it always worked. He smiled to himself as he served his first customers. The Charter-Plackett charm was up to full strength as usual.

As soon as Jimbo saw Harriet pull up outside he poured out two coffees from the pot brewed for the customers, put them on the counter with a couple of special chocolate biscuits and confidently awaited her entrance. But she didn't come in. He played the waiting game while he served two more customers and then, to his amazement, saw Harriet dressed to kill driving past in the Volvo.

'Sadie, Sadie!' Jimbo shouted into the back where his mother-in-law was doing the mail order parcels. 'Where's Harriet going?'

'Jimbo, I have no idea. She flew past me saying "I'll kill him, so help me, I'll kill him." To whom she referred I have no idea. I assume she's driven off to commit a murder. We'll have to hope it's no one we know.'

'It could be me.'

'You? Why, what have you done?'

'Put in a bid for old Phyllis Henderson's cottage and asked for planning permission for a restaurant. I thought it would be a lovely surprise for Harriet and yet she's absolutely flown off the handle.'

Sadie finished addressing a parcel of Harriet's Country Cousin Lemon Cheese – farmhouse-made with free-range eggs – took off her glasses and said, 'Now look here, Jimbo. As mothers-in-law go I think I give you an easy ride but this time I have to speak my mind. I don't want to interfere but I must. Do you realise that Harriet has far too much to do?'

'I work hard, too.'

'Indeed you do, but you don't also prepare meals and look after the children and cook for dinner parties and receptions and meals at Game Fairs and the like. My daughter never has a minute to herself and it's got to stop. Employ more help. Ease the burden. She only objects to the restaurant because she physically can't do any more than she is already doing.' Sadie's index finger poked Jimbo rather sharply on his lapel and she turned on her heel and left him to think.

The day wore on and still Harriet had not returned. The boys and Flick arrived home from school, accustomed to their mother greeting them with food and sympathy, to find their grandma there instead.

'Where's Mummy? I wish my Mummy was here.' Flick did not take kindly to her routine being upset.

Sadie told the children that their mother had gone out for a change, and that she'd soon be back. Jimbo was feeling exactly like Flick but he didn't voice his feelings. By eight o'clock, anxiety took the place of wishing. He sat at his office desk trying to do the VAT return, but too worried to have much success. About eleven the back door opened and in she came.

Jimbo leapt up to greet her. 'Darling, where have you been! We have missed you.'

'Crawled out from under your stone, have you?'

'Now, Harriet, that's a bit unfair. You know I've always wanted a restaurant. If you say no then no it shall be. I leave it entirely to you.'

'That's emotional blackmail.'

'No it's not, I'm simply being thoughtful.'

'Don't, it's too painful. Goodnight, Jimbo. Good luck with the VAT return.'

'Aren't you going to help me?'

'No.'

When he'd finished he went upstairs, only to find that Harriet was not in their bed. He crept round the bedrooms and discovered her fast asleep on the put-u-up in Flick's bedroom. This was the first time they had slept apart since they were married. Jimbo knew he had gambled once too often. Serious amends would have to be made.

Next morning Harriet saw the children off to school while Jimbo started work in the shop. His first job was to write out an advertisement for the local newspaper.

'*Smart young people needed, full and part-time, to help entrepreneur with busy catering business. Excellent remuneration for hardworking lively applicants. Apply Turnham Malpas (0909) 334455.*'

He telephoned the advert to the newspaper and served some customers, all of whom were eager to know about the restaurant. Most of them were thrilled at the idea, but over in The Royal Oak, some, but not all of the regulars, had signed Betty's petition.

'I've said it once and I'll say it again.' Vera Wright was laying down the law. 'Before we know it, this village will be as busy as the M4. Car doors slamming late at night, headlights on full blast. It won't be the same any more.'

'It will mean more jobs, Vera.'

'Oh yes, more jobs for chefs and the like. How many chefs do you know in Turnham Malpas?'

'Well, none actually.'

'Exactly, Willie – *none*. All it'll do is bring people in from outside. Village folk will get the rubbish jobs like cleaning and doing the vegetables. Aren't I right, Pat?'

'Well, yes, I suppose you are, Vera. Who do we know who'd want to work restaurant hours? Not me for a start, though I could manage evenings, I suppose, and fit it in with the school.'

Jimmy Glover, a regular at The Royal Oak, placed his pint carefully on a beer mat, wiped the froth from his mouth and said, 'What about all these tourists coming to see the murals in the church and the stocks and the like – where can they go for a nice meal? Not here for a start. One look at Betty McDonald's face and it's a wonder they don't all run a mile – to say nothing of the rotten food here. I hope he does get permission.'

'You would, Jimmy. That's you all over. No thought for the village green getting churned up 'cos they can't be bothered to park in the proper places. Oh no. It's time that Jimbo was taken down a peg or two anyway. Too clever by half, he is.'

'Vera, that's not fair. He does a lot for the village.'

'Oh yes? Like what – jumping naked into that pool of his? I seed 'im one morning when I was off to work extra early. By gum, Pat,' she nudged her friend and nearly made her spill her lager, 'he's got nothing missing.' They both laughed raucously.

Harriet didn't begin to come round to Jimbo's way of

thinking until she answered the phone to find herself talking to an eager job applicant. After a moment or two of confusion it dawned on her what he'd done. She took the young woman's name and telephone number, and promised that Jimbo would ring her back.

She put the piece of paper down in front of him as he ate a lonely pork pie behind the bread counter. Linda, who ran the post office and the stationery section, was nearly dying of laughter at the sight of Jimbo in the dog-house.

'There's someone who thinks we need extra help on the catering side,' Harriet announced. 'I can't think why they've rung us, can you? That's their number if you think they're needed.'

Jimbo kissed her hand as she turned to go. She hesitated for a moment but then went on her way. She's softening, she's giving in, thought Jimbo elatedly.

As she had threatened, Betty McDonald started a petition, wrote letters, campaigned and spread malicious rumours in an effort to stop Jimbo opening the restaurant, but it was not to be. Plenty of the inhabitants of Turnham Malpas signed her petition, but the majority liked Jimbo and didn't like Betty McDonald. The planning committee met only a month after Jimbo's application had gone in. They could see no reason for withholding their permission and in fact quite welcomed the idea of an up-to-date restaurant, to supply a service to the tourists who visited the village.

Jimbo was beside himself with delight. The three new part-time girls he had employed eased Harriet's burden, while he flung himself into organising the complete refurbishing of his latest project. The whole building required attention: rewiring, replastering, mains water and electricity, decoration, and of course brand-new kitchens.

Jimbo whirled around phoning and writing, cajoling and compelling until within four weeks he had completely changed the cottage both outside and in.

A few people had hazarded guesses as to what it would be called, but he had remained mum on that issue. Harriet knew but she refused to tell. The sign was being put up as Pat Duckett wended her way to open up the school. The transformation from tumbledown house to smart village restaurant in such a short space of time had amazed her.

'It's these Londoners, you know. They don't let grass grow under their feet. Their motto is "Time is money". Get taking money in as fast as you can.' Michael Palmer only half-listened to her. He'd had years of Pat Duckett and he knew she'd waste hours talking, so he never encouraged her.

'He's calling it Henderson's, would you believe! Old Phyllis would be tickled pink having it named after her. Fancy Henderson's. What do you think, Mr Palmer?'

'Sounds good enough to me. I shan't be eating there.'

'Time you got out and about a bit, Mr Palmer. Man your age should be enjoying himself, not be shut up with his books every night. You enjoyed Mr Charter-Plackett's party, didn't you?'

'I did indeed. The children will be here shortly, Mrs Duckett. Could we get on, please?'

'Has it gone through yet about Mrs Meadows and that playgroup thing?'

'The committee meet this week. There shouldn't be any problem. It seemed to meet with a favourable response.'

'I'm not looking forward to all that mess. All them wellington boots from them farm kids. Stands to reason the toilets will be a mess, with them all being so young. They make all these arrangements but they never think about the school caretaker.'

'Well, I am right now, Mrs Duckett – and she isn't getting organised.'

'Sorry, I must say. Only passing all the news on, like,' Pat Duckett said offendedly.

'Thank you.'

Michael stood watching the children arriving in the playground. They really were a good bunch – clean, healthy and eager, except for the ones who came from the Big House. The cards life had dealt them were rotten indeed. He doubted if they would ever get their lives straightened out. Come to think of it, he hadn't managed it yet and he was forty-five. If Stella had lived, his life would have been hell. People thought they should feel sorry for him when she died, but in truth the opposite was true. He wasn't any happier since she'd died, but he would have been a sight worse by now if she hadn't. How he could have married her and not known, he had never fathomed. There was something to be said for living together before marriage. Morally he couldn't condone it, but in their case it would have saved a lot of heartache.

Now he had this problem of Sharon McDonald. She'd struck him as a sly child when she was in the Infants, and he'd been right. He opened the window and called out, 'Close the gate after you, please. We don't want the little ones out in the road, thank you.' Experience taught you which children were truthful and which didn't know the truth if it jumped up and hit them, but Sharon had been unfathomable. Now she'd grown up she was still sly. Fancy her seeing Stella in Culworth and following her. She'd harboured the secret all this time. That demonstrated just how sly she was. How to tackle the problem, though? Say, 'Tell all and be damned'? There'd be no end to it if he began paying her. Or should he give in his notice and disappear? Or have a word with her parents? Then the cat would truly be out of the bag. Betty McDonald would still be spreading gossip from her grave – he might as well put an advert in the paper.

Just then, Toria Clark rang the school bell and his favourite people began pouring into school, laughing and chattering all ready for another day. Thank heavens he'd chosen teaching; he couldn't think of a more rewarding job.

# Chapter 9

Caroline went into the village store to buy a card and present for Muriel's birthday.

Jimbo asked her how Muriel was.

'It's her birthday tomorrow so I'm getting her a card and taking a present in for her. They've put her in a psychiatric ward. I can hardly bear going in to see her. She sits entirely still and speechless. Whoever did what they did to her needs serious psychiatric help themselves. We know about your dear cat, but we think other things happened before that, and Orlando's death was what finally broke her. What can I buy to take for her, Jimbo?'

'My present will be one of my special birthday cakes. We have them already made – they do for birthdays, weddings or whatever. I'll get Sadie to put "Muriel" on one while you wait. Look round while I organise it.'

Caroline chose a card and a box of chocolates. Muriel had lost so much weight perhaps the chocolates would entice her to eat. Jimbo emerged from the back of the shop carrying a smart cardboard box. He showed Caroline the cake before closing down the lid.

'Why, that's beautiful, Jimbo. What a lovely idea! She'll

enjoy giving everyone a slice.'

'Will she be back with us soon, do you think?'

'Not for a while yet, I'm afraid. She won't tell anyone what the matter is, you see. She needs to get it all out of her system before she can get better. Thank you for the cake. I'll remember you when it's Peter's birthday. His is in November. Your restaurant will be open by then – we'll have a meal in it to celebrate.'

'If you see Harriet, don't mention it. It's a sore subject at the moment.'

Caroline laughed. 'See you, bye!'


'Good morning, Dr Harris. You're on the ball this morning.'

Caroline put the carrier bag down on her desk and slid out the box containing Muriel's birthday cake.

'I am – I've a lot to do. Don't make it sound as if it's unusual for me to be here in good time, Anne, I always am.' She grinned at her secretary.

'Well, I meant you were bouncing in more energetically than normal. Sorry.'

'I'll see to my post and then I'm going down to the psychiatric ward. It's someone's birthday and this is a cake for them.'

'Oh, can I look?'

'Yes.' Caroline opened the box and they both admired Jimbo's cake. 'It's from our village store. Albeit a very superior village store.'

'It looks gorgeous. Your friend no better?'

'Unfortunately, no.'

'We're short-handed today. Two of the technicians have got this 'flu thing that's going round, and it's ante-natal clinic day as well, so we shall need to get our skates on.'

'Right, here goes then.' Caroline rolled up her sleeves and began opening her post. Samples, drugs, letters, reports . . . endless paperwork. She loved her work as a doctor. The only event which could stop her doing medicine would be the arrival of a baby. For that she would give up everything. Although Peter reassured her often enough that he wasn't the slightest bit bothered about not having children she knew it would absolutely crown their lives together. She'd just finished her medical training when they met. Full of determination and dedication, having arrived at last at the goal she had pursued for more than ten years, nothing was further from her mind than marriage. On her first day as a GP, taking surgery entirely on her own, he had been one of the patients. The moment they looked at one another she knew he was going to be special. Within three months they were engaged and then married three months later. If he had had a call to go as a missionary to some far-flung primitive corner of the world, she would have followed without a backward glance. When she saw him again at the end of a long day her spirits soared as though she were a lovesick girl instead of a professional woman of thirty-two.

Having sorted through the post and allocated it to different trays she gave Anne her work for the morning and then set off down to the psychiatric ward with Muriel's cake and present.

The ward had been made more 'user friendly' in recent years. The high windows, such a favourite with Victorian architects, had been draped with soft net curtains, each bed had pretty curtains around it, the furniture was modern and one end of the ward had been turned into a sitting area where the patients who felt well enough could sit and talk in comfortable armchairs or watch television.

Muriel sat in one of these chairs surrounded by cards and presents given to her by the staff. She'd lost more weight and her hair hung in lifeless strands down each side of her vacant face. She sat motionless, ignoring the other patients, wrapped in her own world like a very old person who is sitting out the years waiting for death.

'Muriel – hello. Happy birthday!' Caroline put the cake on the table beside Muriel's chair. 'Jimbo has sent you a cake. Would you like to have a look at it?'

Her head nodded assent. When the lid was off she peered into the box. Tears began pouring down her thin cheeks. Silent rivers of release. She made no attempt to wipe her tears away but let them flood down. It was painful to watch her.

Caroline didn't try to stop her; she simply held her hand, feeling that the tears were significant and healing.

The ward sister came by and behind Muriel's back gave the thumbs-up sign. 'That's encouraging,' she mouthed.

When the tears had ceased, Caroline wiped Muriel's face and combed her hair for her. It was like attending to a very young child. For the first time in days Muriel spoke.

'It's got my name on it. It's meant for me, just me. It's really meant *just for me*. How kind of Jimbo, such a thoughtful man. I haven't ever had a birthday cake. Mother thought they were a self-congratulatory luxury. She didn't know how much it pained me not to have one. I'll have a slice right now. Will you have one too?'

Caroline organised tea for the patients sitting round the table and they all had a slice of cake. It was delicious and Muriel enjoyed it more than any food she had been persuaded to eat in all the time she'd been in the hospital.

Muriel leant over to Caroline and asked her if she would get Peter to come in to see her. 'I've got things to tell him I can't tell anyone else. He hasn't been, has he?'

'Yes, he has, several times, but you weren't well enough to talk to him.'

'Oh, I don't remember that.' The shutters came down and Muriel returned to wherever she had been before Caroline came in.

'Dr Harris, have you a moment?'

Sister Bonaventure discussed some blood tests she felt one of the patients needed, and then Caroline wended her way back to the pathology lab, calling in at the ante-natal clinic en route to collect any blood samples they might have.

The clinic was busy. Expectant mothers lined the walls, some with little ones in tow, others alone and staring ahead, bored by the waiting. Some of them were exchanging pregnancy experiences, while others read magazines. Caroline stood looking out of the Sister's office window at the full waiting room wondering whether she might like to change to obstetrics. It would certainly be more lively than pathology. It was then she noticed Suzy Meadows, with Rosie on her knee. Suzy must have sensed someone was looking at her because she glanced up before Caroline could avert her eyes. They looked directly at one another. Caroline raised her hand in greeting and then turned away.

She longed to go and have a word with her but as a doctor, professional etiquette dictated she should remain silent. This was one of the problems of being a doctor in a busy county hospital. One met neighbours and friends but had to keep a discreet silence to preserve their confidentiality. Poor Suzy, with another child to bring up and no husband for support. Still, this one might be a boy and that would be a great comfort. Suzy was a born mother. How sad that Patrick had not lived to see his new baby . . .

When Caroline got home she told Peter about Muriel wanting to see him and nearly mentioned Suzy's presence in the ante-natal clinic, but decided against it. Everyone would know soon enough. It wasn't exactly something which could be kept a secret for long.

Peter went with her to the hospital the next day and called into Muriel's ward. She was sitting as before, wrapped in thought.

'Hello, Muriel. It's Peter come to see you. God bless you.' He shook her hand and then held on to it. 'I see you've had plenty of cards for your birthday.'

She turned to look at him and slowly recognition came. 'Would you like a piece of Jimbo's cake? He sent it for me; it's the first birthday cake I have ever had. You will have a piece, won't you?'

'I can't wait. If it's the same standard as that birthday meal of his, then I'm in for a treat.'

'Oh, it's every bit as good.' She waited until he had tasted it and then asked how he liked it.

'It is excellent, absolutely delicious. Happy birthday to you. Thank you very much.'

'I can't go back to my house. Not ever again. Not after the cat . . . and the other things.' There was a long pause while Muriel found her handkerchief. 'I'm not fit to live by myself, you know. I'm doing such silly things. I know it must have been Pericles who ate the cake but I did— Oh, Pericles – where is he? I haven't thought about him once while I've been in here. Has he been shut in the house all this time? Oh dear, how could I have forgotten him? You see, it is my mind that's going, it is, it is.' The tears began again.

Peter leant towards her and said clearly: 'Your Pericles is having the time of his life. Sir Ronald has taken charge of him and he takes him and Lady Bissett's Pomeranian for long walks every day. The two dogs are the greatest of friends so you've no need to worry on *that* score. And Pericles hasn't eaten the cake because it's here.'

'I don't mean this cake, I mean the one I baked at home. I put it out to cool and when I came back it had disappeared. Then I didn't make the bed and I knew I had. Then the ornaments were all turned round and put in the wrong places. It was one thing after another – such silly things I was doing. It all started the day Pericles ran away because I'd left the back door open. I lost my keys and since then I've been soft in the head. Yes, soft in the head. Mother went like that – didn't know what she was doing. But she still kept her sharp tongue. To be truthful, she didn't really want me. Having me spoiled her figure and she never forgave me. She was mean, so mean. Sitting here I can remember things she did.'

Muriel put up the shutters and Peter, after praying aloud that God would make His face to shine upon her and give her peace, left puzzled but at the same time relieved that at last Muriel had spoken – even if he couldn't understand her.

That evening when Caroline came home they exchanged information about their respective days. Peter told her about Muriel.

'She seems to have been doing such foolish things. Yet it all must have happened very quickly because the night of Jimbo's party she was perfectly all right, in fact on top of the world. She natters on about cakes being eaten and ornaments being moved. I can't understand her.'

'Look, I've got her keys. I'm going to have a look in her house when we've eaten. What shall it be – Spanish omelette or fish with chips, or shall we be completely disgusting and have Chicken Kiev out of the freezer?'

'Nothing you could do would be completely disgusting,

so we'll have Chicken Kiev. I wonder if they do eat it in Kiev? Bet they've never even heard of it.' Peter laughed and Caroline, catching his mood, flung her arms round him and kissed him. She chattered on about her day while she cooked and Peter sat on a kitchen chair enjoying her gaiety. They'd promised right from the start that they would be completely truthful with each other, but it wasn't always the best thing to be completely truthful to one's beloved. Sometimes one needed to be deceitful in order to save them pain, and that left one bearing the pain alone. Peter didn't like himself.

After they'd washed up, Caroline went over over to Glebe Cottages. As she turned the key in the front door of number 1, she thought she heard a noise inside the house. She stood listening in the little sitting room. There was only silence, that kind of hollow silence peculiar to an unoccupied house. She went straight to the back door and opened it. As she looked into the garden she thought she caught a glimpse of something moving swiftly over the wall into the churchyard. Caroline hurried to the wall and looked over, but there was no one in sight. She waited for a moment and then shook her head and went back into the house.

One of the cupboards in the kitchen was open, and as she went to shut it she noticed that there was hardly anything on the shelves. She opened the door wider and saw that it was the cupboard where Muriel obviously had kept her tinned food. Sitting alone was a tin of grapefruit, one of the tiny ones people on their own buy, and a small, partly-used jar of mint sauce. Surely Muriel wasn't so short of money that that was all she had in store? Something told Caroline to search further. The pedal-bin had empty tins in it and an empty biscuit packet. Caroline went into the sitting room and opened the cupboard where Muriel kept her sherry.

There was only a drop left in the bottom, yet Caroline knew that when they'd had a drink together the night she'd lent Muriel a dress for Jimbo's party, the bottle had been nearly full. This all seemed very odd. Back in the kitchen she found two cups standing in the sink; she smelt the remains of their contents and recognised the smell of sherry.

Caroline locked the house and sped home to Peter. She told him all her findings.

'Someone must have access to her house. Perhaps they've had access for quite a while and have intended frightening her with these mysterious tricks.'

'She did say this morning she'd lost her keys.'

'That's it, then! She's lost her keys and someone has found them, said nothing and has been going in and out when they've known she wouldn't be there.'

'Caroline, the only way to put a stop to this is to have new locks put on her doors, then the keys will be useless.'

'Absolutely, but we also need to find out who is so malicious as to want to frighten her – and don't forget, they also have a vendetta with Jimbo Charter-Plackett because they deliberately drowned his cat.'

'You make it sound as if we have a pathological killer in our midst.'

'This kind of thing is only the beginning. We very well could have.'

Peter made a decision. 'First thing in the morning I shall get the sergeant to go with me to the house. Give me the keys and I'll put them on the hallstand ready for tomorrow.'

The sergeant had no answers for Peter but he agreed that it was obvious someone was getting in, and there were no signs of a forced entry. He suggested speaking to Muriel about changing the locks, but Peter said he would go and see her about it. A police sergeant arriving could well do more harm than good.

It was two days before Peter had time to call at the hospital. He took the keys with him.

'God bless you, Muriel, I'm here again.'

'Who are you? I don't know you.' Muriel turned herself so she couldn't see Peter's face.

'Yes you do, Muriel. It's Peter from St Thomas à Becket at home in Turnham Malpas.'

She refused to answer.

'I have something to show you. Will you turn round and have a look?'

Curiosity got the better of her and she half-turned to look.

'In my hand I have the keys to your house. Look.' He opened his hand and let her look.

'I'm not going home.'

'No, I know you're not. When you lost your keys, how did you get into your house again?'

'I used the spare keys I hid in the garden, till the others turned up again.'

'Oh, so they turned up again then? Where did you find them?'

'Mr Palmer found them in the piano stool.'

'So where are your spare keys now?'

She looked furtively round the ward and then whispered, 'Under the pot with the hydrangea in it in the back garden.'

'Does anyone else know they're there?'

'Only you.'

'I see. If I changed the locks on your house, that would mean that no one could get in, wouldn't it?'

'What would I do with all those keys? I wouldn't know which ones to use.'

'We would throw away these keys and you could use the new ones.'

'It wouldn't stop me doing silly things.'

Muriel switched off and Peter could do no more. He debated about changing the locks and decided to go ahead.


A few days later he was sitting in his study reading a book entitled *Why Follow Christ?* when Willie Biggs knocked urgently on his door. He always knew when it was Willie knocking because he didn't give two or three knocks like everyone else. It was always nine or ten, as if his message couldn't wait to be delivered.

'Mr Harris, sir, I've come to report that there's someone living in the churchyard shed.'

'Living in the churchyard shed? Whatever for?'

''Cos they've got no 'ome, I 'spect.'

'Who is it?'

'If I knew that I'd 'ave chased 'em off, sir. Can't catch 'em, yer see. I keep finding crisp bags, tins, a tin opener, a plate and a cup, biscuit packets . . . one thing after another, but I can't catch 'em. When I do I'll beat the living daylights out of 'em.'

'I don't think that would look very good in the headlines, Willie. "*Verger beats hell out of homeless boy.*" Of course, it might be a girl, which would look even worse.'

'I'll keep watch. If I sat on that seat in Miss Hipkin's garden by her rose arch, lovely roses they are, yellow with a fleck of pink, I could keep an eye from there right grand and they wouldn't see me. What do yer think, Rector?'

'I think it's a brilliant idea, but you could be there for ages.'

'I don't care and it won't be upsetting Miss Hipkin, her not knowing, like.'

'On one condition, Willie, that you bring to me un-harmed whoever it is you catch. Unharmed, mind you.'

'Very well, sir.' Willie tapped the side of his prominent bony nose. 'And mum's the word, sir. It's between you and me. Bet Mrs Rector likes the garden a bit better now. I haven't let on it's me who's been doing it, yer know.'

'No – and neither have I. That's another secret we have, Willie.'

'I'll be off then. Wonder who I'll catch?'

# Chapter 10

Willie had a shock when he recognised the person wandering casually up to the shed. Sitting under Muriel's rose arch he'd contemplated who it might be. The children from the Big House were well known for bringing their town ways to the village. Smoking in the bushes down by the beck and shoplifting if Mr Charter-Plackett didn't keep a sharp eye out . . . more than likely it would be one of them, he thought. Several times he'd caught them wandering round the church, but the rector – old Mr Furbank, that is – insisted that the church must be open for private prayer, and also for tourists to visit and admire the ancient murals and the Templeton family tombs. Willie had kept everything locked that he possibly could. No sense in inviting trouble, he'd thought. This new rector, Mr Harris, wanted the church to be freely available too. Sometimes, the verger of St Thomas à Becket wondered which century these men lived in. What had done before didn't do for now. From the corner of his eye he watched Scott McDonald walking quietly between the tombstones – an unlikely occupation for such a one as he. Willie kept entirely still and waited. Scott approached the shed, went past it and climbed the wall into Muriel's garden, Willie, hidden by the lush growth of the climbing rose, bided his time.

From his pocket Scott took some keys and went to Muriel's back door. He put one key in the lock with confidence, then found it wouldn't open the door. He tried the other key, rattled the door knob and stood puzzled as to why he couldn't get in. Willie crept up behind him.

'Got you, my lad!'

Despite his years Willie was very nimble and with the shock of his discovery and the idle life Scott made sure he lived, Willie had him by the collar before he could make an escape.

'We're going straight round to see the rector. One word from you and I'll cuff you one.'

'Willie Biggs, what do you think you're doing? Leave me alone. Wait till my dad hears about this.'

'Yes, just you wait. If he doesn't give you a hiding, I shall. Upsetting old ladies – whatever next.' Willie marched him to the Rectory and rattled on the door.

'Here we are, sir. I've found him trying to get into Miss Hipkin's house with his own key.'

'You'd better come inside, young man, and sit down in my study.' Peter led the way. Scott by now was beginning to feel uncomfortable. Visiting the rector's study was not something he did from choice. He was completely out of his element.

'I didn't do nothing, Mr Harris,' he whined. 'It's the first time I've—'

'First time, my foot,' Willie shouted. 'I could see you knew exactly what you were doing. You've been in there before.'

'Just a moment, Willie. We'll let Scott speak first.'

Scott looked at Peter and kept his mouth closed. Peter continued waiting for him to speak. The silence lasted and lasted, Peter patiently leaving the silence for Scott to fill. Eventually he did speak, worn down by Peter's searching look.

'It was our Sharon. I found the keys that day old Muriel—'

'Miss Hipkin to you, Scott,' Peter interrupted.

'Well, Miss Hipkin then, that day the dog got out and she raced out of school to catch him. Took 'em home I did, and told our Sharon. She took them into Culworth and got new keys cut. Cost her a packet it did, but she said it was worth it to see the old bat's face when she realised someone was getting into her house. What I did served her right. Told me off she did more than once, the daft old faggot. Why won't the key fit? Always did before.'

'Because I've had the locks changed. Do you know that Miss Hipkin is a friend of mine just as she is to lots of people in the village? We all like her very much.'

'Like her? She's an old bat, a miserable old bat, and it serves her right.'

'What have you done in Miss Hipkin's house?'

'Only daft little things to frighten her. Pinched a cake, moved the cutlery about in the drawer, drank the sherry, switched her ornaments around, things like that.'

'What about the cat?'

'What cat?'

'The cat she found drowned in her water butt?'

'Well, Mr Harris, I don't know nothing about a cat. That's not me. I like cats.' His face suddenly changed as if something had dawned on him which he wouldn't be prepared to talk about. Peter realised Scott had made a guess as to who was responsible.

'Well, Scott, Willie and you and I are going to go to your house to see your parents.'

Scott sprang to his feet. 'Let's keep this to ourselves, Mr Harris. I won't go there no more, I promise. I give you my solemn promise, cross my heart and hope to die. I'll swear on your Bible. Honest to God I will. I won't go there any more if you promise not to tell my mum.'

'It's too late for making bargains, Scott. The tricks you've played on Miss Hipkin have made her very ill. She could prefer charges, you know. Stealing, trespassing – you name it. Your mum and dad are going to have to be told. You've done it not once but several times and we must get the matter straightened out. Come along.'

Peter stood up, took hold of Scott's hand, led him from the Rectory and marched him to The Royal Oak, with Willie following eagerly in his wake. The public house stood prominently on the corner of Stocks Row and Royal Oak Road. Scott resigned himself to the inevitable. There was nothing he could do; Peter was too strong and too big for him to wrestle with.

The bar was open and crowded; his mother was busy serving.

'Two ploughman's name of Coster, here we are then, plenty of pickle like you— And what do you want with our Scott, Rector? Put him down, if you please.'

She and not Mac was the licensee for some reason unknown to the villagers, though frequently hinted at. She stood nearly six feet high and was built on Amazonian proportions. Her jet black hair was piled high on top of her head in a beehive design. Mac had once ventured to say he liked it that way and that way it had stayed. The heat of the bar on this humid afternoon had heightened the usual flush on her face. Her low-cut Lurex blouse exposed rather more of her figure than one wished to see. Her dark eyes glared furiously at Peter.

'Let him go then, Rector. There's no call to hold him like that.'

'Good afternoon, Mrs McDonald.'

'Everyone calls me Betty.'

'Good afternoon, Betty. I wonder if we could go somewhere quiet. We need to discuss Scott's behaviour.'

'Been messing about in your church, 'as he?' She brought her arm back and smacked Scott hard on his face. He ricocheted against Peter's legs.

'Well, no, not in the church.'

'Well then, you've no call to be holding him like that. Let him go.'

Peter held firmly to Scott. 'Betty, I really feel you would prefer to hear this in private.'

'I haven't the time, can't you see we're busy? Out with it.'

'Very well. We have been concerned for some time because someone has been using the churchyard shed. Willie here went to keep watch to see who it was and caught Scott attempting to enter Muriel Hipkin's cottage with a key. He has told us that he'd had the key cut and had been using it for some time.'

Apart from Peter speaking, the whole bar had frozen in anticipation of Peter's news. It was as if someone had pressed 'Pause' on a video machine.

Betty McDonald was totally nonplussed. She glared first at Peter, then at Willie, then at Scott. Before she could say a word, however, the whole bar erupted.

'It's you then that's frightened her.'

'Been stealing, have yer?'

'Might have known it 'ud be him.'

'What about Jimbo's cat, how about that then?'

'He needs horse-whipping.'

'Time you got him under control, Betty.'

Their advice incensed Betty. She rose to her full height, brought her arm back and hit Willie a savage punch right on the nose.

'That 'ull serve you right, sneaking about spying on people. A harmless little boy and two grown men frightening him to death.'

Poor Willie sat down in a chair someone put behind him as his knees buckled. Blood streamed down his face. Someone got him a brandy, someone else found some tissues and tried to catch the blood.

Mac came out from the other bar. 'Betty, that's enough! You lay one hand on the rector and you'll be done for. Mind what I say. Man of God and all that.'

Scott crept quietly upstairs out of the way. He'd seen his mother like this before.

'Man of God? I'll give him man of God, picking on a poor innocent little boy!'

'"Poor innocent little boy"? Come off it, Betty,' someone in the bar shouted.

Peter stood quietly watching the scene, hoping she wouldn't hit him because there was no way he could defend himself against a woman of her size, not when he was wearing his dog collar.

'Mrs McDonald, Scott has caused Muriel Hipkin a great deal of pain. In fact, he is the reason why she is in the psychiatric ward in hospital! You had no cause to hit Willie in that manner. He was only doing his duty by trying to protect church property. It was incidental that he found Scott trying to enter Miss Hipkin's house.'

'If he couldn't get in then he can't have had the right keys, so it can't have been him.'

'He couldn't get in today because I've had the locks changed on Muriel's behalf. Scott has admitted to entering and stealing from Muriel . . .'

'More fool him. He should have kept his mouth shut.'

'That is not the advice a responsible parent should be giving.'

'Are you telling me I'm not a resonsible parent?'

'No, I was just saying—'

'Betty! In the back, if you please.' Mac finally made his voice heard.

Betty turned to look at him, and he jerked his head in the direction of the back room. She flounced behind the bar counter and left the field. Willie's nose had almost stopped bleeding. The crowd round him congratulated him on his success as a sleuth.

'Well done, Willie.'

'Serves him right, the little sneak.'

'Muriel will be glad.'

'Drinks on the house!' Mac shouted above the noise. 'What will yours be, Rector?'

'A whisky please, Mac, and the same for Willie. He really deserves it.'

When the hubbub had quietened, Peter asked Mac for a word.

'Here I am, Rector, fire away.'

'Sharon helped Scott, you know. He didn't do it entirely on his own. She went to the key-cutters in Culworth with Muriel's keys and got copies made. I think only Scott went into the house but she definitely aided and abetted him.'

'I am extremely sorry about all this, Rector. The trouble is we're so busy with the bar that the children are left to their own devices too much. We'll have to make a better effort. You know what it's like with teenagers nowadays, they're that headstrong. Our Sharon's like a grown woman and has been for years. You can't say no nowadays.'

'Do your best, Mac. Muriel has the right to press charges, you know, and I wouldn't blame her if she did. I shall have to tell the police, because they came to have a look round the house when we realised someone was getting in. So they might call in here to speak to you even if Muriel doesn't go ahead with a prosecution.'

'I really must apologise for our Betty's behaviour. Sharon takes after her mother – acts first, thinks afterwards.'

It took all of two weeks before Muriel felt able to come home. Caroline took her to the hairdresser's in Culworth and made her feel a million dollars by encouraging her to have a perm at Caroline's expense. Peter presented her with her new keys, which gave her the confidence to go home. Someone suggested a party to welcome her back but then they all agreed she'd feel better just quietly sliding back into her own routine.

Jimbo had restocked her kitchen cupboards for her, popping specialities of the house into her fridge as well. Sir Ronald had taken Pericles for a shampoo and a hairdo at the dog parlour and bought him a new lead and collar, bright red and glossy. Lady Bissett had arranged a bouquet of flowers for the middle of Muriel's little dining table and the mantelpiece was filled with 'Welcome Home' cards. Willie had been keeping her garden watered and the grass cut so that when she went home her world was gloriously restored.

Her confidence, however, was only partly restored but she felt that time would heal that. A few days after getting home Peter called with Scott in tow.

'Good afternoon, Miss Hipkin, God bless you. I've brought Scott to see you. He has something to say, haven't you, Scott?'

Muriel began trembling. Seeing Scott brought back all her anxieties.

Scott wriggled free of Peter's restraining hand.

'He says I've to apologise. And I will, but I didn't do the cat, Miss Hipkin – that wasn't me. I like cats. But I did the other things, and I'm sorry I made you poorly.'

'Well, thank you, Scott.' Muriel held back the tears and turned away, hoping Peter would take him away.

'Good afternoon then, Miss Hipkin. Say good afternoon, Scott, please.'

'Good afternoon, Miss Hipkin.' They both went out and Peter closed the door quietly behind them.

A day or two later there was another knock at the door.

'Why, come in, Mr Charter-Plackett! I intended coming into the shop to thank you for your kindness in filling my kitchen with food. I can never thank you enough, and also thank you for my birthday cake. Do you know, it was the first birthday cake I'd ever had?'

'Only too glad to see you back home again. We've all missed you very much. Can I sit down for a moment?'

'Of course, how remiss of me. Here, sit in this chair, it's the most comfortable.'

'I've come because I'm in a bit of a dilemma.'

'Oh dear, how can I help?'

'Well, I don't know if you've noticed but I've got the restaurant opened now. We've called it Henderson's.'

'After Phyllis? What a lovely idea!'

'That's right, yes. Well, it's kind of two restaurants in one. There's Harriet's Tearoom which sells light snacks and coffees and teas and the like, which opens at ten o'clock and closes at five o'clock, and we also have what Flick calls the "posh bit" – which is a proper restaurant for dinners, open in the evening from seven until eleven. I've got waiters and waitresses and chefs, et cetera, but what I *haven't* got for the tearoom is someone whom I can rely on to take the money every day. No matter how careful we are with our accountancy, there's always a way of stealing money if one's employees try hard enough. I've found someone I can trust for four days a week, but I need someone for the other two days. It would be Wednesday and Friday. What I wondered was, well, would you like the idea? If I've given offence, please forgive me. It is a very genteel tearoom, not all taped music and the like – a kind of thirties-style tearoom, you know.'

'Why is it called Harriet's Tearoom?'

'Because I had hoped to get her interested in it, but she refuses. I went about it in completely the wrong way and she's taken her bat home and refuses to have anything to do with it.'

'Oh dear. I thought you were cleverer than that.'

'So did I.'

'I don't know if I feel confident enough yet to help out. It would mean being sure about how much change I was handing out, wouldn't it? I'll give it serious thought and let you know tomorrow.'

Jimbo went off home, well satisfied with his morning's work. Out and about she needed to be, and this ruse might do the trick. Besides which, he really did need someone. Harriet could be extremely difficult sometimes. Even the sugared almonds hadn't worked their usual miracle this time. She needed a holiday. That was it – a holiday. He'd get Sadie to organise something. He amazed himself sometimes with his fertile mind . . .

Jimbo had left Muriel all in a dither. Three years at home without much challenge and no need to keep to someone else's timetable, had lessened her capacity to cope. But she could see herself sitting at the seat of custom like Matthew in the Bible, except she wouldn't be collecting taxes. It would be fun, though, because everyone in there would have gone to enjoy themselves. Maybe she'd have one of those tills which went Ping! when she opened the drawer. On the other hand, knowing Jimbo, he'd have one of those electric things with lots of buttons to push and flashing lights. Even so, the money she would earn would be very useful. She could always come home in the lunch-hour to take Pericles out, and not starting till ten o'clock would mean she could do her little jobs about the house and take him out before she went. Yes, why not? Was it a come-down for a solicitor's secretary? – a bit beneath her? No. If Jimbo could serve in a shop when he'd had a good post in the City in a merchant bank, why should she quibble about serving behind the till? 'Two toasted teacakes and a pot of tea.' 'Scrambled egg, pot of tea and a cream cake.' Oh yes, she could manage that, and there'd be plenty of people to talk to.

Next day, Muriel hastened into the shop on her way out with Pericles. Harriet greeted her like a long-lost friend.

'How lovely to see you, Muriel. I'm so glad you're home, we have missed you. You are looking well. I love your hair, it does suit you.' And then she kissed her on both cheeks.

'Thank you, Harriet, and thank you also for all the food in my kitchen. Your kindness will not go unnoticed in the Book of Good Deeds. Jimbo called to see me yesterday and I promised him I would give him an answer today.'

'An answer? To what?'

'Well, something he asked me to do. Is he about?'

'Can you tell me and I'll pass on the message?'

Muriel shuffled about a bit, checked on Pericles tied up outside and then said, 'Well, the answer is yes.'

'Yes to what? What's all the mystery about?'

'Isn't he in?'

'No, he's out on business.'

'Don't be annoyed with me will you, Harriet? I couldn't bear that.'

'Of course I shan't be annoyed, but if you don't explain soon I shall be thinking you and Jimbo are having clandestine meetings.'

Muriel blushed. 'Oh, Harriet, it's nothing like that! You're teasing me, aren't you?'

'Yes.'

'Well, he's asked me to take the money in the tearoom he named after you, two days a week. You're not angry, are you?'

Harriet burst out laughing. 'Of course not. He urgently needs someone. I don't mind at all.'

'You know, Harriet, you should support him. Husbands need support. He's very upset.'

'Muriel, leave Jimbo to me, I know what I'm doing. I won't have him riding roughshod over me and that's what he did with this tearoom business. He thought he'd bring me round by naming it after me, but I know his little game. I'll come round in my own good time, never fear.'

Pericles yapped out his boredom at the long delay.

'I must be off. I'll call in later when Jimbo gets back,' Muriel said hastily.

She began work the following Wednesday. Once she'd mastered the till and how to check the little bills, Muriel found herself enjoying her new role. Handing out menus and showing people to suitable tables and passing the time of day with them, she was in her element. Jimbo paid her £25 a day – riches indeed. One day's pay went into the savings bank and the other for living expenses. If she was careful she might manage a holiday next year. The continent, maybe?

# Chapter 11

The following Saturday morning Muriel was taking her turn cleaning the brasses in the church, listening while she worked to Peter playing the organ. Sometimes when she heard him she wished he was the organist instead of Mrs Peel. Mrs Peel played competently but Peter played competently *and* with his heart and soul, which made such a difference to the beauty of it. He finished playing, switched off the organ, went to the altar rail and said a few words of prayer and then came across to speak to Muriel.

'God bless you, Muriel. What the Church would do without its women I do not know.'

'Good morning, Peter. In that case, why can't we be ordained priests? I'm not clever enough to be one, but there are plenty of women who would be and could do good service to the Church.'

'I didn't know you were a militant parshioner?'

'I'm not, but I do get annoyed about the whole subject sometimes. I expect we'll win in the end, women usually do. Have you got out Mr Furbank's costume for Stocks Day? I'll give it a good clean and a mend for you if you like.'

'Stocks Day – what's that?'

'Surely Mr Furbank must have left notes about it? We've been celebrating Stocks Day for centuries. The whole village joins in a procession and we all wear costumes and someone dresses as the Grim Reaper and someone else as an Angel. After dark the night before, the verger has to dress the stocks with dead or dying flowers. Then the next afternoon, always the last Saturday in June, we all walk twice round the green. The first time we carry sticks and we all beat the stocks when we pass them and knock off the old flowers, and the second time round we carry white flowers and lay them all on the stocks and cover it completely if we can. Mr Palmer knows someone who plays the flute and they come and lead the procession, like as if it was medieval times. Then, weather permitting, we all sit down to a big tea on the green. Some say we've been doing it since 1066, some say since before history began – but I think that's a bit fanciful – and some say since the plague. According to the church records, Turnham Malpas was badly hit by the plague in 1349 so I think that's more likely, don't you?'

'What part do I play in this?'

'Oh, you're the Devil.'

She turned away to collect her cleaning cloths and move on to the altar vases. Peter stood appalled. '*The Devil?*' He followed her to the altar.

'Yes, you wear your marriage cassock underneath your costume and when you reach the stocks for the second time you take off your Devil's costume and then you bless the stocks. You're all in white like the flowers, you see. Purity or cleansing or something, I think. The whole village loves the celebration. They used to hold games and competitions on the green after the tea, but since about 1895 there's been a fair on the spare land behind the Methodist Chapel. So, when the tea is finished, the tables are all cleared away and everyone goes to the fair for the evening. It's a wonderful day.'

Muriel didn't notice the effect on Peter of what she had said. She busily rubbed away at the twiddly bits on the altar vases, remembering processions from her childhood and how much she had enjoyed seeing the transformation of the Rector from a nasty horned Devil to a charming harmless figure dressed all in white.

'The Press always come and take photographs and there's always a piece in the paper about it and lots of people come to watch – to see the villagers playing at being quaint, I suppose. There's an old painting of it on the wall in the corner behind that tomb that Willie Biggs says is haunted – you know, the one with the knight resting his ankles on his little dog. I don't know which rector it is but he's there for all to see.'

Peter beat a retreat to the rear of the church and stood gazing at the painting. The gold frame was old and in need of a good clean and so was the painting, but it was possible to discern a rector of indeterminate century dropping his Devil's mask and costume onto the grass and standing there holding up his hand in blessing. Close by him were an angel and a figure he assumed was someone's idea of the Grim Reaper. Pagan. Definitely pagan. Nothing to do with Christianity at all.

Peter called to Muriel: 'Surely we usually dress a well, not the stocks.'

Muriel came up the church to speak to him.

'Well yes, most villages do, but the only well still in existence is that one in Jimmy Glover's garden and that is foul. Over the years he's been throwing all his rubbish down it. It certainly wouldn't be any good blessing that. Besides, which, he wouldn't let you. Something of a recluse is Jimmy and a smelly one at that. Oh, and there's another one in Thelma and Valda Senior's garden too. I'd forgotten that one.'

'I have grave doubts as to whether I can perform this blessing.'

'Oh dear. Mr Furbank never gave it a thought – he loved getting dressed up. We had the procession right through the war. Whatever's going on in the world, the ceremony always takes place.'

Neither of them realised that they were being overheard. The news about Peter's misgivings was all round the village and the outlying farms before he had finished his soup that evening.

As Peter entered the church the next morning he noticed an increase, in fact a substantial increase, in the size of the congregation. For a split second he wondered if he had forgotten it was some kind of special day but knew he hadn't. The difference he did notice was that only the choir was singing. The congregation stood mute to a man. When he announced the first hymn, scarcely a hymnbook rustled. Mrs Peel played the first two lines and everyone stood. From his position on the altar steps Peter could see that Caroline, Muriel and Jimbo and Harriet had got their hymnbooks out , but none of the real villagers had done so.

He conducted the entire service in his normal joyous uplifting manner but by the end the strain was beginning to tell. When Peter stood at the church door to wish the congregation 'Good morning' he found that apart from those same four people, no one appeared to shake his hand. They had all gone out through the vestry door.

Willie Biggs supplied the answer.

'They've all taken their bats home, sir. Heard you were

none too pleased about playing the Devil in the procession on Stocks Day and they is very upset. They've sent you to Coventry till you change your mind.'

'Does it mean so much to them, then? Why can't someone else play the part? Jimbo would do a good job, wouldn't you, Jimbo?'

'No, Peter, indeed I wouldn't. If they gave me the same cold shoulder they've given you this morning, I'd be bankrupt in a week and with a wife and three children to support, I simply can't afford it. It's you they want, Peter. I'd be no substitute, believe me.'

'But it's a pagan ritual.'

Caroline took his arm. 'Let's go home and have a think, darling.'

'Can't you persuade him to do it, Caroline?' Harriet asked as they made their way down the church path.

'I never try to influence Peter where his conscience is concerned. He is the rector, not me. Sorry, Harriet.'

Caroline went straight to the kitchen and began making sandwiches for their lunch, leaving Peter to wrestle with his own conscience. She knew he'd have to fall in with it in the end, but he needed to come to that conclusion himself. This Stocks Day was evidently part of the fabric of village life and sometimes modern theological thinking had to give way when such stout opposition was voiced. She'd been mortified during the whole of the service and had felt desperately sorry for Peter. At one stage she had nearly stood up and told them what she thought about them all, and then she remembered that he was the rector, not she, and that this was a battle he must fight.

During the afternoon she began altering a dress she'd worn in a play at the hospital. It was drab and loose and torn, but just right for a medieval peasant woman taking part in a village ritual.

'Surely to goodness that isn't a dress you intend wearing, is it? It's not your colour at all,' Peter protested as he brought in an afternoon cup of tea as a means of regaining Caroline's favour.

'Yes it is. I'm playing the part of a medieval peasant woman fearful of the plague and trying hard to forget that I've lost my mother, my father, two sisters and three of my children with the dreaded pestilence.'

'Caroline, is this some kind of joke?'

'No, thanks for the tea, no, that's what it's for.'

'Are you joining in the procession, then?'

'Yes.'

'Even though I don't approve?'

'I am not trying to persuade you to change your mind, so you mustn't try to change mine. We agreed on that before we married.'

'But this is something where I need your support.'

'I can't support you when these good people have so vehemently shown you their disapproval. They must feel very deeply about the issue or they wouldn't have been as unkind and rude as they were this morning. It's not in their nature.'

'But this has nothing to do with Christianity. It's a relic of some pagan ceremony, I'm sure it is. The Devil, indeed! There's no such thing, only the evil within ourselves.'

'Who are you trying to persuade now? Yourself or me?' She slipped off her dress and tried on the costume. 'All I need now is to make my hair all drab and disgusting and I shall look a treat. I've got that old pair of Jesus sandals you don't like – they'll come in handy. It's ages since I had my tea on a village green. You'll have to get your own tea that day. I'll leave something in the fridge for you.'

Caroline went into the hall and stood looking at herself in the long mirror. Peter came up behind her and put his arms round her.

'What if I asked you not to join in?'

'It wouldn't work, Peter. I'm part of the village and I must join in. They know it has to be done or things won't be right for them. I look like a too-well-fed peasant, don't I? I'll have to put some shadow on my cheeks and make them seem hollow.'

Peter had a bitter week following his declaration about Stocks Day. Those who did speak to him looked sorrowfully at him; even Muriel was icily polite when he dropped into Harriet's Tearoom for a coffee.

'Good morning, Mr Harris. Would you like a table outside in the garden or do you prefer inside?'

'Inside, Muriel, then we can talk.'

The YTS girl brought his coffee and Muriel sat at the till trying to look busy with her bookwork. Her natural politeness prevented her from being rude but secretly she was very distressed by Peter's attitude.

He chattered on about the playgroup starting and one thing and another of parish interest, and then eventually she could stand it no longer.

'It's no good, Mr Harris. You've got to face up to it, you know.'

'Face up to what?'

'Stocks Day. I knew the village would be upset but I'd no idea feeling would run so high. The ceremony has a great deal of significance for them, you know. It's right there in their bones and they won't feel right if they don't have the rector doing what he should. They'll all be quite convinced that terrible things will happen to the village if they don't keep faith with the past.'

'I've heard what you say, Muriel, but what about my conscience?'

'Pshaw! What's your conscience worth if you lose everyone's trust?'

'It's worth a lot to me.'

'Yes, I know it is, and we wouldn't want it any other way, but please try to see their point of view.'

Other customers came in and she had to break off her conversation with him.

He went across to the school in the hope that he might find some kindred spirit there in Michael Palmer.

The children were all having their dinners when he arrived. The hall was full of laughing chattering children, a sheer delight which lifted his spirits. As soon as they noticed him, however, they fell silent and Peter knew it wasn't out of respect.

'Good day to you, children. God bless you all.'

Michael Palmer looked sternly at the children and told them to answer. Peter got some shamefaced muttered responses and then the children ignored him.

'Mr Palmer, could I speak to you for a moment?' They went into Michael's tiny office, where Michael offered him the only chair whilst he perched on the edge of the desk.

'You've done it now, Peter. The children can talk of nothing else.'

'I don't know how everyone found out I disapproved.'

'You can't catch cold in this village without they know before the first sneeze. It's no good trying to keep anything quiet. Historically, Blessing the Stocks is part of them, you see.'

'Historically yes, but from the Church's point of view it's a no-go area.'

'You do know the origins, don't you?'

'Well, they're pagan, aren't they?'

'Not really. A Victorian cleric with more time to spare than you have nowadays, investigated old village customs and found that the Stocks Day procession in Turnham Malpas originated because of the plague. A vagrant had come to the village and had been stealing food and clothes from the villagers. They caught him at it and the local Lord of the Manor, namely one of the Templetons, had him put in the stocks. Unfortunately, while he was fastened in there they realised he had begun showing the early symptoms of the plague. They released him but he died the next day. In consequence of this, many of the villagers died. The part of the ceremony in which villagers beat the stocks with sticks to get rid of the dead flowers is their way of getting rid of the vagrant who brought death with him. That's why there is someone to represent the Grim Reaper – though where the angel comes in I'm not sure. Then the white flowers represent a new beginning after the plague had passed, and the rector dressed in white blessing the stocks makes everything right for another year. When you do that, the whole village will feel safe from the outside world. So really it's an historical drama commemorating the past.'

'I see. I suppose that casts a different light on it. But they shouldn't need something like this to make them feel safe.'

'I know, I know, but they do. Presumably they felt the Devil had sent the vagrant in the first place, and they get rid of him by turning him into the rector.'

'Thank you, Michael, for taking time to explain. You'll need to get back to the children now. How's the playgroup working out?'

'Extremely well. Suzy Meadows is excellent and we are all dovetailing in very nicely indeed. She was an inspired choice. While Muriel has been ill, Suzy's been playing the piano for us. It's early days yet, but I know the children will benefit.'

'Good, I'm glad. Thank you for your help this afternoon.'

Peter made his way out across the playground, smiling at the children and throwing a ball back to someone, but the children would have none of his overtures. He went into church to meditate for a while.

As he stood before the altar wrestling with his conscience he heard firm footsteps approaching and turned to see who had come in. It was Betty McDonald.

'Thought I might find you here, Rector. Seeing as you've been communicating with His Nibs, perhaps you've decided to change your mind about Stocks Day?'

'No, indeed I haven't. I still feel it's wrong.'

'Well, you'd better think again. Who the hell do you think you are? Have you any idea how much money we shall lose in the bar if you don't do it? Stocks Day is one of our busiest in the whole year. We can't afford to lose money. You're all right, it won't affect your pocket but it will affect mine and Mac's.'

'Whilst I would not wish any harm to come to your business, I'm afraid that your public house is not my responsibility.'

'I dare say, but I'm damned if I'm going to let the village suffer just because of your conscience.' She advanced another step and prodded Peter in the middle of his chest.

'You come here with your posh ways and more money than you know what to do with, and think you can dictate what we do. We may not have been to Oxford but we do know what's right and it's time you did too. Take my advice, play the Devil in the procession, and do it with your fingers crossed behind your back then it won't matter, just like we did when we were telling lies when we were kids. Do it you will, or else I shall want to know the reason why.'

She stormed from the church like a ship in full sail. Peter groaned and said, 'Now, Lord, what do I do?' He went out of the church, crossed the green and stood in front of the stocks. Ancient though they were, they were complete. He'd often seen them in other villages and only the bottom half remained, but Turnham Malpas stocks stood as they had done for hundreds of years. He tried lifting the top half and found it was possible to move it sufficiently to put his own legs and hands through and he decided to sit in the stocks for a moment. The strangest feeling came over him as he sat there. He didn't feel like himself at all; he almost became someone else. He looked round the village and observed that the houses facing the green were just as they had been for centuries. That vagrant must have looked out through the pain of his plague symptoms and seen the village more or less as it stood today.

Here and there a new sign could be seen. The tasteful Turnham Malpas Stores of Jimbo's, and the new sign above his restaurant and tearoom were perhaps the only changes. Peter only intended sitting there for a moment but he became wrapped in his thoughts and drifted away in time. He could see that woman Caroline had pretended to be who'd lost her parents, two sisters and three of her children in the plague. She would have joined the procession in a desperate effort to ward off its return, in case any more of her family died from it. The rector himself must have prayed for it never to return because of the burden he would have had to carry comforting the bereaved and burying the dead. History stretched out before him and behind him, and Peter saw himself as part of a pattern in which he felt compelled to participate. He decided to agree to do the

Blessing; it was only right.

Peter extricated himself from the stocks and went off home satisfied he was doing the right thing. 'I must not let Betty McDonald think she's persuaded me – that would be the end!'

Peter sitting in the stocks had not gone unnoticed. Pat Duckett had seen him on her way to close up the school, Muriel had seen him from the window of Harriet's Tea-room, and so had Suzy Meadows as she set off to collect Pansy and Daisy from afternoon school. Her heart missed a beat as she saw him, for she still found him tremendously attractive. It wouldn't be long now before he knew. She couldn't disguise her situation many more weeks; she'd never been as big as she was this time. Maybe he already knew, perhaps Caroline had told him about seeing her in the clinic, but she felt he didn't know. He wouldn't have been able to stop himself from speaking to her about it. God knew she didn't want this baby. She'd offer it for adoption. Surely people who adopt a child would cherish it. She quite simply didn't want it. No way. No way.

# Chapter 12

Muriel pressed her costume with loving care. She'd worn the same one for four years now. It was made from an old brown coat of her mother's. Every time Mrs Hipkin had worn it she'd said, 'This coat will see me out.' It didn't. She'd bought another one, but refused to throw the old one away. 'It'll come in for something one day,' she'd maintained. Stocks Day was only two days away and Muriel couldn't wait. The fair had already arrived, Willie Biggs had cleaned all the trestle tables and had them stacked in the church hall awaiting the big day. Tradition had it that everyone brought their own food for the tea so there was no catering to do, which made the event a pleasure for everyone.

Thank goodness Peter had decided to do the Blessing. Muriel wasn't superstitious, but she had a sneaking feeling that if he hadn't, all kinds of dreadful things would have happened in the village. Death and destruction, that's what. The costume, hanging up on its hanger from the door frame, blew gently in the breeze from the garden. The hot weather still persisted. Because her plants were so dear to her she'd managed to get over her fear of the water butt, but she shuddered each time she used it. Those weeks in the hospital had gone by in a blur but they still struck terror in her heart. She'd only to see Scott in school and the horror came flooding back – but she mustn't dwell on it. There were so many exciting things happening to her these days. The part of the week she liked best were Wednesdays and Fridays, when she went to the tearoom. She hadn't realised what a gregarious person she was. All these years she'd taken a back seat and she shouldn't have done.

Peter's costume was hanging from the door frame as well. The mask and horns had had to be seriously renovated but she'd taken great joy in the task. How sensible he was to accept what had to be. He and Caroline were the best thing that had happened to the village for years. They'd brought such light and joy to everyone, and in such a practical way, too. If only they'd had a family. Peter's children would have been beautiful indeed, and Caroline would have made such a lovely mother.

She went out into the front garden to water the roses. Glancing up, she saw Betty McDonald going past.

'Good afternoon, Mrs McDonald.'

'Why do you always insist on calling me Mrs McDonald? Everyone but you calls me Betty. Go on, say it – Betty.'

'Well, Betty then.'

'That's better. It was me made the rector change his mind, yer know.'

'I should think that Pe— the rector made up his own mind.'

'Oh no, he didn't. I went to see him in church. Praying, he was. Said he didn't agree with it, but I told him. "Cross yer fingers" I said, "and pretend you're liking it." It did the trick – I knew it would. Just needed someone to tell him what was what.'

'I don't expect he took any notice of what you said.' Muriel said this politely but firmly.

'See 'ere, I'm telling you it was me what made him change his mind. I told him good and proper. "Mac and me 'ull lose money if the Blessing doesn't go ahead," I said. I told him he'd have me to answer to if he didn't. Next day he's doing it.'

'I see.'

'Time you unbent a bit, yer too stiff and starchy. Come in the bar tonight and I'll treat you to a drink. Mind what I say, I shall expect you.'

Muriel had never been in a public house unescorted in all her life. She dismissed the idea and carried on watering her plants. Pericles dug about in the borders and got under her feet in that annoying way he had when he was wanting to go for a walk. Finally she gave in and got his lead. They wandered down to the beck and met Lady Bissett out with her Pomeranian. The two dogs greeted each other like long-lost comrades so Muriel and Lady Bissett joined forces and chattered about this and that as they walked by the beck.

'I'm to be the Angel this year you know, Muriel.'

'I didn't know that. We usually have a – well, a younger person to be the Angel.'

'Yes I know, but the committee said they would choose me on account of all the work I've done in the past for the Village Flower Show and things. It is an honour. I've hired an angel costume from the costumiers in Culworth. Ron . . . ald has gone to collect it this afternoon.'

'Do you think that's wise? After all, it's only a simple village affair.'

'I know, but you must raise standards, don't you think? And what with the Press being there as well, you have to

134

keep up your position. Ronald is delighted. He's the Grim Reaper this year, you know. In fact, if Peter had not changed his mind he was going to volunteer to be the Devil.'

'The verger is the Grim Reaper, by tradition.'

'Well yes, but he has no style, has he? Willie Biggs isn't really suitable for such a part.'

'The verger is always the Grim Reaper – it doesn't matter whether he is suitable or not.'

'Yes, it does. Things must be done correctly. I did consider paying for Peter to have a new costume. It's still not too late. Ron . . . ald could go back tomorrow and get him a real smart outfit.'

'I've renovated Peter's costume. It's the one that has been worn by the rector for something like seventy years.'

'That's what I'm saying – he needs a new one.'

'Well, I disagree. We've all to be thankful he's decided to do it; let's leave it at that.'

'It was me who persuaded him to change his mind, you know. I told him that these small-minded village people have to be humoured. They haven't much in this life and if Blessing the Stocks makes them feel better, then who are we to argue?'

'I think you're being very patronising, Lady Bissett. Just because they live in a village, it does not mean to say they are idiots.'

'Don't take on so. I'll go and see Peter this afternoon and tell him I'm hiring, at my own expense of course, a brand-new Devil's costume for him.'

'You can't. He's away at a Diocesan Retreat all day.'

'I'll ring the company this afternoon and reserve one just in case then, and ask him in the morning first thing and Ron . . . ald can go in again tomorrow morning to pick it up.'

Muriel grew flustered and actually stamped her foot. 'You'll do no such thing! You are an interfering old busybody.'

'How dare you call me that? I'm giving the whole proceedings a bit of style, that's all.'

'A bit of style? If we listen to you we shall all be hiring costumes and that's not what it's about. Some of the costumes are dozens of years old and have been passed down from generations back.'

Muriel snatched Pericles up into her arms as he dashed by, turned on her heel and fled the scene of battle.

Hired costumes, indeed! Whatever next?

Peter declined Lady Bissett's offer. He felt things were in such a delicate state that he daren't trespass so far from tradition. Besides, he didn't want to hurt Muriel's feelings. She'd worked so hard on his costume.

On the Day he put it on over his marriage cassock and stood admiring himself in the hall mirror. Caroline joined him and they both burst out laughing.

Wiping the tears from her eyes, she turned to him and said, 'When I promised to marry you I thought we would be at a university church or a big city church and be all posh and dignified. Now look at the two of us!'

'So did I, but this is much more real and much more fun. I'm going to take you on the dodgems tonight – it's years since I went to a fair. I must say, Dr Harris, you look very authentic. What have you used for the shadows on your delightful cheeks?'

'Just a very little soot from the stove in the sitting room, mixed with some wrinkle cream. I've been quite artistic, haven't I?'

'Indeed you have. Now, where are the words I have to say? Oh, here they are in my cassock pocket. Having given in about this thing I must do it right. I wish Arthur Furbank had been a bit taller. My cassock's barely covered by this costume.'

'Never mind, you look very impressive. Come on, it's time we were off.'

They made their way to the starting point where already three-quarters of the village were waiting and the Press had their cameras at the ready. The down-at-heel local reporter stood wearily watching the proceedings for the umpteenth time. He'd been well primed by Lady Bissett with two double whiskies in her drawing room and in return he had persuaded the photographer to take pictures of her standing by the door of her house, but the feather wings she was wearing caught on the thatched roof where it curved round the porch and she had had to be extricated by Sir Ronald. The reporter forbore to take notes on the language she used as her husband rescued her.

It must have been one of the most successful Stocks Days the village had ever had. Because of Peter's initial decision not to take part, a lot of outside interest had been aroused and the crowds watching the procession were bigger than ever. Betty and Mac had a sensational day in the bar, and the fair took more money that evening than on any Saturday night for years. The brilliant weather, of course, had encouraged the crowds. About half-past nine, Pat Duckett decided that it was time she went home, as the children had already spent most of her money. Dean was clutching a huge turquoise teddy bear he'd won on the little shooting range and Michelle was munching her way through yet another toffee apple.

'There's no more money left now so we'd better go home.'

'Aw, Mum, we want to stay for Mr Charter-Plackett's

firework display.'

'I didn't know he was having fireworks.'

'Well, he is. It's a secret but we all know at school because Flick told us. She couldn't keep a secret, not if you paid her.'

Michelle took time off from her toffee apple to say, 'It's at ten o'clock, she says. Please can we stay?'

'Well, all right then, but after that we must go. We shan't be able to eat all week if I spend much more. Where's the display?'

'On the green. He started getting it ready as soon as Mr Biggs had cleared the trestle tables away.'

'Righto then. We'll walk round a bit longer then we'll go and stand near the school and get a good view.'

It was almost dark when the three of them went to take their places. A small crowd in the know was already in position.

As the first fireworks went up, the crowds in the fairground came running to watch the fun. Oooh! Aaaah! they went as the huge rockets soared into the sky. Pat Duckett watching Jimbo igniting the fireworks thought how lovely it would be to have the kind of money that could afford a display of such magnitude. To have money to spend just for fun. She turned her head to watch a rocket as it flared into dozens of stars above the school. Right mess I shall have clearing the playground before school on Monday, she thought. As she glanced at the school, she noticed that a light had been left on.

'That's funny – there's a light on in the school. You two stay here and don't move. I'll just go and see everything's all right. Do as I say, now.'

Pat dug around in her bag for the school keys. There they were right at the bottom with her fags. 'Have to clean this bag out some time,' she muttered. She put the huge key in

138

the lock of the main door and to her surprise found it was already undone. The rows of pegs in the narrow corridor leading to the main hall were free of the children's coats and they looked quite forlorn. She pushed open the door into the hall. Only the lights at the far end were on. She walked forward to the bank of light switches and kicked against something on the floor.

She looked down to see what she had kicked. She was so distraught she didn't know she was screaming at the top of her voice. Her hand clamped to her mouth, she ran from the hall and out into the playground. The fireworks were still exploding with massive bangs and no one could hear her screaming above the explosions. She ran to the edge of the crowd and found Willie Biggs.

For once in her life she couldn't speak. She grasped his arm and, still screaming, pulled him towards the school.

''Ere, Pat, what's up? Now then, now then, go steady.'

Pat Duckett pushed him through the main door of the school and then stood outside sobbing and gasping for breath. She couldn't bear going inside again.

Willie pushed open the door into the hall and saw what had frightened Pat Duckett. Lying on the floor at his feet was Toria Clark, so badly beaten about the head that she must have died instantly. She still wore the bright red shirt and the close-fitting black trousers she'd put on for going to the fair. Her dark hair was blood-soaked and her face almost unrecognisable from the beating she had taken. By her hand lay the keys which Willie recognised as belonging to the school. He ran outside, turned Pat Duckett's key in the lock, thrust it into her hand for safe keeping and set off for help.

He knew the police sergeant was on fairground duty and he ran as fast as his legs would carry him. He found him at the entrance talking to some boys from the next village.

'Sergeant, you'll have to come to the school. There's been a . . . well, a tragedy. Come quick!'

It was the same sergeant who had come when Suzy Meadows' Patrick had been found dead. The news of Toria Clark's death flashed round the crowd in a moment. The babble of sympathy and curiosity grew in volume as the sergeant arrived. A crowd had gravitated from the finale of the fireworks to watching the activity around the school.

Pat Duckett was being revived with a timely nip from Sir Ronald's hip-flask.

'Terrible sight it is. I shall have to have another nip, my nerves is all shot to pieces. She's laid there dead as a doornail. Can't believe it, always such a nice person she was, nothing too much trouble. There's all that blood. Oh dear, I'm going to faint.'

She slid sideways off the school wall where Sir Ronald had sat her down and fell with a resounding thud onto the pavement.

The sergeant hastened up to the front of the crowd. 'Evening, Rector. Sounds nasty. Thank you for keeping the school locked, Mr Biggs. Can't have everyone tramping on the evidence. You have the keys, sir? Thank you. Stand aside, please.'

Caroline arrived on the scene. 'Sergeant, it's Dr Harris here. Can I help?'

'Would you come in with me, Doctor, please? By the sound of it we're much too late but I should be glad of your opinion.'

'Of course.'

They entered together. Caroline left Toria Clark lying just as she was. She felt for a pulse and listened for any signs of breathing but there were none.

'She's definitely dead, Sergeant. I don't think anyone

could survive such a savage beating. I should like to cover her up but we'd better wait for your forensic people, I suppose. Don't want to confuse the evidence.'

'Certainly not, Doctor. Come here and have a look at this.'

The sergeant was standing in the light at the far end of the hall. Laid out on a table was a huge poster made up of two sheets of the paper Michael Palmer used for artwork. They had been joined together by Sellotape with a partly finished message in large letters scrawled on, saying: *Ask Mr P. he knows she was a Lesbian, that's why she died.*

'Very embarrassing this, Dr Harris. Not quite the kind of thing a village like Turnham Malpas is used to. In your opinion, do you think she was – well, you know – what the poster says?'

'We've only been here a few months, as you know, Sergeant, but I've seen Miss Clark on several occasions and she's been to the Rectory for coffee a couple of times and I have never, not for one moment, thought on those lines. Not even for one moment. Whoever wrote this is quite mistaken. But why did she have to die? I can't understand that.'

'Whoever attacked her certainly didn't intend her to live.'

'What did they kill her with, Sergeant? It must have been something fairly thick and heavy like a rounders bat or a cricket bat.'

They were interrupted by a hammering on the outside door.

'That'll be the inspector now, Dr Harris. Would you stay and have a quick work with him, please?'

'Yes of course, though I can't contribute much.'

After Caroline had said what she had found, the inspector asked her to find Mr Palmer and tell him to come into the school and look for anything missing which might have been used as the murder weapon. She found the headmaster patiently waiting in the playground. Caroline explained why the police needed to see him immediately.

'Murder weapon? She really is dead, then?'

'Oh yes, there's no doubt about that. Who on earth would want to murder Toria? She was such a lovely person and so well liked. Whoever did it is accusing her of being a lesbian. They've written a big poster saying that's why she died.'

'Lesbian? Toria Clark? She most certainly wasn't.'

'Exactly my sentiments, Michael. You'd better go in, the police are waiting for you.'

Pat Duckett had been revived and was sitting surrounded by eager busybodies wanting to hear again her vivid description of the body.

'Now, Mrs Duckett, is there anything I could do for you?'

'Oh, thanks, Dr Harris, but I'm feeling much better now. It was a terrible sight, wasn't it? Oh dearie me. I shall never forget it, never. Where's them kids o' mine? Back on the fairground, I expect.'

'Well no, the fairground has been closed by the police. Here they are, look.' Dean and Michelle appeared, surrounded by children from the school all wishing to bathe in their reflected glory. 'I think it would be a good idea if you had a word with the police, told them what happened and then took these two children home.'

'Shall I have to be questioned, then?'

'Well, it was you who found her, wasn't it? You were the first on the scene after all.'

The sergeant came out at this moment and asked to speak to Mrs Duckett. 'Here I am, Sergeant.'

Much to the disappointment of the crowd he took her inside.

Michael Palmer was questioned for much longer than Pat Duckett. He answered every question with genuine truthfulness and was unable to throw any light on the murder at all. He denied all suspicion of his colleague being a lesbian and could furnish no reason why anyone should want to kill her, nor indeed why his name should be mentioned on the poster. They asked if he and Toria had had a relationship.

'Only that of a headmaster and an assistant teacher and no more. We were simply teaching colleagues, that was all. Ask anyone in the village. Her social life and mine were something quite separate.'

Every person in the village was interrogated by the police. Toria's house was thoroughly searched from top to bottom in an effort to uncover some clues as to her death. The television news crews came and went, the newspaper people came too, but the police were no nearer finding a solution to her death nor even a motive than they had been the day it happened. They'd endeavoured to trace everyone who had been at the fair that night and question them all, with no success. The file was kept open but despite all their efforts her murder remained unsolved.

The speculation in the bar at The Royal Oak kept the regulars fully occupied. Pat Duckett's story was repeated time and again.

'I'm 'aving nightmares about it, Vera. Every time I go into that dratted hall I can see her lying there. It's all right them carting off the body, but who is it who's left with the memories? Me. I 'ave the floor to clean and when I see them dear children sitting there calm as you please eating their dinners or doing that dancing they do with Miss Hipkin playing away on that pianna all I can think about is Miss

Clark and all that blood. I think there was something in it, what was said on that poster. Otherwise why would anyone want to murder 'er? They say there's a lot of it about.'

'A lot of what about?'

'You know, that funny stuff with women.'

'She wasn't a lesbian, Pat. I seed her out with a chap only a few weeks before she died. Nice young man he was.'

'Did you tell the police that when they questioned you?'

'Yes I did, and they found him and questioned him but he'd been away on business when it happened so that ruled him out.'

'I think it's disgusting, people like that teaching our children.'

'I don't think you should talk like that,' Vera bridled. 'She was nice was Miss Clark and you hadn't a word to say against her before she was murdered, Pat, so don't start now. She was lovely when our Rhett couldn't settle down at school and kept running home every playtime. Lovely, she was. She soon got him sorted.'

'It's funny there should be two deaths in that school hall. First Mrs Palmer and then Miss Clark. Course, I know the circumstances were different but we never got to the bottom of Mrs Palmer killing herself, did we, Vera? And what's more, each time it comes back to Mr Palmer, don't it? "Mr P." it said on that poster.'

Jimmy joined in. 'I can think of lots of people called Mr P. What about old Mr Pratt at Bolton's Farm or Mr Planchard what has that cobbler's shop in Culworth?'

'It's hardly likely to be one of them. Can't see Mr Pratt at his age having anything to do with someone as young as Miss Clark!'

Jimmy wiped the beer froth from his mouth before

adding his bit to the conversation. 'You never know; he was seventy-one when his Gerald was born, remember. Married a girl of thirty when he was seventy, and bob's yer uncle – next news they had a baby.'

'So they say, but was it his?' Vera queried sagely.

'Anyways, I reckons Mr Palmer knows more than he's admitting to.'

'That's enough of that, that's not nice, Pat. That's casting a slur. He could have you for libel and then where would you be?'

'There is one thing, the murder certainly put Stocks Day in Turnham Malpas on the map. Nobody will forget us in a hurry.'

But a couple of weeks after Stocks Day, the village had something else entirely to gossip about.

# Chapter 13

Several people had had their suspicions but it was Muriel who first voiced hers in public. 'Harriet,' she said one day when she was the only customer in the shop. 'You know much more about these things than I do, but have you thought that Suzy Meadows, the poor dear, might be expecting another baby?'

'It's funny you should have said that, Muriel. I was thinking on those lines myself, but I hoped I was wrong.'

'Poor dear girl if she is. A posthumous baby – how very sad for her.'

'Well, I'm fairly sure we're right. She's not simply putting on weight. He died at the end of March so the very latest the baby could be born would be the end of December. But judging by the looks of her it will be earlier than that.'

'Let's hope it's a boy. It would be a comfort to her, having lost Patrick.'

'I suppose it would, but a new baby costs money. I don't see how she could afford it.'

'The Lord will provide, I'm sure.'

Peter, busy about his parish duties, having initiated more

schemes than he had time to comfortably oversee, was one of the last to hear the news about Suzy. Also, Caroline had given him food for thought with her decision to resign from her pathology post.

'But why, Caroline? You've always loved working at the hospital!'

'I know, but I feel you need me at home more. Just lately you've looked very much like a little boy lost and have been giving me some searching looks as if you don't know who I am any more. So I've decided to have some time to ourselves. I can always go back to hospital work if I get bored with housekeeping. I've worked all the time we've been married and it's time for a while anyway that I spent more time looking after your needs. The money's not important, with your private income as well as your stipend. So I shall be the dutiful wife sitting at your feet admiring your efforts. I might even manage to finish decorating this place, you never know.'

'My darling, I don't deserve your sacrifice.'

'It isn't a sacrifice, Peter, it's a joy and a pleasure. I'd do anything for you if it made you happy, you know that.'

'What I've just said is true, I don't deserve your love. It's absolutely true. One has to earn love like yours, and I haven't earned it. I've tried to throw it away.'

Peter stood up at this point, turned abruptly away and strode off into his study, leaving Caroline puzzled by his reaction. She'd known for some time that Peter was deeply troubled but she couldn't discover what it was. There was definitely something he was keeping from her. She hoped it wasn't that he was going through that period most clergymen had to confront at some time or another – that deeply disturbing time when they questioned whether their faith was real or imaginary, and doubted if they should have taken up the Church. Whatever it was, whatever his decision, she would stand by him. Nothing and nobody would separate her from him. That was, if he still wanted her. The alternative didn't bear thinking about.

Michael Palmer asked Peter if he could have a private word after morning service the following Sunday.

As soon as he had closed the vestry door, Michael dropped his bombshell.

'Suzy Meadows has told me this week that she won't be able to continue with the playgroup for much longer.'

'Why ever not? She's doing such a good job.'

'For the very good reason that she is expecting a baby. In fact not just one, but two.'

'Two! Oh, good Lord!' Peter turned away and looked out of the window.

Michael, full of his news and plans for coping with the emergency, didn't notice the effect his words had had. Peter stood looking out onto the churchyard but seeing absolutely nothing. What he had most dreaded had come about. Dear God, not one but two. He was blinded mentally and physically. He heard Michael saying, 'What do you think, Peter?' and hadn't the faintest idea what he had said. Still apparently studying the churchyard Peter said, 'I'm sorry, Michael, I didn't catch what you said.'

'I said that the education committee had decided to confirm the appointment of the temporary teacher they sent to replace Miss Clark, and that Liz Neal has said she would like to take charge of the playgroup while Suzy has the twins. Do you think that will be satisfactory? I told Liz I would have to consult you first before I could confirm it, but I was sure you would agree.'

'Yes, of course I agree. You decide what is best. We're

148

lucky to have people who can step in.'

'The other thing is that I am thinking of giving in my notice. Toria Clark dying like she did has set a lot of rumours going and I feel it's time I should move on. I always intended to move after a few years but somehow Turnham Malpas has the effect of getting you in its clutches and you can't get away. However, I've decided that now is the time. I'll go at the end of the school year in July. Mind you, I've said this several times before and then changed my mind.'

Peter turned to look at him. 'I shall be sorry to see you go but we all have to move on some time. In fact, I shall be *very* sorry to see you go. Thank you for coming to tell me.'

Michael left, puzzled by the rector's awkwardness. Peter went back into the church and knelt in torment in the seat Caroline always occupied. He found her prayer book, opened it and read on the flyleaf the words '*To my dearest Caroline on our wedding day. Together from this day unto eternity. Peter.*'

Caroline had his dinner ready and when he didn't come she eventually set off to find him. And there he was, knelt in prayer where she usually sat. He had her own prayerbook in his hand. She sat beside him and took his hand in silence, not wishing to interrupt. He gripped her hand until it hurt. When she tried to release his grip he turned towards her, laid his head on her knee, put his arms around her and wept.

'My dear, dear Peter, what on earth is the matter? My darling, for heaven's sake tell me.' She stroked his hair as she would have stroked the hair of a child of hers. 'Whatever is the matter? There isn't anything that you can't tell me, you know.'

Caroline waited patiently for Peter to speak. His voice came out jerkily.

'Suzy Meadows is having a baby.'

'I know.'

There was a long pause before Peter spoke. 'How long have you known? Did she tell you?'

'No. I saw her at the ante-natal clinic several weeks ago.'

'So you don't know anything really?'

'I would have thought that giving birth to a baby after your husband has died was sufficient to be going on with. What else is there to know?'

'Caroline, you remember you said the other day that you thought I seemed strange and needed looking after? I don't need looking after, I need hanging.'

'Hanging? Oh God, Peter, whatever have you done to deserve that? Surely you're not our phantom killer?'

'In my judgement it's worse than that. I have been totally disloyal and unfaithful to you and I think, in fact I know, the result is what I've just told you. Which you already knew – except you didn't know the whole truth.'

'What are we talking about, Peter? Toria's murder or Suzy's baby?'

'Suzy's babies. She's having twins.'

'Twins? Oh good heavens, the poor girl. Now that really is a problem. I shall have to go round to see her. However is she going to manage? Why has that upset you so much?'

'You still haven't understood. The twins are mine.'

The only sound in the church was the steady drip drip of the tap in the choir vestry. The flowers on the altar looked just the same as they had done two moments ago, the great brass cross still hung gleaming above the altar. The old, old wood of the pulpit and the choir-stalls still glowed softly in the summer sun filtering through the stained-glass windows. Caroline still sat cradling Peter's head on her knee, the clock kept ticking, Caroline's heart kept beating.

Inside herself she had died. Finally Peter spoke.

'It only happened once, a few days after Patrick died. She needed comforting and she begged me, begged me to comfort her and it went on from there. That isn't any excuse, nor a reason. I could still have gone away, but the first time I saw her I was attracted to her. Not loved her but lusted for her, I suppose. After that one time I kept right away I was so ashamed of what had happened. I thought if I carried the burden of what I'd done all by myself I could atone for the sin of it. I didn't want to hurt you, you see. Didn't want to cause you pain. Even though we had promised each other always to be truthful about our feelings. Now of course the greatest harm has been done. I have given someone other than my beloved, a child.'

Willie Biggs coughed loudly as he came in to switch off the lights. Peter stood up and tried to appear normal.

'Sorry to interrupt, sir. I forgot to switch off the electrics. Just started me pudding when I remembered.'

'That's all right, Willie. Thank you for remembering. Must save on the electricity bill.'

'Exactly what I thought, sir. See you about six, Mr Harris.'

'Yes, of course, Willie.'

Caroline stood up after Willie had gone. She turned to Peter and said in a small defeated voice: 'Why should these babies be yours? Why aren't they Patrick's?'

'She told me they hadn't . . . well . . . they hadn't had relations for nearly a year.'

'I see. It's no good pretending that I'm not hurt because I am. I'm going back to the Rectory now. I need to find out where I stand.'

The following morning Caroline told Peter she was going to take a few days' leave and go up to her family home in Northumberland to give herself time to think. She rang the hospital, made arrangements for her work to be covered and then packed a case and left.

From her bedroom window Suzy Meadows watched her go. Caroline's white strained face told Suzy what she needed to know. After the last of the playgroup children had gone home, Suzy took Rosie by the hand and marched off with the firm intention of calling in at the Rectory on her way home to lunch. 'Grasp the nettle,' her mother always said, and this was some nettle.

Suzy could see through the Rectory window that Peter was sitting at his desk. She knocked loudly on the door.

She looked closely at his face when he opened the door and was shocked to see that he appeared to have aged ten years at least. His normally fresh complexion had turned to a strange shade of grey and his eyes had lost all their fire.

'I need to talk to my parish priest.'

'Please come in.' Before, the sound of his voice would have set her heart zinging but no longer. She had lived an age since anything had had the ability to do that.

Peter stood back and made room for her to enter. 'Come in the study.'

'I need to talk.' Suzy patted Rosie's head. 'Can we occupy her somewhere else?' Peter stood nonplussed for a moment and then suggested to Rosie that she went in the kitchen and played with Mrs Harris' cats. 'Do you like cats, Rosie?'

'Yes I do, Mr Harris,' Rosie beamed at him, and confidently put her hand in his and allowed him to show her where to find the cats. When he returned to the study Suzy was sitting on a chair waiting to speak.

Suzy cleared her throat. 'I realised this morning when I saw Caroline leaving and looking so upset that she knows what has happened.'

'I honestly didn't . . .' Suzy held up her hand to stop him speaking.

'There's no need to say anything at all, just let me speak. I have no intention of anyone knowing that these twins I'm carrying are anyone else's but Patrick's. That's what everyone will think and that's what I shall allow them to think. There is no way that I would ruin your life nor Caroline's by telling the truth. To be brutally frank, Peter, I don't want these babies at all and I shall offer them for adoption. In fact, I've already had a word with the adoption people about that. I have it all arranged. As soon as the babies are born they will be handed to the new parents. Then the adoption will go through when they are about a year old. I've picked out who their parents shall be.'

'You have?'

'Yes. It's quite simply sound common sense. I can't possibly feed and clothe five children. I need to get back to work as soon as I can and with Rosie nearly ready for school that becomes feasible. If I keep the twins it would be impossible. In any case, I can't find any more love in my heart at the moment. There is none to spare for two more babies, be they boys or girls.'

'I can never forgive myself for what happened.'

'Why should you feel guilty? I needed you and you, for the moment, needed me. But Caroline is your life's partner, not me. I wouldn't do at all. I know I sound absolutely hard as nails but at the moment that's the only way I know how to cope. The twins are due in December around Christmas-time, but I expect they'll have to be induced so that fits in very nicely with Patrick's death.'

'Thank you for being so totally considerate towards Caroline and me. I don't deserve it.'

'Not another word shall I say to you or anyone else from

now on. What I have said I have said, and that's it. Caroline hasn't left for good, has she?'

A flash of pain crossed Peter's face. 'I don't think so. She's gone home to Northumberland to sort her feelings out. Walking along the coast there has always done her good. If she doesn't come back I shall be finished. I can't go on if I haven't got Caroline.'

Suzy stood up as Rosie came back into the study. 'Some good must come from this, and it will. Two children will have been given life – and what better father could they have than you?'

# Chapter 14

Four days after Caroline had gone to Northumberland Peter had to go to an inter-Church meeting in Culworth. He knew he would be away all day so he fed Caroline's cats, made sure the cat flap was unlocked, patted their heads as being the nearest he could get to kissing his darling girl and left with a heavy heart. Inter-Church services were not foremost in his mind. He'd tried ringing Caroline, though if she'd answered he wouldn't have known what to say. There'd been no reply. He hadn't realised that he no longer functioned as a single person. If he didn't hear from her soon he would go straight up to Northumberland and hang the parish.

He drove back to the Rectory and arrived home about six. There was no letter on the mat as he had hoped. The cats rushed to greet him.

'Cupboard love, that's what it is — pure cupboard love.'

As he hung up his jacket he smelt that special lingering perfume of Caroline's on her coat hanging beside his own. The cats cried for attention and he went to the kitchen to get their food. The table was laid for two. He could smell a casserole cooking.

The cats pestered, so hardly daring to believe that Caroline was back he fed the ravenous beasts while he decided what to do. When he'd put down their dishes he stood listening for a moment and then climbed the stairs. Their bedroom door was open and he could see Caroline unpacking her case. Her back was turned to him and he realised she hadn't heard him come in.

'Caroline.'

'Peter.'

'You're back.'

'I am.'

Caroline turned to face him. 'Mother sends her love. I've put a casserole in the oven. It'll be ready in about twenty minutes.'

'I smelt it when I came in. I've fed the cats.'

'So have I. The greedy things.'

'Shall I get a bottle of wine opened?'

'That would be nice. I'll be down in a moment.'

'I didn't see your car.'

'No, I've had to leave it in Culworth for repair. There's something wrong with the electrics.'

'I was in Culworth. I could have picked you up if I'd known.'

'I caught the bus.'

'I see.'

On a weekday evening they usually made a bottle of wine last two meals but tonight they finished the whole bottle. They exchanged news about the parish, about the weather, about Northumberland, carefully avoiding the major difficulty which consumed their minds. Caroline broached the subject first.

'Peter, I had to get away to get the right perspective on things. Something about not being able to see the wood for the trees, you know. It took me until yesterday to understand how I felt. I stood high up on the cliffs watching the sea coming pounding in onto the rocks, and I thought about the permanency of the sea and that it goes on relentlessly no matter what trivial pursuits Man manages to occupy himself with. I sat thinking about you, thinking about how you are the permanency in my life. I tried to imagine what my life would be like if I turned my back on you now. Sitting there I said goodbye to the Rectory, to the village, to Muriel and Jimbo and Harriet and Willie and all the others. I set myself up in a little flat and got a job in a hospital. I saw myself coming home at night to an empty flat, trying to make new friends, going to evening classes. It didn't work. I thought about you coming home to an empty house. No one to talk your problems over with, no one to love you and make sure you were fed properly, no one actually to care whether you lived or died. And I could see no point in both of us being on our own.'

Peter smiled. 'Are you saying then that the sole reason for you coming back is to make sure the village doesn't sit sniffing the air during the sermon because the rector hasn't washed his socks?'

'Yes, you could say that.' Caroline looked up at him and grinned. 'That's if you want me.'

'A lifetime of washing my own socks couldn't make up for what I've done to you. You make me feel very humble. Could you possibly sit on my knee?'

'Yes.'

They talked well into the night. The cats gave up hoping for their nightly walk around the garden with Caroline and went to bed in a huff. The Aga in need of its usual stoking up went unattended, the Rectory door remained unlocked and the bedroom light stayed on all night.

# Chapter 15

The following Sunday, Peter's sermon dealt with forgiveness. Muriel listened with deep interest. That was exactly what she should be doing to Scott McDonald – forgiving him, even though he had caused her so much pain. She looked round the church to see if there was anyone else who should be listening with particular interest to Peter's powerful, heartfelt words. Well, old Jimmy Glover had put in one of his rare appearances, and he certainly needed to ask forgiveness for the bad language he used when the children threw sticks into his tree to get the conkers to fall. And Vera, who lived next door to Pat Duckett – now *she* needed to ask forgiveness for her disgraceful behaviour outside The Royal Oak on Friday night, when she had had too much to drink. Betty McDonald had had to throw her out – really throw her out, not just ask her to leave. Come to think of it, Muriel supposed everybody had something they needed to ask forgiveness for . . .

After the service, she stood talking to Lady Bissett whose head was full of arrangements for next month's Village Flower and Vegetable Show.

'Well, Muriel, if you go on winning like you do we shall

have to ban you to give someone else a chance.'

'I'm not competing this year.'

'Not at all?'

'No. I haven't the time to devote to my garden like I used to. I'm so busy, you see.'

'Of course – I'd forgotten you'd got a job. I've decided to organise more classes for the flower-arranging this year and some more for the children. If they enter things they're bound to bring their parents. Do you think Jimbo might provide the refreshments?'

'He's already promised Peter to provide the meat for the Harvest Supper. We can't go on asking and asking.'

'Oh, come off it, Muriel! He's making a packet out of this village, what with the store and the tearoom and restaurant. He can well afford it.'

'Can well afford what?'

Lady Bissett hadn't realised that Harriet was standing right behind her.

'Ah, Harriet. I was just saying to Muriel here that you and Jimbo might be so kind as to provide something towards the refreshments for the Village Show.'

'It sounded to me as if you were saying we could well afford to provide the lot. It's not Charity Hall, you know. We do actually run a business.'

'Oh, I didn't mean it like that.'

'How did you mean it, then?' Harriet retorted. Muriel felt very uncomfortable. She hated rows and this one looked as if it was going to be a big one. But Lady Bissett was saved from answering Harriet's belligerent question by a loud joyous shout.

'Moo? It is – it's really Moo! What in heaven's name are *you* doing here?'

Muriel turned round to see who had used a name she

hadn't been called since she was a girl. The owner of the cultured voice stood about five feet six in his socks. He had thick snow-white hair, big bushy eyebrows, a very tanned complexion, a haughty nose and big laughing bright brown eyes. She blushed bright red as she realised who he was.

'Why it's . . . it's . . . Ralphie! I don't believe it.' Before she could say any more he had clasped her in his arms and given her a hearty kiss on both cheeks.

'What are you doing here, Moo? You left the village years ago.'

Muriel tried to restore her equilibrium but didn't succeed; she was quite breathless. Swallowing hard she replied, 'I did, but when I retired I came back here and bought a little house. What are you doing here?'

'Come to see the old place to find somewhere to live. I've retired, you see – fancied coming back to the old roots. Well, would you believe it! You haven't changed a bit. This is wonderful! Won't you introduce me to your friends?'

In a state of total confusion and almost unable to differentiate between everyone because of a sudden mist which had come down over her eyes, Muriel introduced him.

'This is Sir Ralph Templeton. Ralphie, this is Harriet Charter-Plackett who owns the village store with her husband James who's over there talking to the rector. This is Liz and Neville Neal from Glebe House. This is Lady Bissett, who's husband Sir Ronald you might know, with him being a trades union leader. He's been on TV a lot . . .'

'Living abroad, I haven't had that pleasure.' He shook hands with them all. 'Delighted to meet you, how do you do. What a pleasure to meet Moo's friends! There must be a lot of newcomers to the village, I imagine, and very few of the old families left.'

Muriel found her voice again. 'Well, Jimmy Glover's still here, and Valda and Thelma Senior, the twins. You remember them, don't you?'

'Not the twins!'

'I can't think of anyone else at the moment.'

'Come on, Moo, I'll take you out to lunch. We've lots to talk about – more than forty years to catch up on. You will excuse us, won't you?' he said to those around him. 'I'm sure we'll see each other again before long.'

'I don't think so,' Muriel panicked. 'No, I really can't.'

'Have you other plans?'

'No. Well, yes . . . I have. I like to garden on Sunday afternoons in the summer and — '

Ralphie interrupted, 'The gardening can wait, can't it, surely?'

'Well, I suppose it can, but no, I can't come with you for lunch. It wouldn't do.'

'Wouldn't do? I'm not abducting you, Muriel, simply asking you out for a meal. I'll bring you straight back if you like.'

Harriet gave her a nudge. 'Go on, Muriel. You can't say no, you've so much to talk about.'

'Well, perhaps I might then.'

Before she knew it Muriel was whisked off towards Sir Ralph's Mercedes which he'd parked in Church Road.

'Moo, I'm so sorry – I didn't stop to think. Have you a husband we ought to be taking with us?'

Muriel, who was already blushing at the prospect of the entire village seeing her being carried off by this dynamic personage, went even redder.

'No, but I do have a dog and I can't go anywhere until he's been for a little walk.'

'Where do you live?'

'Here by the church in Glebe Cottages.'

'Go and get him, then. I've got a cover I can put on the back seat and we'll take him out for a run. I know a nice place in Culworth where we could have lunch afterwards.'

The congregation mysteriously found reasons for lingering around the lych gate. They weren't going to miss the chance of watching Muriel Hipkin being driven off in such style. Pericles climbed into the car as though he'd been going for rides in a Mercedes all his life, and when Muriel waved goodbye to the crowd at the gate, she felt quite royal.

Lady Bissett was taken aback by the sudden change in Muriel's social status.

'Who the dickens is Ralphie?' she said too loudly, forgetting she was titled.

Harriet laughed. 'I really don't know, but it doesn't matter.'

Caroline supplied the answer. 'He's just introduced himself to Peter. He's one of the Templetons who used to own the Big House. Apparently, Sir Ralph has retired from the Diplomatic Service and is coming back to live in the village as soon as he can find a house he likes. He's rather nice, isn't he?'

Harriet agreed. 'Nice? He's gorgeous. I would never have dreamt of calling her Moo.' Lady Bissett wasn't sure she approved of someone she looked down on suddenly having such aristocratic connections. It rather put Ron's life peerage in the shade.

The news about the return of Ralph Templeton spread through the area in a flash, and there was much speculation about the difference it might make, having a Lord of the Manor in the village again. Would he buy back the Big

House? And wouldn't it be a bit of a comedown, living in an ordinary house after having been abroad, and after growing up on a country estate?

Tucked up safely in bed that night, Muriel gave herself time to think about Ralph Tristan Bernard Templeton. Ralphie was the only one who called her Moo. Her mother used to get furious when he called her that. 'Your name's Muriel and a very pretty name it is, too. Tell him, go on – you tell him not to call you Moo!' she used to nag. But Muriel never did. It was their own special link. They did have something between them, even though they were only children. They were just in their teens when his mother sold up and he went away for ever. She remembered how they'd held hands, on the last bonfire night that there'd been at the Big House. With his father gone, Ralphie had had to light the bonfire himself; the older people, Muriel recalled, had had difficulty in not shedding a tear when they thought about his father, dead in some Burmese jungle and his body not brought home for burial with his ancestors. The two of them had kissed when he left – just a little youthful peck on the lips, but she had carried the memory of it for years. She had been leaving, too, at the time and in the turmoil it had never occurred to her to ask for his address. It all seemed so final, that moving away from their roots. Fancy – she hadn't thought about him for years – and then out of the blue he turns up!

They'd had a lovely lunch, in that posh restaurant overlooking the Cul. He asked the restaurant manager for some bread and they'd gone out to feed the swans when they'd finished their meal, just like they used to when they were children, feeding the swans on the lake at the Big House with bread Ralphie had pinched out of the kitchen.

She wondered if the colleagues who'd seen him as a pillar of the Foreign Office all these years knew what a naughty boy he'd been when she knew him. There was that time when he started the farm tractor and drove right up to the front door of the House, with her stood up on it clinging to his shoulders. Or that time in the war when he switched on all the lights and opened all the blackout curtains as a gesture of defiance to Hitler. The butler had been furious. Until he was eight, Ralphie had gone to the village school. She remembered he'd been very quick to learn but such a trial to poor Miss Evans. He was far too inventive and all the children had followed his lead.

'I shall have to get up and have another cup of Ovaltine,' Muriel murmured. 'I'm not going to get to sleep, I'm in a whirl.'

As she got warm in bed again and began relaxing, Muriel thought about the thick scratchy tweed jacket he wore and how it had rubbed on her arms when he'd kissed her as he left. There was that slight perfumed smell about him, as if he kept himself particularly clean, and she liked that in a man. Scrupulous attention to cleanliness was a commendable trait.

Next morning, she popped into the store. It was her cousin's birthday and she needed a card.

Jimbo was serving. He raised his straw boater to her and said, 'Ah, good morning . . . er . . . Moo. You've got back home, then?'

'Good morning, Jimbo, of course I have.'

'What a send-off! I don't think there could have been many more people to witness your departure. Did you have a good time?'

'I did, thank you.'

'Shall we be seeing more of him?'

'He's looking for a house to buy, but of course there aren't any in the village at the moment so I don't know what he's going to do.'

Harriet came in. 'Hello . . . Moo. What a sensation! The whole village is agog to hear how you got on.'

'We had a lovely lunch at the George in Culworth and then we drove around a bit for Ralphie to see how things have changed – or not, as the case may be. Then we had afternoon tea at that new café by Havers Lake and then he brought me home.'

'I'm so glad you had a good time. He seems very nice.'

'He is, just like he was as a boy except he's calmed down a lot.'

Jimbo, stacking shelves from the top of a stepladder, called down, 'He could always rent until a house comes up for sale. Those people from London who have the cottage behind the pub are off to South Africa for six months soon. They might be willing to rent to such a nice tenant.'

'That would be a good idea, Muriel, wouldn't it? Which one is it, Jimbo?'

'Number three.'

Harriet suggested ringing up Ralph to tell him about the cottage.

'I mustn't presume to ring him up,' Muriel demurred. 'I don't really know him very well. No, I won't ring.'

'Well, if you do decide to ring, come here and use our phone. Don't use the public one – it's always so smelly.'

'I'll put some money by the phone if I do use it.' Muriel left in haste to avoid being persuaded.

'Now who's playing at Charity Hall?' Jimbo said from the ladder.

'This is a good cause. In fact, a very good cause. I've half a mind to have another dinner party. What excuse could I 'think up?'

'Too late, Caroline's already arranging one. She has the date to fix, that's all. She's planning the menu with me 'cos she's no time to cook herself at the moment.'

'Who's she inviting?'

'Yours truly, "Moo" and "Ralphie", Liz and Neville, and you if you behave yourself.'

'What does that mean exactly?'

'Come here and I'll show you.'

He leant down from the ladder, clutched hold of Harriet's hair, turned her face up towards his and began a lingering kiss which would have lasted much longer if Muriel hadn't come in and interrupted.

'Oh, I beg your pardon, I'm so sorry. I left the card on the counter. I'll be off now.' She hastened out covered in embarrassment.

'Tell you what, a good kiss like that is just what Muriel needs. It wouldn't half widen her horizons.'

'Jimbo, not everyone is sex-mad like you.'

'N . o . o . o . o . o . ?'

'Wouldn't it be fun if the two of them got married?'

'Getting like a typical villager you are, a finger in every pie.'

'I shall pull the stepladder away in a minute.'

'Don't you dare! How is the menu for that Twenty-first coming along?'

'Not too good. The mother likes everything I've listed but the son wants something less traditional. I'm waiting to see who wins. There's another two weeks yet.'

The door burst open and in dashed Linda. 'Sorry I'm a bit late, roadworks for miles. Have you been busy?'

'No. The birthday-card order came in first thing and there's a big envelope of instructions from the post office.

It could take all morning, working out what they mean. Something about changes in procedure to make things simpler but it looks a lot more complicated to me.'

'Thank you, Jimbo. Just what I need on a Monday morning.'

Linda's first customer was Sharon McDonald.

'Ten first-class stamps, please, and be quick. I'm in a hurry.'

'Have you got the right money? I haven't unlocked the till yet.'

'No. That's all I've got.' She handed Linda a five-pound note.

'Rightio then, half a mo.' Linda got the keys from Jimbo's pocket, unlocked the till and tore off the stamps.

'There yer go, Sharon. Ten first-class stamps and two pounds sixty change.'

'And then some.'

'I don't understand. You gave me a five-pound note, the stamps cost two pounds forty, and I've given you two pounds sixty change.'

'I gave you a ten-pound note – you know I did. Come on, Linda, pocketing the takings, are you? Nice little earner if it comes off. Jimbo, this Linda of yours is lining her pockets.'

Jimbo strode across the store, his moustache positively bristling. 'That's not a very nice accusation, Sharon. In any case I know exactly how much we leave in the till ready for the day so I can count the notes and tell you what you gave.'

Linda tried to signal a message to Jimbo which, in his annoyance, he failed to interpret.

He sprang open the till and realised that it had not been cleared on the Saturday night, so he couldn't prove anything. He made a pretence of counting up and said, 'Well, by the looks of it the customer's always right. Here you are Sharon, another five pounds.'

'You've been caught with your fingers in the till, haven't you, Linda?'

'It was a genuine mistake. I'm very sorry.'

'So you should be. Don't try it on with me again. It might work with the old bats collecting their pensions, but it won't wash with me.' Sharon bounced out of the shop, her high heels click-clacking on the red tiles.

Linda was very upset.

'Mr Charter-Plackett, I know, I positively *know* she gave me a five-pound note.'

'Don't worry, Linda. I know she did, too, but I couldn't prove it. It was my fault – I forgot to clear the till on Saturday when you were away. It won't happen again, I can assure you. Don't let her upset you, she isn't worth it.'

'She's so rude. One day she'll get her comeuppance.'

# Chapter 16

The police sergeant had never really given up on the murder of Toria Clark. As he said to his wife, his gut reaction was that it was someone local, so he wasn't surprised when he saw what Jimmy Glover brought into the station one day. The sergeant had been watching the news on the television and, through the open door, been keeping half an eye open on the station desk. That was one of the advantages of having the police station and his own home all in the same building.

'Now then, Jimmy, what's this?'

'A rounders bat, Sergeant. Found it hid behind the Methodist Chapel in that long grass that never gets cut. I've handled it careful, like, on account of there being blood on it, like they does on the telly.'

'And what were you doing messing about behind the chapel? Not you been stealing the Scout money, is it?'

'I don't steal from the church. That's lower than low, that is. I was wandering along enjoying the sunshine and decided to sit down on that low wall that's all that's left of the old boiler-house. There it was, tucked down in the corner. Thought your men had searched every inch?'

'We did. I'll enter this incident in my book and pass it on to forensic. Thank you for being so alert and spotting it, Jimmy.'

'I liked that Toria Clark. She allus had a kind word for me, which is more than some people I could mention. If this is what killed her, perhaps it'll help you find who did it.'

'What's that hidden in your coat, Jimmy?'

'Never you mind. I'm off.'

'Hope you haven't been poaching, old son?'

'I have not.' Jimmy was indignant but could not meet his eye. The sergeant laughed. He hadn't been the village bobby for twenty years without knowing about Jimmy Glover's noctural activities.

The rounders bat proved to be the murder weapon all right, but there were no fingerprints on it. Mr Palmer had checked the rounders bats on the night of the murder but had forgotten that Toria had brought her own to school until the office had supplied a spare. That had meant there were two in the stock book but three on the premises.

This find supplied the regulars of The Royal Oak with further fuel for their small talk.

'Here, Betty, you heard Jimmy's found the murder weapon?'

'Yes I have, Willie. Just wish them lazy beggars 'ud find the murderer. We pays their wages, it's time they got off their backsides and earned 'em instead of catching me for speeding last week.'

'Now, Betty, they 'as tried, can't say they haven't. They questioned every living person for miles around. It was made more difficult with it being Stocks Day – there was that many strangers hereabouts. If it'd been an ordinary day, there would have been only a tenth that number about. Seems funny to me that whoever it was knew where to find the rounders bat. Makes me think it's someone local.'

'Local? For heaven's sake, Willie, don't put the wind up us all.'

'Stands to reason. If you never went to the village school, how would you know where to lay your hands on a rounders bat? Especially if you were worked up.'

'Just think, there's someone here in this village who might be coming into this bar night after night and they've got that on their conscience. They might strike again.'

'Well, Betty, you'd better not make too many enemies. Yer never know, it might be you next.'

Jimmy Glover laughed at the prospect. 'Fat chance they'd have of killing Betty. It'd take more than a rounders bat to see her off.'

'Here you, Jimmy, just mind yer manners or I'll turf you out.'

The bar burst into corporate laughter. 'Watch out, Jimmy. She'll be clasping you to her bosom next and out you'll go.'

'Cor, it'd be worth it, though, eh?' someone well out of Betty's reach shouted.

The door opened and everyone's attention was taken by the man who entered.

Jimmy shouted, 'Well, if it isn't Ralphie! I'd heard you were about. How do you do, Ralphie, remember me?'

Ralph held out his hand in greeting. 'Why, it's Jimmy Glover! How are you, Jimmy? I'd know you anywhere.'

'I'm fine, how are you?'

'In the pink. What are you drinking?'

'Best bitter. Thank you.'

'Best bitter and a double whisky, please, landlord.'

Mac attended to his order and welcomed Ralph to the bar. 'I hear you're thinking of coming to live in the village, sir?'

'I am indeed. I'm hoping Jimmy here will be able to put me up for a while.'

Jimmy's head jerked up. 'Eh, what was that?'

'Only joking, Jimmy. Come and sit over here and we'll talk about old times.' They sat at the corner table Ralph had chosen and enjoyed an hour's chat. The rest of the bar marvelled at the sight of smelly Jimmy being made a fuss of by such a personage as the son of a past Lord of the Manor.

Finally, Ralph rose to go. 'I'm off to see if Muriel will come in for a drink, Jimmy. I'd ask you to join us if you were a bit, shall we say – tidier? I'll be back shortly.'

Muriel answered the knock at the door wearing an old jumper and skirt she'd put on to do her gardening earlier in the day.

'Oh dear, I wasn't expecting visitors.'

'I've come to ask you to join me in a drink at The Royal Oak. How about it, Moo?'

'I've never been in the bar before. I don't really think I could, anyway I'm not dressed properly. I've got my old gardening skirt on.'

'Well, pop upstairs and get changed. I'll wait here.'

'Shall I? Perhaps another night.'

'Don't turn down the chance of an hour on the tiles. Please come.'

'Very well then. I'll be as quick as I can.'

Ralph waited, sitting in the most comfortable armchair in the room, while Muriel dithered about upstairs deciding what to wear. Should she put a touch of that lipstick on that Caroline gave her for Jimbo's dinner party, or would Ralph prefer her without? Which shoes should she wear – her 1960s court shoes or her Clark's walking shoes? Oh dear, oh dear. All these decisions when what she had originally planned was to simply collapse in front of the television and watch that nice play.

Ralph stood as she came down the little spiral staircase.

'Come along then, we'll give the bar a big surprise.'

He chatted to her as they strolled through the village, knowing full well she was feeling apprehensive. Sure enough, the company fell silent as they walked in through the door. Miss Hipkin in the pub, whatever next? Jimmy had disappeared.

Muriel allowed Ralph to choose where to sit, and what she should drink.

''Evening, Muriel.' ''Evening, Miss Hipkin.' She nodded to them all, hoping she wasn't as red in the face as she felt. Why did she never have the courage to face new situations?

Ralph put her Snowball down on the little mat and sat beside her. 'You have nothing to fear, you know. You're with me and I have been in bars all over the world so I know what's what.'

'Have you really been all over the world, Ralphie?'

'Not far off. You get sent to all the worst places when you first start in the Foreign Office and then once you've proved yourself and you have a few strokes of luck, like being in the right place at the right time, you find yourself in the better places. Rome was my favourite, I think.'

'Have you been to Rome? Oh, I would love to go there! I always feel it's larger than life.'

'That's a good way of describing it. "Larger than life" – yes, I like that.'

Sharon came into the bar, having been press-ganged by her mother into clearing the tables. She went round languidly picking up empty glasses and limply wiping up any spills.

'Our Sharon, look lively! I need those glasses pronto.'

She queezed between the tables and stopped by theirs. 'Finished, 'ave yer?'

Ralph looked up at her. 'Neither Miss Hipkin nor I have finished, as you can well see.'

'All right, all right, keep your shirt on, only trying to help. Surprise seeing you in the bar, Muriel. First time in yer life, I reckon.'

Ralph showed his anger by snapping, 'Miss Hipkin to you, if you don't mind, young lady,'

'Miss Hipkin then, *Sir* Ralph. She'll need more than a Snowball to get her going, yer know. A stiff whisky would do better.'

'That's quite enough of that.' Ralph stood up to assert his authority. 'Kindly leave us alone.'

'OK, OK. Just giving you some advice, Ralphie.' She turned away with a flick of her pert bottom.

Muriel wished the floor would open up and swallow her.

Ralph ordered, 'Drink up, we're leaving.'

He took her arm and as they reached the door he turned to Mac who was behind the bar and said, loudly enough for everyone to hear: 'Landlord, that girl who collects the glasses needs her manners attending to. See to it or I shall not patronise your bar again. Good night to you.'

'Ralphie, I don't know how you dared to speak like that!'

'She was extremely rude.'

'She's their daughter.'

'I don't care whose daughter she is, Moo, she was rude to you and to me. It simply won't do, I'm not accustomed to it. I'll see you to your cottage and then I'll be on my way.'

When they reached her door Muriel daringly suggested he came in for a coffee before he went. She would quite have preferred him to say no but he said yes so she'd no alternative but to open the door and invite him in.

Pericles growled and barked but Ralph patted him and made a fuss and Pericles allowed him in. He wasn't used to male company and felt Muriel needed defending.

They sat drinking coffee and talking until nearly midnight. Ralph had such an easy way with him, and to her surprise Muriel found herself to be quite an interesting person.

As he left Ralph said, 'I'm renting Derek and Bunny's cottage for six months, possibly a year, while they're in South Africa. They leave on Tuesday and I'm moving in on Thursday. Perhaps you would be so kind as to have a meal with me one evening when I get settled?'

'I should like that, thank you.'

'Good. Moo, be very careful of that girl Sharon. There's something not quite right about her.'

'Sharon McDonald? She's very rude and outspoken, but she's all right really.'

'You're too kind. Just mark my words.' Ralph took both her hands and very tentatively kissed her on her lips.

'Good night, my dear. You are one of the few real ladies left in this world, do you know that?'

Muriel closed the door and stood with her back leaning on it. She felt the same thrill that a girl in her teens would have felt at her first kiss. She'd been kissed in Postman's Knock at Sunday School parties in her early teens but never by a grown man. Now she felt she knew something at least of what that kiss she'd witnessed between Harriet and Jimbo must have felt like. Well, just a little maybe, because Ralph's hadn't lasted very long.

She put an extra dash of oil in before she stepped into her bath – frankincense she chose, to help her sleep. The light from the night sky lit the bathroom and she imagined what it would be like visiting Rome with Ralph. Katharine Hepburn had had that fabulous holiday in – Venice, was it? – when she met that two-timing Italian in that film, *Summer Madness*. Katharine Hepburn had had a wonderful awakening. Muriel could see herself standing by the Trevi Fountain with a chiffon scarf around her throat, the ends blowing about in the summer breeze, and Ralph handing her coins to throw in and her wishing, like you should, that this moment would never end . . . but end it would, and they'd have to go back to the hotel. Abruptly Muriel sat up and began vigorously scrubbing herself with the loofah. Got to get to bed, work to do tomorrow.

On the Wednesday before the Thursday that Ralph moved into number three, Muriel was sitting at her 'seat of custom' as she jokingly called it in her mind. She'd not been very busy but then it was market day in Culworth. She was contemplating asking Jimbo to run off a few new menus, as some of the ones in use at the moment were beginning to look tatty and she did like to have nice clean menus for everybody, when the door opened and in walked Sharon. Did she never work? Muriel thought to herself.

The girl was wearing her usual high heels and skin-tight short skirt. She trotted over to a table. Her peroxided hair had taken on an orange tinge and she wore lipstick and blusher to match. Her Walkman was plugged into her ears.

'Hello, *Miss Hipkin*. A coffee and a slice of chocolate gâteau if you please.'

Muriel did hope Sharon wouldn't be rude while she was in the tearoom; if she was, she'd send the YTS girl for Jimbo. But Sharon sat quietly, reading her magazine and listening to her music. Muriel busied herself checking her bills and sorting out which menus she would throw away.

She contemplated going to find Jimbo to get him to do them, but decided she wouldn't leave Sharon on her own – for you never knew. There was a lovely smell of burning wood in the air, she noticed.

Muriel had just shown three customers to a table and settled them with a menu when Sharon shouted: 'Oh, look, Miss Hipkin! There's smoke.'

Muriel looked out of the window cautiously; she anticipated that Sharon was playing a joke on her. But sure enough there was smoke billowing into the sky. They must be having a bonfire, though it seemed the wrong time of year.

Sharon leapt to her feet. 'I'm off to see where it is. Get ready to phone the fire brigade.'

She dropped her Walkman on the table and rushed out towards The Royal Oak. Muriel could see her standing in Stocks Row looking up behind the pub.

She came racing back. 'Ring the fire brigade! It's one of the cottages belonging to them London people. It's got a right hold. Hurry up!'

'Oh dear, what do I say?' Muriel dropped the phone in her agitation.

'Here, give it to me.' Sharon dialled 999 and asked for Fire. She gave the address and explained what had happened. 'Cool and calm in a crisis' were the words which sprang to Muriel's mind. How glad she was, that Sharon had been there. She would have been incoherent if she'd had to phone.

Sharon rushed out again and went round warning everyone. It seemed an age until the fire brigade actually arrived. Someone had rigged a hose up and was trying to wet the thatch to stop the roof burning. Mac and Betty came out to help, as the cottage was very close to the back of the pub and they didn't want their thatch on fire as well. Jimbo hastened across to give a hand. Muriel stayed in charge in the tearoom, thankful for an excuse to keep out of the way. The water from the fire-brigade hydrant soon put the fire out. It was only then that Muriel realised it was the cottage Ralphie had hoped to move into the next day. Then the police came to investigate and the tearoom was kept busy with teas and toasted teacakes and soup for the Press, the firemen and the police. All on the house, of course, for in his inimitable way, Jimbo knew free publicity when he saw it.

Sharon, of course, was the heroine of the hour. Muriel spoke highly of her, saying how calm and level-headed she had been and how well she had explained to the fire brigade about the location of the cottage.

The fire meant that for a while Ralph had nowhere to stay. Caroline suggested that he didn't go back to the hotel but stayed with her until the cottage was sorted out. He jumped at the chance.

'How very kind of you to invite me. I shall be delighted. I'll try to be a model guest, and keep well out of your way.'

'We shall enjoy your company, won't we, Peter?'

'We shall indeed. Bring your things round tomorrow morning as you've planned, but move in here instead of the cottage. We've plenty of room if you need to store anything, haven't we, Caroline?'

'Acres. Anyway, I intended inviting you to dinner on Saturday night, as we're having a few friends in, so you'll be on the spot so to speak.'

'It's extremely kind of you. I do appreciate it.'

'I hope you like cats, because I've got three Siamese.'

'That's fine, I like animals. Never had a chance to have any of my own with moving around such a lot, but when I get settled I shall have at least three cats and a dog.'

'A poodle perhaps?' Caroline's smile was wicked and Ralph had to acknowledge it.

'You never know.' He smiled gently, turned on his heel and thereby terminated the conversation.

Peter was outraged. 'Caroline, you take the biscuit for absolute cheek!'

'It was only a bit of fun. I've decided I'm inviting Suzy to our dinner party.'

'Suzy?' There was a pause.

'I know you might find it difficult but it won't be half as difficult as I shall find it. If I leave her out, tongues might wag. If I invite her I shall have a devil of an evening, but I can't do otherwise. I'll invite Michael Palmer as well, then she'll have a man to partner her. You don't think they might . . .'

'Caroline, between you, you and Harriet Charter-Plackett ought to be running a marriage bureau.'

'It's only kindly interest. Do the police know how the fire started?'

'They assume it was faulty wiring but they haven't had time to be sure. I expect these old houses have had bits of wiring done here and there over the years and most of them could do with a complete fresh start.'

It wasn't until she was in bed that night that Muriel remembered Sharon hadn't paid for her coffee and chocolate gâteau. Well, in the circumstances, Muriel couldn't really remind her about it. She'd have to put it down to experience.

# Chapter 17

'Good evening, Michael. Come in, please. Have you met Sir Ralph Templeton?' Peter was greeting his guests whilst Caroline was performing miracles in the kitchen with the food Jimbo had organised for her.

'I haven't had the pleasure. Good evening.'

Michael Palmer shook hands with Ralph, then followed the two men into the sitting room. Jimbo and Harriet were already there with drinks in their hands. 'Hello, Michael. How are you? Glad the school holidays have started?'

'Not really, Jimbo, no. I love school. There isn't another job in all the world I would rather do. I know people think that being a schoolmaster is some sort of soft option and a skive, but it is the most interesting and rewarding work anyone could hope to do.'

'I don't know how you cope with our little lot.'

'Your little lot as you call them are very very bright, well behaved and a great challenge. They keep me on my toes.'

'That's nice to know.' Jimbo turned and laughed at Harriet who raised her glass to Michael and dropped him a mock curtsy. 'Harriet will live on that recommendation for about a fortnight.'

'Jimbo, that will do.'

Caroline appeared, trying not to look too flustered. She loved dinner parties but worried herself to death about how they were going to work out.

The doorbell went and Caroline answered it. On the doorstep stood Suzy. She was wearing a pale lavender dress with a scarf of a deeper shade draped across her shoulders. Her long blonde hair was brushed back and held up in a comb on the top of her head.

She smiled nervously at Caroline. 'Thank you for asking me.' Suzy spoke in a soft voice so no one else would hear.

'Thank you for coming, you look lovely.'

Caroline slipped her arm through Suzy's and drew her into the sitting room. 'Here we are, everybody, Suzy's arrived. You know everyone, of course, except Sir Ralph. Ralph, this is Suzy Meadows our next-door-but-one neighbour.'

'How do you do.'

Peter stepped forward and asked as naturally as he could what she would like to drink.

'Orange juice, thank you. No alcohol.'

As he handed the glass to her he caught her eye and smiled cautiously. Suzy looked up at him and gave that Madonna smile which had so captivated him. 'Thank you, Peter.'

In order to make conversation with someone he had never met before, Ralph innocently asked whether her husband would be coming along later, or was he abroad or something?

There was a brief silence and then Suzy answered steadily: 'No, my husband has died. To add to my troubles he left me expecting this baby – or should I say babies.'

'I'm so sorry. I had no idea.'

'Please don't be upset – I'm not. He's dead and gone and

I've the future to think about. He wouldn't have wanted anyone to feel sorry he'd died, would he, Peter?'

'I didn't know him, Suzy.'

'No, of course not. He never took part in village life. The only good he did with his life was to give me thr— *five* children. Being a nuclear scientist isn't exactly commendable, is it? I understand you're wanting to settle in the village, Sir Ralph?'

'Yes. I'm staying with Caroline and Peter at the moment because I was to have moved into number three behind the pub, but it caught fire, as you know.'

'Oh yes, of course. It doesn't look too serious.'

'No, fortunately it isn't. Sharon McDonald spotted it before it got too much of a hold.'

At that moment Muriel arrived. She was late, breathless, and very tense. She was wearing a slim-fitting black dress, long-sleeved with pearls filling in the neckline.

'Why, good evening, Muriel. How absolutely charming you look!' Peter drew her into the circle and offered her a drink.

'A sherry, please. Sweet, if I may.'

Ralph took it across to her. As he put the glass into her hand he smiled and said, 'You look lovely.'

Harriet and Caroline winked at each other.

When they sat down for their meal Caroline put Michael between herself and Suzy. Though she was feeling desperate about Suzy, she made the greatest possible effort to be a hospitable hostess.

Jimbo came up with an idea for Ralph's consideration.

'I've just had a thought. Toria Clark's house must be coming up for sale soon, Ralph. It would be a good buy if you like it.'

'Where is that?'

'Next door to here.'

'Why ever didn't we think of that? Of course – what a good idea!' Caroline exclaimed.

'Where is Toria Clark going to live?'

Jimbo cleared his throat. 'She isn't. She was found dead a few weeks ago, the night of Stocks Day to be exact. Her house must be going to be sold, I would have thought.'

Harriet, finishing the last of her soup, put down her spoon and gave Ralph a résumé of the accommodation.

'It sounds ideal,' he responded. 'A little on the large side, but then I don't like poky little rooms. Would I be able to have an open fire?'

'Well, Toria had a wood-burning stove so I suppose yes, you could have an open fire. Have you ever been inside it, Muriel?'

'No, never.'

'It's very nice.'

'Stop playing estate agent, Harriet, and let Ralph make up his own mind.'

'Jimbo, you're bossing me again.'

Jimbo apologised and they all laughed.

Muriel was having the greatest difficulty in enjoying herself. Being actually partnered with Ralph made her very self-conscious. This dress she'd bought was so slim-fitting that in fact it was almost tight, and it showed every inch of her figure. She hardly dare bend over to eat because she felt sure the dress would drop forward and reveal her cleavage. She caught Ralph smiling at her and she went bright red. To cover her embarrassment she took a deep drink of her wine and within a few minutes was feeling quite light-headed. Ralph asked her a question and her words slurred as she answered.

She was one of the first to leave, excusing herself on the

grounds that Pericles would be needing to go out. Ralph offered to escort her to her door.

'Oh no, thank you, don't come out. I can manage quite well. Please, no thank you.'

'Of course I shall, It's very dark with there being no street lighting. I couldn't possibly let you go by yourself at this time of night.'

He stood up and, taking her elbow, guided her towards Caroline. Muriel kissed her hostess and thanked her confusedly for a lovely evening.

'Not at all, Muriel. I'm glad you could come. See you in a minute, Ralph.'

After the pair had gone, the rest all looked at one another and speculated about them.

Ralph held tightly to Muriel's arm as they picked their way along the path.

'Moo, you've got some very nice friends.'

'They are, aren't they, Ralph? I'm very lucky.'

'Have you thought that they are lucky, too, having you as a friend?'

'They give me far more than I give them.' She put her key in the door, and out of politeness offered Ralph a drink before he went back. The lateness of the hour had persuaded her he would refuse but he accepted. He followed her into the kitchen and helped her fill the kettle and get out the cups. Muriel felt invaded. Her very own space was being taken over. She'd created a safe world, a place for everything and everything in its place, and now here was this masculine person touching her very own belongings. It was an effrontery. Her natural graciousness held her back from being rude and asking him to go, but it was all very disturbing. She'd have to wash all the kitchen things tomorrow, to make them all hers again.

'Moo, sit here. Here's your cup.' They chatted for a while about Toria's house and whether Ralph would like it or not and then out of the blue he asked her a question.

'Have you enjoyed yourself tonight?'

'Yes, thank you.'

'I thought you seemed ill at ease.'

'No, I wasn't.'

'Is it me? Am I crowding you too much?'

'No, it's not that at all.'

'What is it then?'

'I haven't had a real friend since I was a girl. I've known people well but not had friends, and there is a difference, isn't there? Mother never encouraged me to make friends, always afraid they would take me off somewhere and I wouldn't be there to look after her, I suppose. Your coming back has mixed me up.'

'I hope it's a nice mix-up? I know at our age we can't expect to have rich passionate relationships like one does when young, but there's no reason why one can't be happy together, is there?'

'No, I enjoy your company.'

'Good, because you won't get rid of me easily.'

Ralph stood up and pulled Muriel to her feet. 'I'll say good night now and leave you to go to bed. You must be tired. I have to say that you were the smartest lady there tonight. Good night, Moo.' Ralph put his hands on her shoulders and very gently kissed her lips. She stood, arms by her sides, not responding.

'Moo, don't keep people away, let them draw near.'

He left, giving Pericles a pat as he went.

Muriel sat down when he left and cried.


Caroline was crying, too. Peter held her in his arms

trying to soothe her distress away.

'My dearest girl, it all went absolutely smoothly. I was so proud of you. The table was lovely, the food was great, they all enjoyed themselves and you carried it all off so well.'

Caroline dried her eyes and tried to gain control of her voice. 'It's not that. Oh, Peter, I *do* wish I could have a baby. Why does someone have the chance to have five and I can't have any? I am so envious of Suzy. It's not fair. Not fair.'

'If it's any consolation to you I love you more than ever and I wish I could take away the pain, but I can't.' She burst into a fresh flood of tears.

'Caroline, Caroline, please, darling, try to stop. How about we try to adopt? That would be a solution, wouldn't it? We're still not too old and we couldn't have better credentials, could we? Now you're leaving work it is a possibility.'

Caroline dried her eyes, laid her head on Peter's shoulder and contemplated a wholly new idea which Peter's suggestion had triggered in her mind.

'What a brilliant idea. What a *very* brilliant idea. I'll think about it.' She turned her face to Peter, looked him straight in the eyes and asked: 'Do you not love her just a very tiny little bit because she is carrying your children?'

'Despicable though it is, no I don't. You're the one for me. Never forget that.'

'Thank you. Ralph's taking a long time to come back.'

'Stop matchmaking and go to sleep. Feeling better now?'

'Yes, thanks.'

'Good night, my love.'

'Good night, Peter. Sometimes you do hit upon some very good ideas.'

Peter slid his arm around her waist and hugged her. 'I am

some use then, sometimes. What's the good idea I've come up with?'

'Never you mind. I'll tell you when I'm good and ready.'

# Chapter 18

Never one to let the grass grow under her feet, Caroline asked Suzy the next time she saw her if she could come round to her house for a chat when the children were in bed.

'You want to see me?'

'Yes, if that's possible.'

'Yes, it's possible but why?'

'Well, I can't speak about it now, it's just something I need to discuss with you.'

'About Peter?'

'In a kind of a way.'

'They're usually all in bed by eight at the latest so come round any time after then.'

'I'll come tonight if I may.'

'Very well.'

Caroline knocked on the door by two minutes past eight. Suzy gave her a glass of wine and they both sat in front of the fire. Suzy waited to hear what Caroline had to say.

'I was extremely upset when I found out about . . . about your pregnancy. When I saw you in the clinic quite naturally I assumed it was Patrick's baby. Peter didn't know about you being there because of course I don't discuss patients at home – not by name, anyway. He only found out when Michael told him you wouldn't be able to keep on with the playgroup. That was the day before I went up home to Northumberland.'

'I saw you leaving. I knew from your face you'd heard. It was only the once, and entirely my fault. I was so shatteringly lonely that day. I needed comforting and before we knew where . . . well, anyway, you know what I mean.'

Caroline took another drink of her wine and tried hard not to mind about what Suzy had left unsaid. She had more important things on her mind.

'I've given in my notice at the hospital.'

'Oh, I didn't know that. Whatever for? I thought you enjoyed it.'

'I do – or rather I did. I gave my notice in because Peter and I have never had much time together. I've always worked long hours, ever since we were married, so I decided that I would spend some time at home and then perhaps go back to hospital work when I got fed up with keeping house.'

'I see. Is that what you wanted to discuss with me?'

'No – well, kind of. How are you going to manage with the twins?'

'Do you mean financially?'

'Well, yes – and also, how will you look after them? I mean, two babies and three little girls is an awful lot for one person.'

'Are you fancying being mother's help, Caroline?' Suzy smiled when she spoke.

'No, I'm not. Look – I find it hard to know how to say this.'

'Well, say it and then I'll tell you if you've done it well.'

'Peter knows nothing of what I am about to propose – it's all my idea.'

'Right.'

'I wanted to say: if at any time you found you couldn't face coping with the twins, I would be more than willing to . . . well, I would be more than willing to have them.' Caroline gulped nervously.

'Have them for the afternoon, you mean?'

'No, I didn't mean for the afternoon. I meant for – for always. To keep. That is, if you could part with them, if that was possible at all.' Her voice trembled.

'Caroline, has Peter not told you what I said to him?'

'No. I didn't know you'd spoken to him about them.'

'The day you left, I told Peter that no one – and I mean *no one* – would ever know that these twins were not Patrick's. I told him that I intended to have them both adopted, and that I had already chosen the parents.'

'Oh, I see. Then there's no more to be said. I'm sorry if I've caused you pain. I'll be going.' Caroline rose blindly.

Suzy took hold of Caroline's hand and told her to sit down again.

'I know I sounded as if I was being very difficult, but I wanted to hear it from you, absolutely and completely from you without any help at all, that you, Caroline Harris, wanted to have Peter's children. I had to be sure, you see.'

'But it's no good! You've just said so. Oh please, let me go.' The pain and disappointment were tearing her apart.

'It is, that's the point,' Suzy insisted. 'You've told me, with no help from Peter and no prompting from me, that you want to adopt them. That was what I wanted to hear! You and Peter are the parents I've chosen. I told him so in a roundabout way, but he was so upset about you leaving that he didn't understand what I was saying.'

Caroline sat down again slowly, unable to take in what Suzy had just said. 'You mean you want Peter and me to have them? Is that what you really want? Truly want?'

'Yes. I've no love to spare for anyone at the moment, least of all for two new babies who'll need loving attention for years. I've got to get back to work, Caroline. With three children to feed and clothe, the money Patrick left is rapidly disappearing. I've gone quite dead inside. I don't want to know about obligations to anyone else at all. I just want to get on with working and looking after my three girls. As soon as the twins are born I'm leaving here, so there won't be any worry about me billing and cooing over the pram. They'll be yours completely.'

'As long as I live I shall be entirely in your debt.'

'I won't tell you where I'm going. I shan't want photographs – nothing at all, and I mean that.'

'Suzy, how are you going to tell the girls?'

'Daisy and Pansy can't help but notice things aren't quite what they were. I've explained to them that though I'm expecting two babies, we are not going to keep them because I have no money to feed and clothe them. So what better way is there but for us to give them to someone who has no babies at all? They've both cried about it and said could we keep one and let the lady with no babies have the other one, but I've said you can't separate twins as that would be cruel. Bless their dear hearts, they do appear to understand. Rosie doesn't even seem to have noticed that she can't sit on my knee easily any more, so I'm leaving that till she says something. They won't forget, but at least it will stop hurting after a while.'

Caroline stood up, put her arms round Suzy and kissed her. 'Thank you, thank you so much, so very much.'

'When the twins are due I shall want you there. Right

there helping.'

'There aren't any words to tell you how grateful I am.'

'What about Peter?'

'I'll tell him in my own good time.'

'We won't let anyone else know what we've planned, Caroline. They gossip so much in this village that all kinds of stories will do the rounds.'

'No, that's right, we'll keep it our secret. Good night. You may say you have no love left for anyone, but I think you must have.' She closed the door and tried hard to walk normally into the Rectory, but it was so difficult, so very difficult. She wanted to skip.

Peter was in his study with a couple who were asking to be married in the church. She took coffee into them, then went off to have a bath. She lay there planning which room she would choose for the nursery and how she would need to buy a twin pram, as well as nappies and cots and . . . then a cold drip from the tap fell on her toe and seemed to chill her through and through. What if the twins were premature and didn't survive? What if Suzy decided to keep them both? What if Peter didn't want them?

She heard him coming up the stairs. He came into the bathroom and sat on the edge of the bath.

'Someone else taking the plunge. They seem as if they'll be very happy. Sometimes couples come and you want to say to them, "Look, it won't work," but it's very difficult when they're convinced they're doing the right thing. Where have you been?'

'Talking to Suzy.'

'What about?'

'About you not understanding what she was trying to tell you.'

'I don't know what you mean.'

Caroline sat up and began rubbing soap onto her face flannel. She didn't answer immediately. She held up a leg and soaped it right from her toes to the top of her thigh and did the same with the other one. Then she looked up at him and said: 'You know, the twins. Well, she doesn't want them.'

'I know – she told me.'

'She's going to have them adopted and she . . . I asked her if I could have them and she said that was what she had been waiting to hear, and that yes, I can – *we* can. Now I'm frightened they'll die or something, or she'll see them and change her mind. And I'm frightened in case you don't want them.'

'I don't.'

Caroline sat up, startled at the vehemence of Peter's reply. 'You don't? You can't mean that!'

'I do. I most definitely do.'

'Peter, it's what I most want in the world. Please don't do this to me. *Please.* I have never pleaded with you in all the time I've known you, but I'm pleading now.'

'I can't face day in day out the evidence of my unfaithfulness. Do you hear me? I can't do that! It would destroy me to watch you loving and caring for my children, ones that were mine and not your very own. I couldn't bear it.'

Caroline stood up quickly, making the water surge over the edge of the bath onto Peter's feet. She took the towel she'd propped on the edge of the washbasin and wrapped herself in it. When she'd climbed out she stood facing him and looked up at his face. He was in the deepest depth of despair.

'Caroline, you don't realise what you're asking of yourself.'

'So I can care for children who are not mine and not yours

193

– strangers' children – but I'm not allowed to care for yours. Have you no idea how bad I feel about not being able to have your children? Have you any idea what being barren means? What if things were reversed and it was you who couldn't have children? Would you feel a complete person? Because I certainly don't! Suzy *wants* us to have them. She sees it as a very right thing to do. She's told the adoption people all about us and we are the parents she has chosen. Don't break her heart by making her have to give them to people she doesn't know.'

'Caroline, please don't bring Suzy into it. This is for you and me to decide. We have to get things straight between us. Get dried and we'll talk later when we've both calmed down.'

Peter turned and left the bathroom. He went down to his study and sat at his desk with his head in his hands. He'd suffered so much since that day with Suzy that he didn't think God could ask any more of him. To have them here in this house and watch Caroline loving them was too much. No matter how he longed for children of his own, he mustn't agree to adopt them just because of that need. He could only agree if he felt Caroline truly forgave him for his infidelity. If he knew that, then he could accept adopting them. But he'd no right to ask forgiveness of that magnitude from her.

She was in the kitchen making coffee for the two of them when he sought her out.

'I'm deeply sorry for shouting like I did just now. It was unforgivable.'

'I can understand, I was too precipitate. It must have been a quite dreadfully unexpected announcement.'

'I could adopt the children if I knew with my head and my heart that you have forgiven me my infidelity. That's the only way, but I haven't the right to ask such a thing. So that's the end of it.'

'If I tell you that I had forgiven you when I came back home from Northumberland, would you believe me – *really* believe me? You see, I wouldn't have come back if I hadn't forgiven you.'

'Caroline, I don't deserve you.'

'We must wipe the slate clean, Peter. You can't spend the rest of our life together being grateful to me – it would turn me into the most insufferable person. Please don't do it to me.'

'Very well. It would make things very right, wouldn't it, in all sorts of ways if we took the children?'

'Yes, of course it would – and thank you.'

'No, I need to thank you for the immense generosity of your spirit.'

# Chapter 19

Muriel stood stark naked in front of her bedroom mirror looking critically at herself. Her skin appeared to be too big for her: there was a sagging around her bottom, definite sagging down the back of her arms at the top, and her breasts, always small, appeared smaller than ever. How could she possibly imagine for one moment that Ralph, sophisticated, well-travelled Ralph, could have the slightest interest in her? She was sixty-four, heaven help us. Sixty-four! Was it too late for happiness? Ralph had really hit home when he'd told her to let people draw near. That, of course, was half her problem, fending people off all the time. He'd wanted to draw near and she didn't know how to let him. She promised herself that if he kissed her again, she would do as they did on the television – put her arms round him and hold on. She'd watched Jimbo kiss Harriet and Peter kiss Caroline and noticed they fitted each other like a glove; all she'd done was stand completely still. Dare she invite him to dinner, then perhaps he might kiss her again and she could try harder. She'd been to number three after he moved in, but those friends of his from Culworth were there as well so there'd been no opportunity.

She called round with a little note and popped it through the letter box of number three. '*Dear Ralphie*,' she had written. '*Would you care to come for a meal Thursday of next week? Perhaps seven for seven-thirty? Yours sincerely, Moo.*' It was brief because there wasn't anything else to say.

She got a note back accepting. '*Dear Moo, I shall be delighted to come for a meal. See you just after seven o'clock on Thursday. Many thanks, Ralph.*'

It was no good attempting to cook something she wasn't familiar with. She laboured over the menu, trying to plan something which wouldn't keep her tied to the kitchen and yet would be tasty – after all, he was accustomed to eating exotic meals all over the world. The menu she finally settled on was Baxter's Tomato and Orange soup, followed by chicken and broccoli in white wine sauce, with new potatoes, baby carrots from the freezer and peas, followed by her own speciality – home-made chocolate mousse. She debated about the mousse; maybe a lemony dessert would be better for the palate. Yes – lemon passion, that's what she'd make.

Muriel asked Jimbo about which wine to choose.

It cost her £4, but would be well worth the money, he told her. She bought most of the ingredients for the meal from Jimbo and he had the greatest difficulty in not enquiring whom she was entertaining. When she got into bed Harriet complained, 'Why ever didn't you ask her?'

'Because she was in a dither and she has a perfect right to invite whomsoever she pleases. It's nothing to do with us, we just sell her the goods.'

'I bet it's Ralph, I bet it is.'

'It very probably is, but don't say a word. For people their age, romance is a very delicate thing. People our age take it for granted.'

'I wonder if he's kissed her yet?'

'Harriet, you are the limit. Turn over and let me show you a bit of romance of my own.'

'Certainly not! I'm an old married woman and I've decided to live a celibate life in future. It's the modern thing to do, you know. Leaves time for one to contemplate the world and its meaning, instead of clogging up one's thinking processes with all that emotional see-sawing.'

'That's what you call it, is it, emotional see-sawing?'

'Jimbo, stop it, please. Oh, that's nice. *Mmmmmmm*. I do love you.'

'I am forgiven then about the restaurant?'

'You know you are and have been for some time, but don't pull a trick like that again. I might not be so forgiving next time. I wonder how Muriel's feeling tonight? It's a big step for her, to invite someone into her home, did you realise that?'

'Harriet, concentrate on me for a while, will you, please?'

Muriel lay awake unable to sleep. She too was contemplating the dinner. The time-table for the preparation of the food was pinned on her little noticeboard and she was planning what they could talk about afterwards. She should never have asked him. Why *had* she asked him? Yes, why indeed? Did she actually want to get involved with him? What did 'involved' mean? On those Australian soaps, they call it 'being an item'. Did being an item mean you were going to get married?

Muriel hastily hid her head under the bedclothes as though by doing so she could hide from the consequences of the question she had posed herself, but it was no good evading the subject. If Ralph Tristan Bernard Templeton asked her to marry him, would she? Give up her solitude, her privacy – her own personal space? And in return for what? Companionship, more money, a better life-style? And dare she say it, SEX? Did one have sex at her age? Ralphie seemed to be a very virile kind of person, but maybe they could marry for companionship – yes, that would be it – companionship. He could take her abroad and drive her about in that beautiful Mercedes and she would have a wedding ring on her finger and that would be that. Better without SEX. If he asked her, that is what she would say: no SEX. Bit late to start with that now.

The only problem with that decision was that by the time they had finished their meal and Muriel had cleared away, leaving only Ralph's brandy and the coffee on the little table, she was actually wishing he would kiss her. She put it down to the wine.

'Moo, shall I light the fire for you? I think you look cold.'

'If you like, yes. Now the evenings are drawing in, a fire is welcome. It's all laid – we only have to find the matches.'

Ralph pulled the sofa round closer to the fire when he'd got it going and the two of them sat on it watching the flames flicking up the chimney.

'I missed an open fire when I was abroad. If I get Toria Clark's house I shall keep her wood-burning stove. They warm the whole house and there's a lovely crackling sound and a nice woody smell.'

'You're looking forward to your own home, aren't you, Ralphie?'

'Yes. It will be the first real home I've ever had.'

'That will be nice for you. Would you like some more coffee?'

'Yes, please.'

They sat in silence watching the fire. Ralph put down his

cup, swirled the last drops of his brandy round the sherry glass, which was all Muriel could find to put it in, and then took hold of her hand.

'I should very much like to kiss you, Moo.'

'Oh, I see.'

He put his arm around her shoulders and drew her closer. She shut her eyes and waited. Ralph burst out laughing. Muriel's eyes sprang open. 'Moo, you're not in a torture chamber! Kissing is supposed to be fun.'

'Fun?'

'Yes, fun. Come here.'

Muriel did most of her deep thinking in bed. Reflecting on the evening's events, she arrived at the conclusion that yes, Ralphie was right – it *was* fun. They'd progressed from little pecks to touching each other's tongues as they kissed. She recollected the stirrings of feelings she hadn't known existed, feelings which went all over her body and were quite incomprehensible. Ralphie certainly seemed to know what he was doing. But what had given her the most food for thought was his suggestion that they went to Rome together.

'I want to say this right now before we go any further, Moo. It will be all above board. Separate rooms, no obligations of any kind. We shall go as two friends each in need of companionship.'

'Oh yes, that's right, I understand. Companionship. That's how I would want it.'

'I don't wish to give offence but I have plenty of money. What with my bachelor existence and my family money, I've managed to save all my life and I know that things might be difficult for you, so if I may I should like to pay for the flights and the hotel myself. Absolutely no strings attached. There's no pleasure in travelling alone and having no one to share, and it would give me great delight to show you Rome.'

'I'll think over what you suggested and let you know tomorrow.'

As he left, Ralph kissed her hand and said, 'Don't be afraid of what life offers you, Moo. It's too short for letting chances pass you by. Do say you'll come.'

She'd have to ask Jimbo for time off and tell Mr Palmer she couldn't play the piano for him that week. Oh dear, and what about Pericles? He'd have to go into kennels, that's what. Second fiddle he'd have to play for a week. She'd give him his favourite chicken meal when she got him back. No, she'd better not go, it wasn't fair to Pericles. He'd never been in kennels before. She'd tell Ralphie. It wouldn't do at all, going to Rome with a man. It simply wasn't done. But she would have loved to see the Coliseum, and the Trevi Fountain and the Sistine Chapel, and to have walked in St Peter's Square. Well, it wasn't to be. Pericles was her staunch friend and she couldn't desert him.

Ralph was very disappointed. 'I don't wish to be intrusive, Moo, but are you saying no because of me?'

'Oh, not at all. You said as two friends and for companionship and that's how I would want it. But it's Pericles, you see. He's never been in kennels before and he's too old to start now. It would be cruel. I'm so sorry, I would have loved to have gone. I've got to go. It's time I was at the tearoom. Thank you for asking me, though.' She trailed off towards Harriet's Tearoom with a heavy heart. It was no good, you couldn't cast off old friends just because you'd found new ones. One must be loyal.

Jimbo came bustling in about eleven. 'Come to hearten the troops. How's things this morning, Muriel?'

'Very good, thank you, we're having a very busy day.'

'You sound as if you don't enjoy us having a busy day.'

'Oh, I do, I do.'

'Well then, what's the matter?'

'If I told you something in absolute confidence could I rely on you not to tell a soul?'

'Of course. Cross my heart and hope to die.'

'Ralphie – you know, Sir Ralph – has asked me to go with him to Rome. We'd be going as friends and for company, you understand, and I've said no and I wish I didn't have to say no.'

'Well, why do you have to say no?'

'It's Pericles. I'd have to put him in kennels, and that would be cruel.'

'Ah, right. Now, if I could solve that for you, would you go then?'

Muriel stopped to think for a moment. 'I don't know if I should.'

'Why not? Why not have some fun! He's a lovely chap.'

'Yes, then I would.'

'Right.' He dashed out of the shop and left her on tenterhooks wondering what he was going to do. Jimbo couldn't have Pericles because the children had got two new kittens to replace the one drowned in her water butt. There – she'd said it without flinching. She must be improving.

Jimbo returned after half an hour. 'Right, that's settled. I've told Sir Ronald that you've got the chance to go abroad and would it be possible for him to have Pericles like he did when you were in hospital and he jumped at the chance. Says Lady Bissett's Pom loved the company. So that's sorted. I'll look after the till while you go and make your arrangements.'

\*

Ralph and Muriel spent five days in Rome. In her whole life she had never had a holiday like it. Never even been abroad. Mother always wanted to go to Eastbourne or Torquay, when Muriel in her soul had longed to visit far-distant lands. Ralph treated her like a queen, and to his sophistication she brought genuine childlike delight to everything they saw. They dined in pavement cafés, followed in the footsteps of the Christian martyrs, nearly had her bag stolen by children at the Trevi Fountain, stood in St Peter's Square and saw the Pope appear at the window, and held hands as they wandered through the Basilica. He bought her anything she took a fancy to. She felt like a child being indulged in some kind of fairyland. On the last night they had dinner in a smart restaurant and then went walking by the Tiber.

'This is a far cry from Turnham Beck, Ralphie.'

'It is indeed. One day we'll go to India and see the Ganges. That really *is* a sight.'

'I don't know if I could bear to see the poverty in India. That would upset me dreadfully. All those children with flies crawling on their faces.'

'You would have made a lovely mother, Moo, if you'd had the chance.'

'It's too late to be crying for the moon.'

'Too late for children, but you could still have happiness and friendship.'

'You've given me that and spoiled me quite dreadfully. I shall never forget this holiday, not if I live to be a hundred.'

'There could be more like this – Paris, Venice, New York, Hong Kong . . .'

'Oh, don't, Ralphie, I couldn't possibly go to all those places. I'm quite satisfied to have come here. Thank you, thank you, thank you.'

Muriel leant towards Ralph and placed her lips on his. It was the first time she had chosen to make contact with him and she felt she might develop quite an appetite for it.

# Chapter 20

The bar of The Royal Oak hummed with the news of Muriel's return from Rome.

'Have you seen 'er, Betty?' Jimmy Glover enquired.

'Not likely to, after what he said about our Sharon last time he was in here. Flipping cheek.'

'Could be a good customer of yours if she apologised.'

'That's as may be.'

'Well, your Sharon is rude. And them clothes she wears leaves a lot to be desired.'

'Listen who's talking.'

'I'll have you know I've turned over a new leaf, haven't you noticed?'

Willie, seated at a table close to the bar shouted, 'Well yes, I've noticed. I've stopped wearing a peg on me nose when I come in 'ere.'

Jimmy went over to sit with Willie. He took a draught of his best bitter and leaned confidentially towards him. 'Reckon he'll make an honest woman of her then, now they're back?'

'I'll let you know if they put up the banns.'

'By gum, I bet Muriel's had a surprise. Spinster good and

proper all these years, and then this. She must be sixty-three or four, I reckon.'

'Must be – on the other hand, it could be purely platonic. "Just good friends" like all them film stars say.'

'That's likely, I don't think. Our Ralph looks to me like a man who would enjoy a bit of that there 'ere.'

'And what do you know about it in your vast experience?'

'Well, Willie, I have been married, which is more than can be said of you.'

'True, true, but even so I might have had more experience than you have. They say there's some married men who never find out what it's like. Their wives put their foot down on the honeymoon and *finito* – they never even get started. D'yer remember old Fred Armitage? He once told me his wife had ne—'

Their confidential exchange was curtailed by the sound of Betty shouting in the back.

'You're *not* going to an acid-house party! I don't care where it is, you're *not going*! For a start I need you in the bar tonight, we're short-handed, and for another you're not staying out all night.'

'Bit rich, you starting to take notice of me after all these years. Since when have you ever bothered about me and Scott? It's been "the bar, the bar" all my life. I'm off and that's that.'

'You're not. I shall tell your dad.'

'Some good that'll do. He's been under your thumb for years. He's forgotten he's got a mind of his own.'

'That's enough, our Sharon. Do as I say.'

'Who the hell do you think you are, telling me what to do? I'm nineteen and can do as I like.'

'Not under my roof you can't.'

'Under your roof, is it? Well, in that case I'll find somewhere else to live.'

'Right, you do that – and good riddance to yer!'

'And good riddance to you too.' The sound of furniture falling and the distinct noise of flesh on flesh resounded through the bar.

'Mac, hadn't you better go and see what's happening?' one of the women shouted.

But Mac carried on stolidly washing up glasses. 'They'll sort it out without me,' he grunted.

Obvious sounds of a fight were now filtering through.

'Mac, get round there and do something!'

The door from the house into the bar burst open and Sharon and Betty appeared, wrestling with each other. Glasses and bottles on the bar and the shelves behind began cascading onto the floor. Willie and Jimmy leapt up and went to help Mac separate them. Eventually mother and daughter were forced apart. Betty was breathing heavily, her carefully structured hair awry and her gold chains in complete disarray around her throat. Sharon was laughing.

'What a sight you look – mutton dressed as lamb. You won't get away with this. I'll have my own back, just you wait and see. You're welcome to 'er, Dad.'

Sharon trotted back into the house, leaving the inmates of the bar scandalised. The hubbub continued for some time. Betty went to reconstruct her hair and Mac cleared up the mess. He was philosophical. 'They've had rows like this before. It'll all blow over.'

Michael Palmer, absorbed in listening to *Aida* on a new CD he'd bought at the weekend, jumped when he heard the hammering on his front door.

'Drat it, I wonder who that is at this time of night.'

His heart sank when he saw Sharon McDonald standing at the door with her case. A large bruise was making itself noticeable all down one side of her face, and there were tears brimming in her eyes.

'Oh, Mr Palmer, please can you help me? I've nowhere to go and Mum's turned me out. Please help me.' Tears began to fall and she sniffed helplessly.

'Whatever are you doing with a bruise like that on your face?'

'Mum did it and I'm too frightened to go back home. I've packed my case and climbed out of the window. I've always tried to do what she wanted but I can't please her. Could I stay the night while I decide what to do? Please let me in. She'll never think to look for me here.' The tears trickled down her bruised cheek and she fumbled unsuccessfully in her pocket for a handkerchief.

'Here, come in. I'll find you a tissue.' Michael's immediate reaction, that he mustn't have anything to do with this girl, was overridden by his schoolmasterly instincts to care and protect children in distress. 'We'll have a cup of tea and talk things over. Perhaps if I come back home with you we could sort it out with your mum and dad. It's not right for you to have nowhere to go.'

He found a box of tissues and went in the kitchen to put the kettle on. Sharon followed him in. 'I'm scared to be on my own. Can I sit in here while you make the tea? Oh, Mr Palmer, all my life my mum's been hitting me. Now I'm old enough to leave but that means our Scott will be left on his own. She's terrible to live with, you know. I have thought about going to the Social about 'er but who'd believe me?'

'Well, of course they would, Sharon. You've got the evidence now.'

'Yes, that's right I have, and they couldn't make me go back 'cos I'm nineteen. But who'd protect Scott then? He's the one I worry about.'

'That's very commendable. Let's go and sit down by the fire and see what we can sort out.'

'You are kind to me, Mr Palmer. I always liked you when I was in school. I know I gave you a lot of trouble but with all the rows at home it was hard to behave right.' The tears began falling again.

'Now, now, Sharon. Drink your tea up and you'll feel better. I've only got digestive biscuits, will they do?'

'I love digestive biscuits, Mr Palmer. They're so homely and that's something I've never had, a real home.'

Michael pondered the predicament in which he found himself. He'd no idea that the girl had experienced such a difficult childhood. She'd kept it to herself all these years. No wonder she'd been such a trial! He had really misjudged her . . . Sharon adopted a brave smile. She touched the bruise on her face and grimaced.

'I'll get some ice for that, Sharon. At least we might keep the swelling down.' They sat chatting for a while and as it grew later and later, Michael realised he had no alternative but to put her up for the night. He didn't fancy tackling Betty McDonald until the clear light of morning. No one would know, anyway.

'See here, Sharon, just for tonight you can sleep in the spare bedroom. It's downstairs next to the bathroom. So you go and use the bathroom and I'll put clean sheets on the bed. There are fresh towels in the airing cupboard in the bathroom.'

He kept well out of the way while she got ready for bed; he didn't want her to think he had any designs on her – which he hadn't, heaven forbid. He called, 'Good night,

Sharon,' through her closed door as he went up to his bedroom. He'd never got rid of the double bed he and Stella had used, and as he got into it he suddenly felt quite lonely. Being a widower had its compensations, but sometimes it would be nice to have someone sharing the bed, even if it was only for keeping warm and conversation. Despite the events of the evening he fell asleep almost directly, firmly convinced that in the morning he would go across to the McDonalds' with Sharon and lay down the law.

During the night, he turned over and woke with a start. Close beside him was a female form. Convinced he was dreaming, he put out a hand to assure himself he was alone, but it came in contact with another hand which guided his to a warm ample breast. He leapt out of bed. There was a soft chuckle and Sharon's voice.

'Oh, come on, Michael, I'm used to this kind of thing. A handsome widower like yourself must be in need of some hanky panky. Come on, get back in. I'll give you a good time. Don't be shy.'

'Sharon, get out immediately – this minute! Go downstairs to your own bed.'

'It's cold and lonely down there, and I need someone to hold my hand. Come on, no one will know. It'll be our secret. I bet I can teach you things you've never even dreamt about. Let's face it, that Stella of yours wouldn't have given you much joy, so take your chance now while you can.'

'Do as I say. Get out of my bed this instant!'

'Don't waste your breath coming the schoolmaster with me. You want me, so for once in your life let go and enjoy yourself. I don't kiss and tell and I'm panting for you. Come on.'

'Absolutely not. Get out.'

'Well, in that case you can be cold all night because I've

got cosy. Good night. If you feel in need of a cuddle, climb in any time.'

Defeated and unable to get her out without dragging her out – which would give her the chance she wanted – Michael went downstairs. He found an eiderdown and wrapped himself up on the sofa. What a blithering idiot he'd been. He should never have let her in in the first place. She'd totally deceived him. Her acting abilities merited an audition with the RSC. He woke a couple of hours later needing to go to the bathroom, and saw that the spare bedroom door was open and Sharon's case had gone. Oh God, had she moved into his bedroom – surely not? But she hadn't, she'd disappeared. Thank heavens for that. At least no one would know what a fool he'd been. And he had been right all along – she *was* sly.

All that boasting about knowing about sex, a girl her age! On the other hand, she'd been in Culworth very late at night and seen Stella there; she'd already threatened him with that. From the back of his mind pieces of a puzzle began coming together. Pieces were missing and he could be wrong, yes of course he *must* be wrong, unless it was that Toria Clark had found someone writing the pos . . . That was it! Sharon had been writing the poster to leave in the school, and had been interrupted by Toria Clark. But Sharon wouldn't kill someone, would she? How could she? She was a village girl who'd gone to school there, grown up there . . . No. No. No! But it fitted. Sharon was the only one who knew about Stella being lesbian. It was Sharon who'd driven Stella to suicide with her threats of exposure. The poster referred to Stella, not to Toria Clark. That was the mistake they'd all made. They'd all thought the poster meant Toria. He'd have to tell the police what he thought, and a right fool they'd all take him for. He wouldn't be able to hold his head up any more; he'd have to resign. Would he need to tell the police that Sharon had stayed there all night? He could say he'd been thinking things over and had decided to tell them what he knew.

Betty and Mac went to the police the following day.

'Our Sharon's missing.'

'How old is she now, Betty?'

'Nineteen.'

'Well, she can do as she likes, you know. It's no crime at nineteen not to come home one night.'

'Look, Sergeant, me and our Sharon have had our differences but she'd no money with her when she went – we've found her purse in her bedroom. She was only doing it to frighten me. She didn't intend going any distance at all. You've got to do something for us, Sergeant, no messing.'

'I'll make some enquiries in the village and see what I come up with. But if she's decided to leave I can't bring her back.'

'She's always led such a sheltered life. I won't let her go to these all-night parties or anything like that. We've always been so careful with her, haven't we, Mac?'

'Yes. Well, fairly careful.'

The sergeant questioned everyone in the village. The row in the bar came to light and also another factor which caused the sergeant's pen to hesitate for a moment as he took notes.

'You saw her going inside?'

'Oh yes, Sergeant. He opened the door and he closed it behind her. I saw him with my own eyes.'

'This is very serious, you know. Mr Palmer is a well-respected gentleman in this village, so you'll have to be very careful about this. Are you absolutely certain it was Sharon McDonald?'

Pat Duckett nodded her head in agreement. 'Who could miss that cheeky backside and those sticking-out boobs of hers? And I couldn't be mistaken about the house, could I? It's the only one in the school playground. It was only because I was going out for a drink and knew I'd left my purse in the school kitchen that I happened to be there. I thought, "the dirty old man," so I did.'

'That's enough, Pat. Nothing's been proved about anything. Keep mum about this; you might be needed to give evidence and if I hear you've been spreading this story around I might remember about that shoplifting your Dean's been getting up to in Culworth. Remember that.'

Muriel went into school the following day at her usual time. The atmosphere was tense. Suzy came out of the playgroup room and told her that Mr Palmer was helping police with their enquiries so Mrs Hardaker the new teacher would be taking the children for singing and she and Liz Neal were going to keep an eye on the children in the playground for her.

'Helping the police with their enquiries? Whatever do you mean?'

'I'm not quite sure, but the poor man has not been himself for a day or two and now he's at the police station in Culworth. Also, Sharon McDonald's gone missing.'

'Oh dear, whatever next is going to happen in this village? When I was a girl nothing happened, apart from Jimmy Glover's father being caught poaching and someone once setting fire to a farmer's hayrick when they were up to naughty things with a girl. Well, I never.'

She told Ralph about what had happened when he collected her to go into Culworth for some shopping for his house, and asked him what he thought.

'I never cease to be amazed at what goes on in this village now. Do you suppose it all happened before and we were too young to hear about it?'

'I don't know, but I can only think it's all connected with his wife's death, and Toria Clark's murder and Sharon's disappearance. Where shall we go for lunch?'

'I do believe you're beginning to enjoy all this tripping about we do.'

'I am. It's opened up a whole new side of my nature.'

'I haven't decided yet. Where do you fancy?'

'I don't mind. Somewhere quiet where we won't meet anyone and we can talk.'

'So be it.'

Ralph chose the restaurant by the River Cul where they'd first had lunch together. They'd reached the coffee and liqueur stage when Ralph cleared his throat and began to speak. Muriel, enjoying her After Eight mint – she never could resist them – brought her head up with a jerk when she realised what Ralph was saying.

'I know we can't expect to have a mad passionate affair, but why should the two of us live, one in one house and one in another, when we could share so much?'

'Why can't we have a mad passionate affair?'

'Moo, my dear!'

'Why should we miss out on it because we're older? We'd appreciate it a lot more than when we were younger, wouldn't we? We'd be so grateful to have the opportunity. In fact, you can kiss me now in front of everybody.'

'It hardly seems the place to be kissing.'

'I'm feeling daring. All my life I've held back, been too quiet, not said what I felt, let everyone else have all the fun and it's time I came out of my shell. It's like you said, I've been fending people off and not letting them get near. All these old fuddy duddies will be jealous of me. You're such a handsome man, Ralph. I'd be proud for you to kiss me.'

They neither of them noticed the scandalised looks they got from the other diners. Ralph's hands were trembling as he signed the credit card voucher and Muriel, hiding in the Ladies from this new person she had become, could hardly control her hand long enough to renew her lipstick. Ralph took her to a department store and insisted on buying her some new perfume. She dillied and dallied choosing first one and then another till she couldn't distinguish which perfume she liked the best. Finally Ralph chose on her behalf – Obsession, the largest bottle he could find. He then marched her purposefully towards a jeweller's.

'I'm buying you a necklace. Don't argue, I am.'

They emerged after an hour with Muriel carrying a box in which was laid a beautiful pendant of garnets and seed pearls on a long gold chain. They went back to Turnham Malpas without the furniture they had gone for.

Ralph made afternoon tea for them both, and they sat together on his sofa holding hands. 'Put your necklace on, Moo.'

'It's much too good for everyday.'

'No, wear it now – I want to see it on.'

He helped her with the clasp and kissed her throat before leaning back to see the effect. 'Excellent! It looks lovely.'

'My only regret is that I am not young and beautiful, Ralphie. I never have been, come to think of it. I've always been Plain Jane all my life, even as a young woman.'

'I'm not exactly an Adonis, am I? You wouldn't give me a second look if you were as young and beautiful as you would like to be. Oh, I'm so sorry, that didn't come out very well. I do beg your pardon.' They both laughed and Muriel caught hold of his hands and held them to her chest.

'That's what's nice about us. We can laugh, can't we?'

'Oh, my dear.' Ralph took her in his arms and they kissed as they had never kissed before. They fitted like a glove. Ralph's fingers traced the line of her collar bone and then the line of her jaw and he kissed her ear and then her forehead and then her mouth again. He began to undo the buttons of her blouse. She very nearly protested but didn't. Modesty had got her nowhere in the past and it seemed right for Ralph to do as he did.

He suddenly said, 'We must stop.' He rebuttoned her blouse and stood up. 'I must be absolutely truthful with you, Moo. It pains me to say it, but I do not come to this relationship as pure as you do.'

'I thought not.'

'I felt you should know. I've got to be quite open about it to you. I don't mean I had frequent casual one-night stands, but there have been others. Not that I am asking for a serious relationship with you.'

Her eyes began filling up with tears. 'I can't understand what you mean, Ralphie.'

'I mean, I'm not going to expect a sexual relationship with you, Moo. I want something better than that.'

'Oh. I thought you meant you didn't – you wouldn't be seeing me . . .'

'When the time is right I shall ask you to marry me.'

'Oh, I see.'

'I'll see you to your door.'

'No, don't do that. The village is gossiping quite enough about us as it is and it's not dark yet. Pericles will be needing a walk.'

*Marriage*. Heavens above. And she wouldn't be plain Mrs Templeton, she'd be Lady Templeton. She couldn't marry him – could she? Whoever heard of a solicitor's secretary becoming a titled person? It was perfectly ridiculous. It wasn't five minutes since she'd been promising herself no SEX and yet today she'd been saying, 'Why can't we have a mad passionate affair?' What had come over her?

Ralph was so generous, beyond anything she had imagined. Maybe that was part of the attraction – maybe she wanted financial security. That was it, she liked him because he could provide her with the things she had never had. She wouldn't accept anything more from him and next time they went out it would be her treat. No more kissing and holding hands and gifts, strictly platonic till she'd had time to sort her feelings out. Play it cool, as the Americans would say.

# Chapter 21

Michael Palmer was allowed home by the police. He asked for leave of absence from school and the Office agreed that it would be for the best. He'd explained all he could when he was questioned; what hurt most was having to let Stella down by telling them about her secret life. He told them about the threats which Sharon had made and how she had duped him by pretending her mother had treated her so badly. He felt as if his whole life had been laid bare to satisfy his interviewers' insatiable appetite. Finally they could hold him no longer, but he knew they would be keeping a close eye on his movements. The police also had another problem in Turnham Malpas. From being a sleepy, well-regulated village carrying on its life as it had done for centuries, it had become a thorn in their flesh. Peter had discovered that some items of the church silver plate had been stolen. It happened the night Sharon went missing.

Willie, ever mindful of the need for security, always locked the Communion paraphernalia away immediately after use. They didn't have a safe as such but he had a very strong cupboard bolted to the wall with thick doors and a stout lock. In the past that had been all that was needed.

Peter had spoken of buying a safe for the valuables but had decided the expenditure was not possible. The village sergeant sighed at the prospect of yet another problem on his patch. The beautiful eighteenth-century chalices had been given by the Lord of the Manor at the time, a Sir Tristan Templeton, in memory of his wife and daughters who had drowned on board a ship which had gone down in the Channel in a violent storm. The vessels had been in constant use for two hundred years.

'Whoever took them, Sergeant, cannot have realised that if they tried to sell them they would be instantly recognised. It was an amateur for certain.'

'Not necessarily, sir. Organised crime can find outlets abroad for items like Eucharist chalices. You know the story – "Church short of funds must sell to survive" kind of thing and they were beautiful. Some families have been taking Communion from those chalices for generations. The whole village is very upset.'

The habitués in The Royal Oak concluded that no good would come of it.

'Stealing from the church, how could anybody do it? Talk about the wrath of God, it's a wonder they weren't struck dead as they forced the cupboard open.'

'Believe you me, Willie, whoever's took 'em will come to no good. Their lives'll be blighted. Might not happen this week or this year, but as sure as I sit 'ere they'll have a bad end.'

Jimmy leant closer towards Pat and Willie, checked Betty wasn't within earshot and whispered, 'I reckon it's that Sharon, night she disappeared.'

Pat agreed. 'Bad lot, she is. I haven't told a living soul but if you promise me not to breathe a word I'll tell you what I saw the night 'er and Betty 'ad that row in here.'

'Go on, then. We won't split, will we, Jimmy?'

'Definitely not.'

Pat took a long drink of her lager, settled her bottom more securely on her stool and told them what she'd said to the police.

Willie shook his head. 'I don't believe it, Pat. Mr Palmer's a gentleman. He wouldn't have that Sharon calling at his house like that. He's not that kind.'

'You calling me a liar?'

'No, I'm just saying you're mistaken.'

'I'm not. Is there anyone else roundabouts who looks like Sharon? How many houses is there in the schoolyard? One – and that's Mr Palmer's.'

'Let's face it, he must have been the last to see her, that's why the police have been questioning him.'

'Exactly, Jimmy. Exactly.'

Betty strode across. 'Finished with your glasses, 'ave yer, and yer tittle tattle? Pity you 'aven't got something else to talk about. I can see the glances yer keep giving me, making sure I can't hear yer. Yer ought to be feeling sorry for Mac and me with all the worry we have with our Sharon missing, not gossiping about us.'

Willie stood up. 'Right, that's it. I'm coming in here no more. If I can't talk about what I like when I'm having a quiet pint with me friends then I'm off. You're an interfering old buzzard you are, Betty. I've drunk in this pub for forty years and more but I've reached the end of me tether. Good night, Pat. Good night, Jimmy.'

Betty was incensed. 'That's right, cut yer nose off to spite yer face. Now where will you go?'

'I shall cycle down to Penny Fawcett and drink in The Jug and Bottle. Landlady's a sight more welcoming there than you are, or so I'm told.'

'If yer 'ad a tandem I'd come with yer, Willie.'

'Well, I haven't, Jimmy, so yer can't.'

Peter was very distressed by the theft of the chalices.

'If only I'd bought the safe!'

'Well, you didn't because the finance wasn't there so you can hardly be blamed.'

'I shall buy a safe myself, Caroline, and the Church can pay me back when they can manage it. These treasures are priceless in the life of a small parish like this one. They belong not only to the Church but the parishioners as well, simply because their families have used them for so long. Think how you must feel if you can take Communion knowing that your grandfather, your great-grandfather and your great-great-grandfather and further back than that in some cases, have all drunk from the same chalice. I can never forgive myself.'

'Maybe a dealer will be offered them and he'll contact the police.'

'Let's hope so. I must get on, there's a thousand and one things to be done this week.'

'Is there anything I can help you with, now I'm not working?'

'Are you enjoying your freedom?'

'Yes. My mind is obsessed with the twins. I can't think about anything else. If it's two boys, what about Thomas and Joshua? If it's two girls, what about Elizabeth and Sarah? If it's one of each what about Thomas Joshua and Elizabeth Sarah?'

'Don't build up your hopes too much, Caroline. I can hardly dare to think about it. I expect all prospective parents get the shivers sometimes worrying about whether the baby will be all right, and that's the phase I'm going through at the moment.'

'Peter, you mustn't. I know in my heart of hearts that this will all come right.' There was a loud knocking on the door. 'I'll answer it, it sounds like Willie knocking. Hello, Willie, the rector's in his study. Come on in.'

'Mrs Harris, the police is here. They've found the chalices. Can the rector come, please?'

'Thought it was a bomb, sir, they did – as if they'd plant a bomb on Culworth Station. Got the bomb squad in and found it was our chalices. You've to formally identify 'em, they say.'

'I would think you'd be better at that than me, Willie. You've been familiar with them a lot longer than I have.'

'Never mind that, sir. You're the official person as yer might say.'

Inspector Proctor from Culworth was waiting for them in the vestry.

'Good morning, Rector. The cups have been tested for fingerprints, sir, so it's all right to handle them. They are yours, are they, sir?'

'Yes, indeed they are, Inspector. Thank goodness we've got them back – undamaged, too. Where did you find them?'

'In a case on Culworth Station. Left there by the thief. Might I suggest, sir, that when you're allowed to have them back they are kept either in a bank vault, or that you provide better security for them than a stout cupboard?'

'Certainly, Inspector. I shall deal with it as soon as you leave. Thank you very much indeed for all your efforts. No news of Sharon McDonald, I take it?'

'None at all, sir. I wish there was, for there's a few loose ends that she could tie up for us if we could find her. No need to say this, sir, but if you should hear anything of her wherebouts, you will let us know?'

'Of course, Inspector. We are most indebted to you, thank you again.'

The inspector went round to The Royal Oak after leaving the church. He was carrying a small case. He hammered on the door. A voice called through, 'We're not open yet.'

'Police here, can we come in, please?'

The bolts shot back and the door was opened by Mac. 'Have you found our Sharon?'

'No, I'm sorry to say we haven't, but we wonder if you recognise this case?'

'I'll fetch Betty. She'll know better than me.'

Betty came through from the other bar still wearing her dressing gown.

'Mrs McDonald, do you recognise this case?'

'Oh, have yer found her?' She clutched the bar counter for support.

'No, we haven't, but we've found this case and we wonder if it's hers?'

'Well yes, it certainly looks like one I bought a few years back. I'll go and check.' She nodded to the inspector when she returned. 'That's right, mine isn't there, so I expect our Sharon borrowed it to put her stuff in. Have you no clues where she went, Inspector?'

'We know she went to Culworth Station in the early hours of the day she disappeared and left this case under a seat in the Ladies, and we expect she caught the first London train but we can't trace her after that.'

'London? She doesn't know anybody there.'

'Lots of young people go to London. Think they won't get found, with it being so big.'

'Anyway, Inspector, I've a bar to run so you'll have to

excuse me.'

Mac asked the inspector if the case was empty when they found it.

'No, Mr McDonald. Inside were the two chalices stolen from St Thomas à Becket.'

Mac sat down heavily on the nearest stool. 'Is there no end to it? What will that girl do next! I'm right sorry Mr Palmer's been involved. It wouldn't be him, you know. It'd be our Sharon – man-mad she's been for years. I daren't think what she used to get up to in Culworth.'

'Well, we've a pretty good idea. But don't trouble yourself with that at the moment, Mr McDonald. If you hear or see anything, let us know straight away, won't you?'

'Of course.'

Jimbo was surprised to find that Muriel had not turned up for work. She had never been absent before, except when she had gone to Rome. Harriet promised to go round to make sure she was all right.

'Maybe she's forgotten it's Wednesday. I've got one or two things to do and then I'll pop across. Have you seen my action list anywhere? I always put it here by the order book and I can't find it. Dammit, I'll have to start remembering all over again. I'll go and see Muriel first and then make a new list when I get back.'

Harriet knocked on the door and stood admiring Muriel's winter pansies. However did she find the time to keep her garden so lovely! Every flower was meticulously manicured and all the flowerbeds were so neat and tidy, not a single weed. When Muriel didn't answer the door she decided to go round the back and knock on the kitchen door. There was still no answer, though somehow she felt sure there was someone about. Round at the front door again she knocked once more. The door opened a little and there stood Muriel in her dressing gown.

'Yes? Oh, good morning, Harriet.'

'It's only me, come to ask if you're all right. It's Wednesday, you see, and you haven't come to the tea-room.'

'I've got a tummy upset and I'm afraid I can't leave the house.'

'I'm so sorry. Look, is there anything I can get you?'

'No thank you, I've got everything I need.'

'I'll call again tomorrow and see how you are. Are you sure you don't need a doctor?'

'Oh no, thank you, not a doctor.'

'Hope you'll soon feel better. See you tomorrow.'

Muriel closed the door and stood with her back to it. The knife Sharon was holding was only a foot away from Muriel's chest.

'Well done, Moo. We'll make an actress of you yet.'

'I'm going to get dressed now.'

'Oh no, you're not. You stay like that. Make me some breakfast now.'

There was absolutely no alternative, Sharon had the upper hand. Neither of them had slept all night and Muriel genuinely felt ill. Her mind struggled round and round her problem. She'd called Pericles in from the garden last night and left the door open for him to come in. She'd turned from making her Ovaltine to find Sharon – dishevelled, grimy, without make-up and desperately cold, standing in her kitchen. To think the girl had been hiding in the shed in the churchyard all day, waiting for the village to go quiet before coming to the door. Sharon had taken one of Muriel's Sabatier knives they'd given her at the office when she left, so there was no alternative but to do as she said and hope. During the night Sharon had told her the whole story. It was the hot chocolate and the piece of ginger cake which had weakened Sharon's armour. Muriel made it about two o'clock, more for something to do than any real need.

'This is nice, Moo. Real homely. That's what you like, isn't it, things comfortable and homely, not too challenging? Me, I like change and excitement. Poke the fire a bit, it's getting cold. Put some more coal on. Neat and tidy, smart and clean, that's you all over. Mind – there's a bit of coal-dust on the rug. Whoops, that won't do, will it? It was a good fire I made at number three, wasn't it? Nice mess that created. Your Ralphie shouldn't have told me off that night in the bar. That Ralphie of yours, has he been to bed with you? Don't be embarrassed, Moo, it's what makes the world go round. Men – that's all they want, yer know. King Street in Culworth, you should see the kerb-crawlers there. Nice market town, real piece of Olde England but they're all at it. I should know. I've earned more money there in one night than in a whole week at Tesco's.'

'Sharon, I don't believe you.'

'No, well, you believe the best in everybody. You won't find any best in me. I'm rotten through and through.'

'No one is as bad as that.'

'Oh yes, I am. You won't believe the things I've done. Climbed into Michael Palmer's bed night before last, really fancied him but he jumped out like a frightened rabbit. Cor, you should have seen him. Remember his wife Stella? Lesbian, yer know she was. Followed her one night in Culworth, saw her go into a pub there what specialises in people like her. I told her I'd tell good and proper about her goings-on. She gave me money to shut me up. Then she

226

hanged herself. Good riddance to her, who wants rubbish people like that.' She moved the knife into her other hand and pointed it at Muriel.

'No one ever found out it was me who'd threatened her, police running round like chickens with their heads cut off.' She flicked the knife sharply as though decapitating one. 'But I kept mum. Who'd think a girl of sixteen could bring off a coup like that, eh? They ran round like two chickens with their heads cut off when they found Toria Clark. She was a bloody idiot, challenging me and trying to stop me writing that poster. She didn't know what power I had. That night I was so full of power nothing and nobody could stop me.'

'Sharon, are you making all this up?'

'You stupid old cow, don't you believe me? Someone's got to believe me. You've got to take notice of what I say, or you'll be like all the others. My mum never listens to what I say. My dad never listens and our Scott's not even worth bothering about, the little toad. All my life I've heard other children at school saying "This weekend, mum and dad are taking us to Weston for the day and my dad's promised to take me out in a boat" or they were going to the zoo or up to London. What was Sharon doing? Sitting upstairs with some chocolate watching telly and looking after our Scott. Weekend after weekend. So when I got older I found my own entertainment. I made that Jimbo sit up though when I drowned his cat. He treated me like dirt in his shop, so I paid him back. All the money in the world he has, and thinks he's so superior.'

'He works very hard all day and every day. He earns every penny he gets.'

'More fool him. I like easy money. Have you got any money?'

'Only a few pounds. I don't keep money in the house.'

'When I go I'll take that.'

'Where are you going?'

'I don't know but it'll have to be a long way away because they'll be after me.' Sharon's eyes became crafty. She looked about the room. 'Where's Pericles?'

'In his basket asleep.'

'Fond of him, are you?'

'Of course.'

Sharon's mind darted from one thing to another. 'If you steal from the church, will something evil happen to you?'

'Was it you who stole the chalices?'

'What if it was?'

'Where are they now?'

'Under a seat in the Ladies in Culworth Station. Got worried, yer see, stealing from the church, so I thought if I left them there the police would think I'd gone to London, put them off the scent like they do in detective stories.'

Sharon stood up and taking the knife with her, went into the kitchen pushing Muriel in front of her.

Pericles was asleep in his basket. 'See him? One peep out of you and I shall stick this right through him, right the way through and you'll be able to hear him screaming.' She put the point of the knife close to his ribs and prodded him with it. Pericles jumped up and snapped at her.

'See – even the dog don't like me. Come back here for a pat, you nasty little thing. *Come here!*'

'He won't come if you shout, he's not used to it.'

The girl changed her tone to a wheedle: 'Come on, then, little Pericles. Come to Sharon, there's a good boy, there's a good boy.' She grabbed his scruff and pointed the knife close to his eyes. 'Remember, remember, you little sod.' When she released him Pericles scrabbled along the floor towards Muriel. She bent down to pick him up, but Sharon grabbed at her arm. 'Oh no, Moo, he doesn't deserve a cuddle. He tried to bite poor Sharon, he did.'

Muriel ignored her and scooped him up. The knife quickly arrived at her throat.

'Put him down, Moo. Do as I say – now! That's better. I've murdered once and I can do it again. The second time is easier, they say.'

She motioned to Muriel to return to the sitting room. They both sat down and remained in silence. If I can keep awake, thought Muriel, she might drop asleep and I can creep out. Oh dear God, if she kills Pericles whatever shall I do? Ralphie, why aren't you here? This would never have happened if you had been here. Please, Ralphie, come and find me. You'd know something was wrong. If he comes to the door how can I let him know, without Sharon understanding, that something is wrong? Shall I blink my eyes? Talk rubbish? My word, her eyes are beginning to close. I'll count to one thousand before I get up. It's three o'clock. No one will be about. The phone box, that's it – the phone box and 999. *One hundred and four. One hundred and five. One hundred and six.* She didn't actually murder Stella Palmer, *one hundred and fifty.* Killing with a rounders bat, that was vicious. How dreadful. The clock ticked, *two hundred and two*, the fire crackled and Sharon still sat with her eyes closed.

The counting in Muriel's head went on and on. *Two hundred and forty, two hundred and forty-one.* I shan't wait to one thousand, I'll have a try at five hundred. *Three hundred and seven.* It's so hard to keep awake. *Four hundred and fifty-nine.* She still hasn't opened her eyes, but is she asleep or playing with me like a cat with a mouse? *Four hundred and seventy-six. Four hundred and seventy-seven.* A coal in the fire dropped suddenly and sparks flew up. *Four hundred and seventy-nine*. She didn't move; she didn't hear it. *Five hundred*. Muriel placed her feet slightly apart on the carpet, checked where the rug was so as not to trip over it and slowly, slowly stood up. A knee cracked as it straightened. No movement. No movement. Inch by inch she walked forward. Please God, don't let Pericles decide to get up and come in. Inch by inch. Don't breathe, don't breathe. Two more feet and she'd be at the door. When the door opens run like the wind. Slippers won't make a sound. One more step. She turned to check that Sharon was still asleep and bumped into her, nose to nose. Muriel screamed.

'Thought you'd escape, did yer, Moo?' Sharon had Muriel's hair in a tight cruel grip. She'd spent the rest of the night tied tightly by her dressing-gown cord to Sharon's wrist. 'One move and I shall know. Just one itsy bitsy move and Pericles will be a gonner.'

'You'll have to come to the bathroom with me. I want to have a bath. I haven't washed for two days.'

'Very well. There's plenty of hot water. I'll sit outside the door.'

'You won't, you'll be in there with me.'

'But you'll be having a bath.'

'So? Never seen a woman in her birthday suit before? Something new every day when you're with me.'

She made Muriel run the bath for her.

'No bubbles? I like bubbles.'

'No bubbles, only oil.'

Sharon dropped her clothes on the floor and stood in front of the mirror.

'Cor, I do need a bath. Got yer eyes shut, have yer? You

daft old cow. Moo, that's the right name for you. Moooo. *Mooooo.*'

Muriel did open her eyes and wished her body looked like Sharon's. It was a pity Sharon had abused it so.

When the bathing was over Muriel was forced into the bedroom and made to get out fresh underwear and a skirt and blouse and a cardigan. When Sharon had the outfit on she stood in front of Muriel's mirror and laughed.

'Oh God, what a sight. It looks awful on you, but on me it's a disaster area. Time that Ralphie bought you some clothes with a bit of style. That's what you lack – style. We'll go downstairs now and you can make me something else to eat.'

They were halfway down the spiral stairs when a knock came at the door.

The knife-point pricked Muriel's back very slightly.

'They might go away. Keep still.'

'I'll have to answer. It's probably the postman with a parcel. I am expecting one.'

Sharon whispered, 'Answer it then, but I'm right behind you. Where's Pericles?'

'Shut in the kitchen.'

They walked like two halves of a pantomime horse towards the front door.

Sharon hid behind the door and Muriel opened it slightly. Thank God it was Ralph.

'Good morning, Moo. I've just been in the tearoom to see you and have a coffee but Jimbo says you're ill this morning. Is there anything I could get for you?'

'No, nothing . . . thank you.'

'Would you like me to come in and make you some camomile tea or something?'

'No, thank you. I shall be all right. Ralphie, you know

you asked me about going to the theatre tomorrow night to see *The Waiting Game*? Well, yes, I'd like to go. It's a thriller, isn't it?' She managed to wink.

Ralph looked puzzled, hesitated and then said, 'Right, I'll try to get the tickets. I'll let you know tomorrow. Hope you'll soon be better.' He looked her full in the face, waved and went down the path.

The knife-point prodded Muriel somewhere around her kidneys. 'What you playing at?'

'I had to tell him. He asked me to let him know and we don't want him back again asking if I've decided to go, do we?'

'No.'

Ralph had backed off, puzzled by Muriel's suggestion. He'd never asked her to go to the theatre. What on earth was she talking about?

He went round to see Jimbo again and told him what Muriel had said.

They checked the paper and could find no mention of the play being performed locally.

'She winked, you see. She didn't really mean it.'

'Muriel was ill a few months ago. I do hope it's not starting all over again.'

'She wasn't dressed, which isn't like Muriel, is it? – even if she's not well. I know this sounds mad but I had the feeling that Muriel was being overheard.'

The problem unsolved, Ralph went off to find Peter. He'd decided to agree to becoming a church warden. Time he got involved. He wandered up the church path hoping the rector would be about, and when he couldn't find him, he had a walk around looking at the gravestones. He was trying to decipher a very ancient one near the churchyard wall when he saw how conveniently the wall was situated for seeing into Muriel's house. Looking around to make sure he wasn't being watched, he walked along the side of the wall to find the best spot for seeing easily into the back windows of her house. He propped himself on an old headstone and sat with his head barely visible above the wall.

He'd only been there a few minutes when he spotted Muriel, still in her dressing gown, obviously beginning to prepare food. Then he saw what he had suspected: someone else was in the kitchen, and that someone else was wearing Muriel's clothes. Someone as fastidious as she, did not lend their clothes willingly. For a moment only, the other person came close to the back window. Peroxided hair . . . where had he seen that before? Who on earth was it? It was that daughter from The Royal Oak, Sharon what's-her-name. Suddenly, Muriel's odd behaviour became absolutely clear to Ralph. Sharon was hiding in her house and Muriel was very frightened. Ralph felt terribly cold and very afraid. *The Waiting Game*. Of course, that was what Muriel was having to play! 'The Waiting Game'.

When the sergeant heard Ralph's story his insides did a somersault. He'd have to appear calm, but this really was above and beyond the duties expected of a village police-man. Metropolitan police, yes, but not the Turnham Malpas village bobby.

'I shall need to get on to my inspector, Sir Ralph. Would you take a seat for the moment while I contact him.'

'Whatever you do, you mustn't have them barging up there with their big boots on. That girl is dangerous. I've warned Muriel about her before.'

Sharon sat in front of the fire eating her lunch of scrambled egg on toast with two rashers of bacon and baked beans, and tea and a piece of gingerbread for afters.

'This suits me down to the ground, Moo. Once it gets dark I'm going. Waiting here is getting me nowhere. I've got to get away. Pity you don't drive, then you could take me in the car in the dark and drive me away. When I tell you to, you must fetch me all the money you've got.'

Muriel tried to eat her lunch but it would keep sticking in her throat. If only it would get dark right now, but there were another three hours before sunset. Could she keep her nerve until then? Oh, Ralph, please understand what I was telling you, please. *Please*.

'I'll wear a coat of yours and a scarf and get myself to Culworth on the tea-time bus. There's never no one on it going to Culworth.'

'I shall have to let Pericles out or he'll be wetting the floor.'

'I'll come with you when you open the door. I don't want you running out.'

She picked up the knife, took hold of the back of Muriel's dressing gown and marched her to the kitchen. Pericles dashed out of the door. They both stood, Muriel in front and Sharon holding the knife to her ribs, watching the dog in the garden. For one brief moment Muriel thought she saw a head move behind the wall. She glanced at Sharon but she was standing a bit behind and didn't get quite the same view as Muriel did.

A small flame of hope flared in Muriel's heart. Pericles came back in.

'Well now, Sharon, shall we wash up?'

'You can, I'll watch.'

Talk to your captors, make a relationship with them. Be friendly, be sympathetic. Where had she read that?

'I'm sorry I haven't got much money in the house, my dear, but there'll be enough for the bus and something to eat. Would you like me to make a picnic for you to take with you?'

'What's this – trying to win me round? You won't get me to give myself up, you know. Couldn't bear being locked up. Got a thing about it, you see. I've got to have freedom, that's me. Yes, you can make me a picnic. Put some of that gingerbread in and a nice jam sandwich.'

Sharon sat on a stool watching Muriel wash up. The small kitchen made her proximity hard to tolerate. Muriel didn't like people in her house at the best of times but this was suffocating. They watched television during the afternoon and then had another cup of tea. Before it grew dark Muriel made the picnic, found Sharon a coat and a big scarf for her hair.

'You'll miss the tea-time bus, Sharon, if you don't hurry.'

'Right. I'll go over the wall and round the back of the church through the graveyard and wait for the bus behind the wall, then no one will see me.' Sharon put the knife in the plastic bag holding her picnic.

'Sharon, don't take the knife. You don't need it.'

'Oh yes I do. It's a big bad world out there.'

Muriel opened the back door and said, 'Good luck, Sharon.' The girl tossed her peroxided head and without another word ran into the garden and headed for the wall.

The terrifying scream which tore across the night sky as Sharon disappeared over the wall shattered Muriel's self-control. She collapsed unconscious.

# Chapter 22

Ralph thought his heart would burst with fear. Surely, surely, she wasn't dead? Not when they were about to find happiness together after all these years.

He gently rolled her over, fearing the worst. She was ghastly white and scarcely breathing, but not apparently hurt in any way. He needed a phone. 'I shall put a phone in for you, Muriel, immediately,' he whispered.

A constable followed him in. 'Is she all right?' Ralph demanded.

'I think so, sir – just fainted with shock. But she'll need to be checked over all the same. I'll call for another ambulance.' While the constable did this on his radio, Ralph covered Muriel with his coat, gently rubbed her hands between his warm ones, and spoke her name, desperate for her to come back to life.

'How's Sharon?'

'Dead, sir, I'm afraid. The knife went straight through her as she fell, and the blood just pumped out. She was dead in a moment. There was nothing we could do to save her.'

'Poor girl, what an end. Have her parents been told?'

'Someone's gone to tell them now.'

When Muriel came round she was neatly tucked up in bed with Ralph sitting beside her holding her hand. Caroline was there too and they both sighed with relief when she spoke.

'Sharon – I heard her scream. Is she all right? That poor girl.'

'Don't you worry about her, Muriel. Let's be thankful you're OK.'

'She died, didn't she? *Didn't she?*'

'Yes, I'm afraid she did. She saw the police waiting for her and she was so startled she slipped and fell on a knife she was carrying. She died almost instantly.'

'Can I have a drink of water, please, Ralph? I'm so terribly thirsty.' Caroline supported her head while Ralph held the glass for her. She took a few sips and then lay down again.

'You understood then what I meant about *The Waiting Game*.'

'It took me a while but in the end I did. You've been very brave, Muriel . . .'

'You've called me Muriel. You must be growing up.' She smiled.

'And you've called me Ralph.'

'So I have.'

'The police will need to see you when you feel better.'

'Sharon made Mrs Palmer kill herself and then she killed Toria Clark. And it was Sharon who set fire to number three. It's perhaps as well she's died, she couldn't face being locked up. She was only a little girl really, you know. She needed an awful lot of love and she felt she never got it from anyone. I felt quite sorry for her when she left.'

Caroline said gently, 'That's because you have a very kind heart, isn't it, Ralph? Harriet is devastated that she didn't cotton on.'

'She couldn't help it. Sharon said I was a good actress. It wasn't Harriet's fault.'

A nurse came bustling in. 'Message for Dr Harris. Ah, there you are. You're needed in Maternity as soon as you can make it, Doctor.'

'Oh, am I? Right, well, I'll come then. Bye bye, Muriel. I'll leave Ralph to take care of you. Perhaps I could pop in to see you tomorrow if you're still here?'

'Of course, Caroline. Thank you for coming.'

Caroline arrived in Maternity, puzzled about why she should be required.

'Good evening, Sister. You've sent for me?'

'Yes. Mrs Suzy Meadows from Turnham Malpas has insisted we inform you she's been brought in. She says you're a friend.'

'That's right, I am. Ah, the twins are on their way then? Will it be in order for me to be here? Her husband has died and she did say would I be here to support her, purely as a friend.'

'Of course, as a friend. I appreciate you asking my permission.'

Suzy lay in bed pale and anxious.

'Oh, Caroline, you've come – I'm so glad. What's all this about Muriel and Sharon McDonald? I saw the police about during the afternoon but I wasn't feeling up to going out to find out why and then Mother arrived and I came straight in.'

'At the moment it's nothing for you to worry about, but Muriel is quite safe and they're taking care of Sharon. This is earlier than expected, isn't it?'

'Yes, but I'm glad, I couldn't have coped much longer. I do not want to see the babies at all. I shall have my eyes closed and don't let them give them to me, please. You take them. Promise me, will you promise me?'

'Suzy, I shall quite understand if, when it comes to it, you want to keep them.'

'I don't. Oh, please, you mustn't let me weaken. I mustn't weaken. I don't want them, but I'm not strong enough to see them and hold them and then not want them. Tell the Sister, please. Tell her that you're looking after them, not me.'

Suzy closed her eyes and began breathing steadily. She drew a self-imposed wall around herself and concentrated on giving birth and getting it over with. Caroline felt excluded. She went in search of Sister.

'It's all most irregular,' the woman frowned, 'but of course there is no law which says a mother has to love and want her babies. If she is getting them adopted then I can quite understand her not wanting to see them: she's too vulnerable at the moment to be emotionally strong. But it's preferable for the babies to relate to someone immediately. That's how I like to work. It's not only the mothers who have rights, you know. Babies are not parcels.'

'Well, that person is me. She wants my husband and me to adopt the twins and has been making arrangements with that in mind.'

'I see, you and the rector. Well, highly suitable parents I must say. What does your husband think about this?'

'He is delighted. We can't have children of our own, you see.'

'Proper arrangements must be made before the babies are allowed out of the hospital. I can't let them go off willy-nilly with anyone.'

'Of course not.'

Peter sounded anxious when he answered the phone.

'My darling girl, where are you?'

'Sorry, Peter, I learnt about Muriel and Sharon before I left so I've been to reassure myself Muriel's OK, so if anyone asks you can tell them she's conscious and quite unharmed apart from shock. But Suzy has been brought in in labour so she wants me to stay here till the twins are born. Darling, I'm terrified.'

'Oh God, this is it then. Shall I come to the hospital?'

There was a pause and then Caroline said, 'I don't think so, do you? It wouldn't look right somehow. Look, I'll ring as soon as there's any news. Do you love me?'

'You know I do. Take the greatest care, my darling, and keep a rein on yourself. There's always a risk, you know. I don't want you to be heartbroken.'

'I know, I know. I am trying hard to be sensible. I won't leave the hospital without ringing you so take the phone to bed, won't you?'

Peter went into the church. It was about eight o'clock. He stood in the darkness before the altar. His tall figure, topped by his thick, bright-bronze hair, was quite motionless. In the darkness his black cassock made him almost disappear as though only his head was present. Inside he was in turmoil. This day perhaps or at least within a few hours his children, please God, would be born safe and well. He daren't let Caroline know what it meant to him. All these weeks he had been trying to play the role of bystander, the cautionary man, the detached onlooker, when all the time these new powerful emotions were coursing through him. His gut reaction, his primitive instincts were that of pride that he had reproduced, that his bloodline would continue. He knew now what was meant by the words 'my own flesh and blood'. To hold in one's arms the product of oneself

240

must be an unbelievable experience and one for which he was not altogether sure he was equipped.

He knelt before God and prayed, for forgiveness for his sin, for the life of his children, and for the life of their mother. He prayed for his darling Caroline and the wonderful way in which she had decided to take his children into her care. Then he rose from his knees, bowed his head and went across to the organ, where he began playing a sad piece by some obscure seventeenth-century composer that exactly fitted his mood. The music poured from his soul and he concluded with a triumphant Bach Fugue.

As the last note finished he heard someone clapping.

'Wonderful, wonderful. You should have been a musician, not a clergyman. You played from the heart, Peter.'

Ralph stepped forward into the light.

Peter, in a strange mood and not welcoming company, switched off the organ, swung his legs over the organ seat and went towards Ralph.

'I didn't realise I had an audience,' he said quietly. 'How is Muriel?'

'Very well, all things considered. She's had a dreadful time. I'm sorry Sharon has died, but there couldn't have been anything other than a bad end for the girl. Have you seen her parents?'

'Yes. I spent half an hour with them. Betty is distraught but Mac is fairly calm. What a terrible thing for a parent to have to face.'

'Well, that's something we aren't likely to know anything about – not me, certainly. Bit late now.'

'That's right. What's the time?'

'Half-past nine.'

'I'd better get back to the Rectory. I'm expecting a call.'

'Good night, Peter. What an eventful life I've led since I came back here. I thought it would be peaceful in Turnham Malpas. Some chance of that.'

'Too true. Good night then, Ralph. You know you and Muriel could be very happy together.'

'Perhaps. We'll see, we'll see.'

The phone went at 1 a.m.

'Hello, Peter. You're a daddy. Peter, are you there?'

'Yes, I am.'

'They're both fine, a bit small but both fine.'

'I see. I see.'

'Peter, you sound funny.'

'No, I'm not. What are they?'

'A perfect family – a boy and a girl.'

'That's wonderful. Are you all right?'

'I'm in seventh heaven.'

'Is . . . is Suzy . . . ?'

'Yes, she's fine. She's very upset but still determined that she doesn't want the babies.'

'I see. That's good, isn't it? Are you coming home now?'

'In about an hour, when the babies have been weighed and washed and everything. I held them as soon as they were born. They are beautiful, just beautiful. Wait till you see them. You could come tomorrow, couldn't you?'

'I can't wait.'

When he held Alexander and Elizabeth in his arms, Peter had tears in his eyes. His own two, very own two children. He'd thought that joy like this would never be his and yet here he was. Caroline stood looking down at him. He glanced up at her and smiled.

'Aren't they beautiful, my darling?'

'Absolutely. We are blessed.'

'We are indeed. God be praised. Caroline, my darling girl, thank you from the bottom of my heart.'

'You've got two darling girls now. Muriel's coming down to see them before she goes home. I couldn't wait to tell someone that they are going to be ours.'

'They seem very tiny.'

'Well, they only weigh just over four pounds each so they won't be coming out until they get a bit bigger.'

The midwife had given Alexander to Caroline as soon as she'd cut the cord. The tiny tiny being lay bawling and squawking in her arms, his weeny arms waving in indignation at the disturbance his birth had caused him. She'd pulled aside the sheet Alexander was wrapped in and examined his ten little toes, touched his minute fingers, admired his fingernails, stroked his wet, blood-streaked hair which looked as though it would be the same colour as Peter's, and noticed how very long he appeared to be, with what seemed like two quite large feet fidgeting away as he cried. She'd smiled to herself. What else could she expect from a baby of Peter's, but long legs and big feet and bright, almost strawberry-blond hair? There was no mistaking whom Alexander belonged to. She laid him in a cot, carefully placing him on his side, and covered him over. When the midwife handed the second baby to her, Caroline found herself holding a neatly made, composed little girl. She'd lain in Caroline's arms stretching and occasionally opening her eyes but mostly preoccupied with sucking her thumb. She had perfect little feet. Elizabeth – that's it. Elizabeth, she'd decided.

Sister interrupted her reverie. 'What a wonderful job you've done, Suzy. Absolutely brilliant. No complications like we'd anticipated, you've been a model patient.'

'I'd like to have the babies taken out, please. Now.'

'Of course. Nurse, jump to it, if you please. Dr Harris? You too – out you go, please.'

Caroline went across to Suzy, bent over her and kissed her and said: 'Thank you from the bottom of my heart. God bless you.'

Suzy nodded as silent tears began trickling down her cheeks. She made agonising choking sounds as she endeavoured to control the pain rising in her chest. All she could think was 'I mustn't weaken, I mustn't weaken.' Surely when she was so positive that she didn't want these children, surely the pain wouldn't last? She mustn't ask what they were. Mustn't ask who they looked like. Treat it like a miscarriage, a late miscarriage – that was it. That was how she'd solve it. She'd go straight to her mother's from the hospital and then there'd be no chance she might see or hear the babies. Twenty-four hours, that was all she'd stay in this place. Mother would see about moving their belongings and selling the house. Then she'd make a new beginning away from memories of Patrick and Peter. A completely new life. Oh God, please take away the pain.

When Muriel came down to the ward to see Alexander and Elizabeth her feelings were confused. Delight for Caroline and Peter. Distress for Suzy. Anticipation at seeing the two tiny babies, and fear of returning to her own home with all the memories of the last forty-eight hours so fresh in her mind.

Peter and Caroline were both there when she walked in. They greeted her and then she walked over to the cots. The shock she received as she leant over Alexander's obliterated her own anxieties, for there, nestled in a hospital shawl, lay an exact replica of Peter. Fond parents go on about how like their father or their mother a baby is, yet no one else can detect much likeness at all. But there was no doubt here. She stood touching his tiny clenched fist and stroking his bright hair whilst she composed herself.

'Why, he's beautiful! So perfect.'

'And this is Elizabeth.'

Muriel bent over the second cot and saw a tiny, perfectly angelic-looking baby sucking her thumb. Her mass of blonde hair and her fair peaches and cream complexion made a beautiful picture and Muriel loved her from that moment. Had Caroline realised how like Peter Alexander was? Muriel raised her eyes from the two cots and looked straight at Caroline. Their eyes met and without speaking Muriel knew she was right. Caroline dropped her gaze to the cots and said, 'Aren't we lucky, Muriel, to have been given these two babies? A family all at one go.'

'Indeed you are. Congratulations.' Muriel kissed Caroline and then turned to Peter.

'Congratulations, Peter. These two children couldn't have hoped for better parents.' She reached up and kissed him. 'If you don't mind, I should like to get home now. Any time you need a babysitter, just ask me, I shall be delighted. I don't feel up to seeing Suzy yet, but she does need support so you won't forget her, will you?'

'No, of course not. Thank you.' Caroline patted her arm and saw her out of the nursery.

When she'd gone Peter and Caroline stood holding hands looking down at their children.

'Mr Harris, I think that Suzy's parish priest should go to see her. It's only right.'

Peter took his hand from Caroline's and said, 'Yes, of course. Are you coming with me?'

'No.'

Peter knocked on the door of Suzy's private room. She'd

been put in there in preference to the general ward. Sister had insisted on that in the circumstances.

'Come in.'

He felt as if his entrails were being burned before his very eyes; he deserved it too.

'Good morning, Suzy. May I come in for a minute?'

'Of course, Peter, find yourself a chair. If you've come to tell me how grateful you are, and what a heel you feel, and is this really what I want, because you would quite understand and so would Caroline if I changed my mind, don't bother.'

'I won't, then.'

'Good. What I don't need is sympathy. I intended being out of here tonight but I've got a slight infection and Sister refuses to let me go home. Well, I'm not going home, I'm going to Mother's – and I never want to hear the words Turnham Malpas ever again. It has been a disaster for me from the word go. Is Muriel all right?'

'Yes. She's just been to see— She left hospital this morning.'

'Poor Muriel. I would love to know whether or not she marries Ralph, but that's something I shall have to speculate on because I never want to hear another thing about the village.'

'I can understand you wanting to sever your ties. How are you of yourself?'

'Better than can be expected, in the circumstances. Take hold of my hand. Don't worry, I'm not going to go all sugary and weepy. Peter, I won't be putting Patrick's name on the birth certificate – that wouldn't be right. I'm putting yours on, you are their father after all. When they are old enough you will be truthful to them, won't you? Don't deceive them. Children can't cope with parents who lie, they see it as a betrayal. Will you give me your blessing and then go?'

'Of course.' Peter stood with his head bowed for a moment. 'Dear Father God, bless this precious child of Yours, standing at the crossroads of her life. Take her into Your loving care and watch over her in the task she has set herself. Bless her little girls, Daisy, Pansy and Rosie, ensure that they will be a joy to her throughout their lives. Bless her for her generosity of spirit, her courage, and her moral strength. Make Your face to shine upon her and give her Your peace. Amen. May God bless you, Suzy.'

'Take care of them for me, won't you? Go now while my eyes are shut.'

'Thank you, Suzy, for your blessed gift.'

Peter bent over, kissed Suzy's forehead and left.

# Chapter 23

The village bubbled with the news of Suzy's twins going to the Rectory.

Pat Duckett treated Michael Palmer to one of her monologues the first morning he was back at school.

'The rector and the doctor will be delighted. Only right, too. How could Suzy Meadows feed and clothe all them children? Very sensible. Funny her not coming back to empty her house, though. Still, what with Mr Meadows committing suicide and then the twins being born, 'spect you can understand. The twins might be home by Christmas, so I hear. Mighty busy Christmas Rector'll have. Busiest he's had for some time, I reckon. Dr Harris should know how to manage, I daresay. Plenty of offers for babysitting they'll be having, mind. Alexander Peter and Elizabeth Caroline – nice names they are. Going to call 'em Alex and Beth, apparently. Old-fashioned, but nice. You glad to be back, Mr Palmer?'

'I am indeed, Mrs Duckett. The school seems to have managed very nicely without me, though.'

'Don't you believe it. Oh, nothing's gone wrong, it's just that something was missing and it was you. That Mrs

Hardaker, hard by name and hard by nature she is. Told me off good and proper about the boys' lavatories. I said, if you can kill that smell then you go right ahead and do it. I does my best, Mr Palmer, but that smell won't go. I reckon the drains isn't right. Shall we report it to the Office?'

'I'll check them out myself and see what I think. Isn't it a lovely morning, Mrs Duckett? Nearly Christmas but quite mild still.'

'Muriel Hipkin's gone back to her house, yer know. Never thought she would. Thought she'd be living it up at Sir Ralph's. He asked her but she put her foot down and said it wouldn't be right. I ask yer, at their age. Makes yer laugh. They're not likely to get up to anything, are they?'

'I wouldn't know, Mrs Duckett. I'll go and tackle the boys' lavatories, while you get done in here. The children, the best people of all, will be in soon.'

'Don't know about best people of all, they makes a lot of work.'

'Children are the whole reason for the school's existence. Remember that.'

He went off whistling to his appointed task. Life felt a great deal better than it had done for years. A whole load had lifted off his shoulders. Sad that it had taken Sharon's death to do it, but there you were.

When he went to his house at lunch-time there was a letter on the mat. He didn't recognise the handwriting, so when he slit it open he looked first at the signature. Marjorie Vickerman. Who on earth was she? He went back to the beginning of the letter and read,

*'Dear Mr Palmer, I know you will wonder who this is writing to you, but I am Suzy Meadows' mother. I feel very upset that Suzy wishes to cut all ties with the village. People have been extremely kind and helpful to her and you especially. She loved*

*being with you in the school because, as I am sure you realised, she is a born teacher. She is at home with me now and will be for some time. She is going to apply for teaching jobs shortly. Her address certainly for the next year will be 24, Little Orchards Lane, Beckhampton, Nr Gloucester, GL 14 9PJ.*

'*I can't help but feel very sad that I shall never know what happens to her and Patrick's twins and I would be so grateful if from time to time you could let me know. I am a loving grandmother, you see.* DON'T *write to Suzy, write to me at the address above. Many thanks for your kindness to her. Yours sincerely.*'

His heart skipped and danced. He was glad he'd not lost contact with her. She must be heartbroken, giving her babies away like that. Poor girl. He could see in his mind's eye her charming round face and her long silvery-blonde hair. She was small in stature but big in personality and in heart. They'd had some good talks when she'd been leading the playgroup. Real communication, not simply talk.

After lunch he was launching himself into football practice when he saw Betty McDonald coming through the school gate. Oh no, not just now, Betty.

'Good afternoon, Mrs McDonald. Keep going, boys, I'll be back. Come into my office, won't you?'

He propped himself on the edge of the desk and waited for Betty to speak.

'I've come to tell you our Scott will be leaving school soon. We're moving. It won't be for a month or two but move we must. Our Scott and Mac can't stand it here any more so we're off to make a fresh start. Thought I'd better let you know. Sorry you've had all this trouble. She was a bad girl, was our Sharon, and we didn't help. But there we are, it's too late now. Thank you, Mr Palmer, for all you've done.'

'Mrs McDonald, I've only done what a good school-master should have done. Your Scott is a very clever boy, you know, if he'd only let himself do some work. He is actually university material – I don't know if you realised that? With encouragement from you, he'll make it, believe me. Thank you for coming to tell me.'

Betty stood up. Michael opened the office door for her and she went out. He watched her walk across the playground between the footballers, looking like someone who, as his mother would have said, had had the stuffing knocked out of her. The edifice she called hair was not so high, her shoulders were slumped and she'd definitely lost weight.

'Right, where's that goalie? Watch out then, here I come down the right wing. And here we go – and it's a goal!'

'Cor, Mr Palmer, that was a good 'un!'


Muriel stood leaning on the school wall watching the boys. She applauded Michael's goal and then carried on behind the chapel towards Turnham Beck.

Pericles scampered about as though he'd never been there before. He was ten now and still full of life. What a dear little friend he was. She must keep an eye on the time, Ralph was coming for her to go Christmas shopping in Culworth. Not that either he or she had much to shop for. She'd buy something for Suzy's twins. Oh dear, she must stop thinking that. *Caroline's* twins, and a nice gift for Peter and Caroline. How on earth had that strange situation come about? Suzy and Peter, and there stood Caroline knowing all about it. Muriel knew she knew, even though Caroline had said nothing. 'If I know,' Muriel mused, 'how about everyone else? Surely they'll notice?' They were beautiful babies though, and Caroline had got her heart's desire. So had Peter, come to that.

Pericles needed a new basket. What on earth could she buy for Ralph? He had enough money to buy anything he wanted. 'Only one hour to go and he'll be here,' she hummed to herself. 'I can't wait. He's so lovely. Such good fun and so charming and well-mannered. I can hide behind his *savoir faire* wherever we go. He knows exactly what to do. I do wish I had better clothes, though. It isn't that I don't know what is good taste, it's that I can't afford it.' She turned for home.

'Come, Pericles. This way.' Out of the bushes ran Lady Bissett's Pomeranian. 'Oh, hello, PomPom, where's your master? That will do, Pericles, don't be so silly. Calm down now, you're upsetting PomPom. Oh, hello, Sir Ronald, lovely day, isn't it?'

'It is indeed. Not going away again, are you, Muriel?'

'No, why?'

'Well, your Pericles and our PomPom get on like a house on fire. When Pericles isn't there, we've all on to get PomPom out of his basket, but when they're together they race about all day long.'

'Well, not for a while that I know of. I did appreciate you having Pericles for me when I went to Rome; it was a relief to know he didn't have to go into kennels. Any time you and Lady Bissett want to go away I would gladly have PomPom for you.'

'Thank you very much. I keep hoping you might be going away on a honeymoon.'

Muriel blushed. 'I really don't think so. We're quite simply old friends from the past – there's nothing like that in it.'

'If he asks you, you accept. What's the point of not taking hold of life and getting on with it? You can be too retiring and then spend your last years regretting it. Don't let opportunities pass you by, remember that.'

He raised his tweed hat to her as they parted. How dare that man advise her what to do!

Ralph arrived on the dot, eager to be off. Muriel put on her new winter coat, well, it was three years old but it was her newest. The Mercedes had been polished to within an inch of its life and Ralph looked particularly sparkling. They drove to Culworth and started their shopping by having an early lunch.

Ralph had kissed her in the car before they set off. He kissed her when they parked in the multi-storey car park and held her arm tightly as they crossed the road. Muriel's heart began doing head-over-heels. She felt most odd.

He'd emptied the last drops from their bottle of wine when he said: 'Muriel, I have something special I want to say. You don't have to answer me now if you don't want to, but please give it your utmost consideration.'

She mopped her mouth with her napkin and paid attention.

'I want to know if you would like to visit Australia with me.'

'Australia?'

'Yes, but not as my companion, like when we went to Rome. As my wife.'

Muriel clasped her hands together on her lap to stop them shaking. 'I . . .'

'Don't answer yet, think about it. I have various friends in Australia and they have suggested I go out there in the spring and visit them and I thought it would be nice, well absolutely perfect, if I could tell them that my wife would be coming, too. I don't want to rush you. I want you to give it your utmost consideration.'

'I see.'

'Muriel, I hope I haven't rushed my fences.'

'No you haven't, and I am very honoured that you should want to marry me. It's just that . . .'

'What?'

'When I retired I made up my mind that I was quite satisfied with living on my own. I had had years of caring for Mother and being at her beck and call night and day. When I got my own house it meant I could do exactly what I liked when I liked and furnish my home as I wanted it, not as someone else had chosen. I don't know if I can give up that freedom. I've got my life nicely sorted out and I don't think I want to change it. Don't think I haven't thought about what it would be like being married to you, because I have.'

'I see.' Ralph took a long sip of his wine and sat staring into his glass.

'I enjoy your company so much. I can't imagine what it would be like not to see you and go out with you, but that's as far as I want it to go. I'm very sorry. It's not you, it's the whole idea.'

'You mean the whole idea of being truly married?'

'Yes, I think so. Oh dear, I'm not doing very well here, am I? I'm so sorry.' Muriel got out her handkerchief and dabbed at her eyes.

Ralph still sat staring at his wine. He looked up from his glass.

'I thought, you see, we would be able to make a go of it. Marriage for companionship's sake isn't actually marriage at all, you know. It's simply a piece of paper. That's not for me, Muriel – it's all or nothing. I'm sorry I have embarrassed you by jumping the gun. Shall we go?'

They sat in silence all the way back to Turnham Malpas,

Muriel staring fixedly out of the window, wishing she could bring herself to say yes. But there was no two ways about it: she couldn't bring herself to think about being in bed with him. Going out and enjoying a little kiss now and again, or going on holiday as companions was fine but that final commitment . . . No. No. No! That was the truth of it – it wasn't because she preferred to live on her own, she didn't, not any more. She couldn't face up to being 'married'. If she made a list when she got home of the pros and cons of marriage she wondered how many points there would be on each side. Muriel glanced at Ralph's profile as he drove. It was a handsome one, but there was no way she could wake up each morning to find that profile laid at the side of her. Imagine actually getting into the same bed! She preferred her neat white single bed in her neat and tidy room in her neat and tidy cottage. No, she'd done the right thing. It was only fair to be truthful and refuse straight away.

Ralph parked the Mercedes outside Glebe Cottages. He got out and went round to open Muriel's door. She stepped out of the car and led the way to her front door expecting that Ralph was following as usual. But he wasn't.

'Aren't you coming in, Ralph?'

He was standing halfway between the car and the front door. She went back down the path and stood beside him.

'God, what a mess, Muriel. I won't come in, thank you. I'll be in touch.' He spun on his heel and went straight back to the car. She stood watching him drive away, expecting he would turn round and head for his own house down Church Lane, but he didn't. He drove off in the direction of Penny Fawcett. What was he doing? Didn't he know where he lived? She worried about him all evening and wished she'd had more sense and insisted that he came in. When she took Pericles for his evening walk she deliberately went past Ralph's house. There were no lights on so he must have either gone to bed early or not yet got home.

The following morning she found a note from Ralph in her letterbox.

'*Dear Muriel, After your refusal yesterday I have decided we both need time to ourselves, so I am going abroad for a while – at least for a month. After that my plans are vague. I may go to Australia during the summer as I have lots of friends there whom I would like to visit, as I told you. Take care. Ralph.*'

She burst into tears. Hot scalding tears ran down her cheeks and fell into her lap. She hadn't cried with such abandon since her childhood. Like Ralph had said, what a mess. What a stupid, blindingly disastrous mess. She rushed up her little spiral staircase and into the bathroom, turned on the cold tap and splashed her face time and again with the torrents of cold water till her hands and face were numb. Then she dried her face and the edges of her hair where the water had caught it. She combed it vigorously with no attention to style, ran downstairs, pushed Pericles out of the way and fled down Church Lane to Ralph's house. It was all locked up. She was already too late. He'd gone. She couldn't even wish him a good holiday or offer to water his plants or anything. He wouldn't be home for Christmas and that nice little surprise she'd had of inviting him for Christmas dinner wouldn't materialise.

# Chapter 24

A few days later, Caroline called in at St Thomas à Becket.

'Willie, are you there?'

'Yes, Dr Harris, I am.'

'Ah, Willie, have you found my gloves yet?'

'Picked them up this morning. You'd left them in the vestry when you were waiting for the rector to finish. I'll get them for you.' Willie's cassock beat a rhythmic tattoo as he strode briskly down the aisle into the vestry.

'Here we are, Doctor. Safe and sound.'

'Thank you, they are my favourite pair.'

'Will you be having the twins home for Christmas, do you think?'

'Well, I think it's going to be after Christmas now. They've been slow at putting weight on and the hospital want to be sure they're thriving before I get them home. Inexperienced as I am, I'm quite glad in a way, though the rector would have loved to have them home for Christmas, whatever weight they were.'

'Never mind, you have the rest of their lives to enjoy them. By this time next year they'll be running around and wearing you out!'

'Heavens, Willie, of course you're quite right, they will be!'

As Caroline headed for the door she saw Muriel polishing the brasses.

'Hello, Muriel. Soon be Christmas. Have you got your Christmas shopping done?'

'Yes.'

'I'm off to the hospital this afternoon to sit with the twins and give them their feed. I'm getting quite nervous about looking after them all by myself. Still, I can't wait to get them home.'

Muriel sat back on her heels and looked up at Caroline. 'You've taken hold of life and got on with it, haven't you?'

'What do you mean?'

'You knew those babies were Peter's, didn't you, and yet you decided to take them into your home for his sake.'

Caroline sat down with a thump on the pew nearest to Muriel.

'I realised you'd guessed when you saw them in the hospital. I love Peter more than life itself. It took a great deal of agonising on my part before I could cope with what had happened, and then when I got the idea of adopting the twins it seemed to put everything right.'

'That takes courage and that's what I haven't got.'

'What do you mean? Is there something the matter?'

Muriel put down her dusters and sat on the pew next to Caroline. 'Have you noticed that Ralph isn't home at the moment?'

'No, I hadn't. Where's he gone?'

'I don't know.' Muriel got out her handkerchief, blew her nose and took a deep breath. 'You see, he asked me to marry him and I said no. I didn't even say I would think about it. I said no. Unequivocally, no.'

'Ah, and now you wish you'd said yes?'

'No, well, I don't know! He's gone away and won't be back until after Christmas. He put a note through my door. I ran round to his house but he'd already gone, so I couldn't even say goodbye or anything.'

'Oh, Muriel, he must have been very upset.'

'He was. You see, I made the excuse that I'm perfectly satisifed with my life as it is. Now he's gone I'm not so sure.'

'It's being actually married that's your problem, isn't it?'

'To be honest, yes. I've been a spinster for sixty-four years. It's such an invasion of one's privacy sharing a house and a . . . a bed.'

'I'm sure that such a well-travelled man has had plenty of experience. I'm absolutely certain that Ralph would be the most wonderfully considerate lover.'

'Lover? Oh dear. Oh dear.' Muriel got out her handkerchief and blew her nose again to cover her confusion.

'Isn't that what you mean?'

'Yes, I suppose so. It's a big step, isn't it, at my age? He has had experience – he's told me that.'

'Well, there you are, then – and being married to him would make your life so exciting. All that foreign travel and that nice house he's bought and all his money. You would have a wonderful life, so rich and full. Think hard about your decision, Muriel. Life can be very lonely in old age.'

'It's lonely now with him away. He may never ask me again.'

'Perhaps you'll have to orchestrate that yourself.' Caroline stood up, patted Muriel's hand and bent over and kissed her. 'Come for dinner on Christmas Day. It may be my last dignified Christmas dinner for years – thank goodness!'

★

When Caroline got back to the Rectory she found Peter checking his action list for the midnight service.

'Peter, I feel as if I have lived a thousand years since last Christmas.'

'We have come a long way since then. Are you happy, my darling girl?'

'I am indeed. I thought I would miss being a doctor but I don't. I simply can't wait for the twins to come home.'

Peter reached his hand out towards her and pulled her on to his knee. 'This Christmas Service is going to be the best they've ever had. Ralph has bought all the boys new surplices and Sheila Bissett has massive plans for decorating the church and Mrs Peel is practising like mad for the big day. Things have improved, haven't they?'

'They have and all thanks to you. I've invited Muriel for dinner on Christmas Day. Ralph has gone off into the wild blue yonder and won't be back until after Christmas and Muriel's upset because she's to blame.'

'Why, what's Muriel done?'

'Refused to marry him.'

'Oh dear, what a lot she's missing.'

'That's what I told her.'

Muriel was getting ready for the Christmas Eve service in the church. There'd been rather a lot of secret meetings and enigmatic smiles from people about this service but she'd been so obsessed by the dilemma of Ralph and his disappearance that she'd been too self-absorbed to take much notice. She did know that Peter had completely transformed the whole concept of the midnight service and she was looking forward to it. Last Christmas Eve she'd been getting ready to listen to one of Mr Furbank's lacklustre sermons. Well, she didn't think they were at the time but when she looked back she had to admit that was exactly what they were. Heavens above, if she'd married Mr Furbank, oh dear, oh dear, what a tepid life she would have lived!

She got out her new coat: a warm wine red, with a thick black fur collar and a matching black fur hat. Not real fur, of course, she wouldn't have liked that. Her new black court shoes pinched a little but they would soon get better when she'd worn them a few times. Her pride was the beautiful black leather handbag Ralph had brought her back from London. It had clasps and pockets and zips all over the place and in it she put a clean handkerchief and her purse. She drew on her new black leather gloves. When she looked at herself in the mirror she wished Ralph had been coming to collect her and they could have walked to the church together and sat side by side and had Christmas dinner to look forward to. She'd had long days and nights to think about her decision. She was much nearer saying yes than she had been when he'd first proposed, but now of course she had missed her chance. Sometimes she had to admit she stood back from life far too much and she ought to grasp chances with both hands. Maybe that dreadful Ronald Bissett was right. She realised she was ready about half an hour too soon. Would she never learn! She sat down to read the paper for a while.

She glanced at the clock. Mother's clock. Whatever would she have said if she'd been here? She'd have said, '*No! At your age, you stupid girl? And what about me? How would I manage?*'

That could have been one very good reason for saying yes.

The phone interrupted her thoughts. Oh no, she'd never get used to answering the phone. Ralph had insisted she had one, but she knew hardly anyone who would ring her anyway. Who on earth could it be at this time of night?

'Hello, it's Turnham Malpas 23235 here.'

'Muriel? It's Ralph.'

'Ralph? Oh, Ralph, you've just caught me. I'm getting ready to leave for the midnight service. Where are you?'

'In Singapore.'

'Singapore, oh my word. How are you?'

'Not nearly as well as I should like. How are you, my dear?'

'Not nearly as well as I should like.'

'I see. What are you doing tomorrow?'

'I'm having dinner at Caroline and Peter's. What will you be doing?'

'I'm about to have my Christmas morning breakfast. I've been awake a long time in the night thinking about the village and what you'd all be doing. I should never have gone away so abruptly.'

'I've bought you a little present for when you get back.'

'Thank you, Muriel. I might decide to go home earlier than I planned.'

'That would be nice, Ralph.'

'Would it?'

'Yes, it would. I should enjoy seeing you back again.'

'Good, so be it. Happy Christmas, my dear.'

'And to you, Ralph. Bye bye.'

'I won't say goodbye. I'll say, see you soon. Sleep well, my dear, and give everyone Christmas greetings from me.'

The phone went dead. Muriel snatched up her bag and gloves, patted Pericles on his head, slammed the front door shut and raced with a glad heart to the church.

She stood in the doorway full of surprised delight.

St Thomas à Becket had been transformed. In every window were huge, bright-red candles burning; at the foot of each candle were circular arrangements of holly and fir cones. Each of the stone columns supporting the roof had a necklace of ivy and artificial poinsettias around the top, and trailing downwards were long strands of ivy interspersed with shiny red curls of holly-red ribbon. The altar was ablaze with red candles and at the front stood two beautiful flower displays made up with the blooms Willie had got from the hothouses at the Big House. At the foot of the lectern a marvellous artificial display of poinsettias and Christmas roses and holly had been placed, with red ribbons looping their way to the floor from the top of it. Standing to one side was a beautiful Nativity scene – not one of those tinsely things one saw in shop windows, but splendid carved creatures and lovely painted figures of Mary and Joseph. Even the font had not been forgotten: it had pure white ribbons and small white chrysanthemums in a kind of crown around the top, with a large fat white candle in the centre illuminating the display. Over all was the faint smell of frankincense. All the lights had been turned out so that the church was lit only by the candlelight. Mrs Peel was playing completely new pieces and putting her heart and soul into it, quite different from her normal mechanical playing.

Harriet and Jimbo were there with the three children, and Sir Ronald and Lady Bissett, she dressed in her rather alarming leopardskin coat, he in his usual tweeds. Even Jimmy Glover had come and he was wearing a new suit. What had come over everyone? How lovely the church was and full to overflowing, too. Willie had to bring some extra chairs in from the Sunday School. When was the last time we had to do that? Muriel thought.

The organ rose to a crescendo. The choir processed down the aisle looking extremely pleased with themselves, for they were wearing their brand-new bright-red cassocks and new surplices with stiff white ruffs around their necks, which transformed a raggle taggle group into angels. Peter was smiling triumphantly at his flock. They all sang the first carol: 'All my heart this night rejoices'.

She caught Caroline's eye and they both smiled.